SEEDS
OF
POTENTIAL

an anthology of positivity

By Pat Grayson

Heart Space Publications
PO Box 1085
Daylesford, Victoria, 3460, Australia
Tel +61 450260348

www.heartspacebooks.com
pat@heartspacebooks.com

ISBN 978-0-6485828-6-1

Published in Australia

F O R E W O R D

by Graham Williams

Scientist Martin Reese, the Queen of England's astronomer, recently referred to the world we live in: "*… the gulf between the way the world is and the way it could be is wider than it ever was*". *Perhaps as a result, the world that lives in each of us is similarly, and increasingly challenged.* In Christmas 2014, talking to administrators of his church, the Pope mentioned "*existential schizophrenia*" – the danger of forgetting who we are, and living a double life.

Pat Grayson helps to bridge these gulfs. In this book he has planted thirty-three seeds for readers to nurture and bring to fruition. An alchemic mix of wisdom that turns dross to gold. In numerology, you see, thirty-three is an auspicious, mystical, spiritual number associated with energy, creativity, ecstasy, harmony, positivity, a growth mind-set, possibility and transcendence.

These seeds traverse our thinking, feeling and acting. They address the whole, interconnected person – physical, intellectual, emotional, social and spiritual – and engage us in facing our inner demons, letting go of what pulls us back, taming our egos so that soul emerges, appreciating what we have and who we are (including our potential), and reaching out to others with acceptance and love.

Pat astutely and profoundly conveys his own experiences and learning in story, anecdote, imagery, metaphor, analogy, symbol, and aphorism – to open us to awareness, engage our senses, memory, intuition and imagination; and put our fallibilities, fragility, foibles and protective barriers into perspective. His touch is unpretentious, gentle and wise as he does this work – never judgmental, never preaching. Always sharing, inviting, and encouraging – from the heart. Always down to earth.

Storytelling and listening has been around for at least 150 000 years and has the power to connect, engage, inspire and move us, trigger action. As neuroscience continues to confirm through phenomena, such as neural coupling, mirroring and transporting, story enables memorisation, learning, the accommodation and assimilation of new thinking and beliefs. The power of story will wax not wane as we become even more immersed in the digital world. I think this is what prompted singer/songwriter Pete Seeger (do you remember *We shall overcome, and Where have all the flowers gone?*) to say, "*The key to the future of the world is finding the optimistic stories and letting them be known*".

As we read and mull over each of the thirty-three seeds, we go through a process of adopting a positive stance (which is not blind faith and unbridled optimism), learn to avoid being weighed down and held back by our natural, hard-wired negativity bias. We confront, "life is not fair", "I'm not good enough", and other limiting beliefs and hurting places. We see that there are opportunities to break the cycles of foreboding, anxiety, fears, self-doubt and regret; and learn to perceive hard times as a fashioner of character.

After spending time with Pat in this book, some of what I "take-away" are:

- Our thoughts and ideas are not inert but instead are a mental energy that can be a most important factor in the bringing about of a new reality

- Wisdom is acquired in our lives by us being open to learning experiences and events and accepting of new perspectives; having a reflective attitude and practices; getting to understand ourselves and becoming humble, yet confident, authentic, appropriately vulnerable; and learning to be giving and loving towards others

- (In fact, this revelation is very much in line with Austrian developmental psychology professor Judith GlÜcks' research to identify characteristics of wisdom that are developed over the lifespan events and challenges of individuals. She has shown that, when these inner resources are used wisely when facing challenges, then wisdom is reinforced as a result).

- Living purposeful, ecstatic and caring lives demands that we are not fragmented, but integrated 'whole persons'. Thinking, feeling and acting congruently, being true to our true-selves, is a process. Answering the velveteen rabbits' question on how one becomes real, the skin horse replies: *"It doesn't happen all at once. You become. It takes a long time"*.

We all desire to latch onto and live what is noble, consistent and energising. Pat's thirty-three seeds of wisdom are a great resource for us. He makes no clichéd, patronising promises. Rather, he encourages the slow but sure, hard work that we need to do. And, he introduces enjoyment and encouragement into our endeavours.

The overall sentiment of this book is not unlike the biblical metaphor:

"The Kingdom of Heaven is like a grain of mustard seed, which a man took, and sowed in his field; which indeed is smaller than all seeds. But when it is grown, it is greater than the herbs, and becomes a tree, so that the birds of the air come and lodge in its branches".

A final exhortation from another tradition:

"When I run after what I think I want,
My days are a furnace of stress and anxiety;
If I sit in my own place of patience,
what I need flows to me and without pain.
From this I understand that what I want also wants me, is looking
for me and attracting me.
There is a great secret here for anyone who can grasp it".

Rumi

Graham Williams Author of: Ancient Wisdom for Modern Workplaces, Building Your Bounce-Back-Ability, Centreing Customer Satisfaction, Revelling in Transition, Reflections for Head, Heart and Hands Leaders. And Co-Author of: The Halo and the Noose, The Virtuosa Organisation, From the Inside Out (the human dynamics of sustainability), Story Matters @ Work

ABOUT PAT GRAYSON

Pat Grayson is a writer. He writes to make sense of the world that he finds himself in – writing brings clarity. He teaches writing and has helped many shape their manuscript to fruition. It brings joy to him when he sees the smile on the faces of those who receive their printed and published book.

Yet, Pat is dyslexic, and severely so. Because of this, and the anger that he felt, he left school on literally his sixteenth birthday, almost illiterate (more about this further on in the book). One would not think so when you read his stories and hear his wisdom. Pat would be the first to say that each person has a skill, and the trick of life is to find and work that skill. Experience is the best teacher because with direct experience comes empathy. Pat's early life was difficult: being dyslexic; spending time in an orphanage; mental abuse as a child; and because of the anger from these things, for many years he was his own worst enemy, whereby he orchestrated a life of alcohol, was financially and emotionally broke, and where nothing worked.

When this book is published, he will be sixty-seven years old. Within these pages are sixty-seven years of that experience. Every seed within these covers was learnt through experience. He gives you this experience (mostly) in the form of stories. Stories, without doubt are the best inspiring method, as the tens of thousands of years of information sharing by indigenous people of the past reflects. The stories though, must be interesting, and as Pat is a natural storyteller you can receive the seeds of wisdom, and be entertained at the same time.

C O N T E N T

THE FIRST SEED

Preface

Compare your life to that of a tree;

The tree, at first a seed – you a foetus.
The seed germinates – you are born.
Strong green shoots search for sunlight,
you reach for your mother's breast
and experiences.
The sapling gets stronger, firmly burying
roots in nurturing soil,
while you walk, speak, and start to express
individuality.
Years pass;
the tree has grown, and although
not full height,
does not blow or wash away.
You have grown to fend for yourself, life is
spread before you.

STOP!

What happens next?

The tree can remain in shadow, scrambling
for sunlight,

it has a choice – remain stunted or
express itself.

You have the same choice, grow or
remain unfulfilled.

It is in the tree's evolutionary genes to shrug
off inadequacy;

to grow strong, tall, and ever upwards,

arcing towards the sky and taking its place in
the sun.

And you?

Can you claim your natural right and shrug
off imperfection,

or do you languish in the shade of others,

stunted and withered?

I am Pat Grayson, and I am Man. I am ecstatic to be given this life on this planet – what a blessing.

Moreover, as a human, I have been given a wonderful device that gives me the capacity to have either a good life or one of little worth, just as the above poem suggests. How I use this device will determine if my life is joyous or arduous – it is up to me. This device is called the brain, or mind. Its method of use is called thinking or thought. Each thought is a seed of potential.

This device is like a clock, it starts ticking the minute you are born, and only stops when you die. With each tick, 86 400 each day; it directs you to a good or bad life. It is these millions of thoughts that make you the person you are – happy or sad, smart or dumb, with riches or broke, sick or healthy? Do you have friends or enemies, stress or no stress, time on your hands or no time, happy or disruptive relationships? Do you do the work that you want to do, or work an inferior job? Thoughts guarantee or removes a life of stimulus, a life that is full and satisfying. Alternatively, the thoughts guarantee a life of sameness, boredom, unstimulating – one of vibrancy and expansion or contraction and inadequacy? Do you conduct yourself with confidence or with a lack of self-esteem? Do you apply yourself with valour or fear when living your life... and, are you creative or prosaic, interested or disinterred, interesting or boring? All these things in the life of a human are governed by thoughts.

A second capacity that we have been blessed with is free will. There is no force of nature, universal law, god, spirit, demon or fate, person or parent, schoolteacher or employer that determines how you create and process your thoughts. Again, it is up to you. Free will is a blessing, in as much as it gives you the capacity to direct the thoughts to a life of value – conversely, free will also allow laziness of thought direction, where the thought process is slovenly and governs itself, producing what it happens to stumble on, and the invariable inadequacies.

A scientific knowledge of thought is a good thing to have. Thought creates vibration. Vibration leads to energy, energy equals potential. Potential equals outcome. It is vibrational energy that created the universe that sustains us. It is the same vibrational energy that directs the outcomes of your life. Vibrational energy is the potential; of either positive, neutral or negative outcome. You, and only you determine which outcome of the vibrational energy you create. Therefore, thought is a seed.

A seed has a promise or a capacity. The seed becomes the mighty oak tree, another seed becomes an apple. Another produces a monkey. Man's sperm is a seed and produces humanity, and so on. Every thought is a seed. Every building that was ever built started as a seed of thought. The same with everything, and all companies, all constructions, all discoveries – all started as a seed. Seeds can sow discontent, or gratitude, abundance or poverty.

Another law of life is that there will be challenges along the way. There is no person, or animal that has never had challenges thrown at them along their way. It is the way of life that there are challenges. There is the death of loved ones, accidents, disease, war, crime, rape, loss of innumerable varieties.

Our life is like a piece of string with many knots tied at various intervals, where each knot represents a challenge. Knowing that there will be challenges should give one the fortitude to endure and then overcome them. Again, it is the thought process of the owner that determines the result or how we overcome these challenges, or if they overcome us.

As we have all been given challenges, we have also been given the ability to endure, through the way we think. It is not the challenge however that is the issue, it is the thought of the challenge that determines the outcome. There are those who have been given so many challenges that seems unfair. Yet, many of these people still have a joyous and worthy life. There are others who were given few challenges, but their life is one of misery. In both instances, their thought process determined the result.

There may be times of adjustment, as I had… but as Charles Darwin said, *"It is not the strongest of the species that survives, nor the most intelligent. It is the one that is most adaptable to change."*

Moreover, how do I know all these things? Well, I am getting towards the end of the string of my life. I have had many of those challenges at regular intervals. There have been times when I have been happy, and times when I have been sad, times of poverty and times of comfort. I have grieved the death of loved ones, had disease, accidents, and unfair treatment from others. I have been bullied and pummelled by life – perhaps, just as you have been.

I have the capacity to observe, and observe I did, and what I found was that it was my predominant thought that determined if my life was one of happiness or sadness, of poverty or comfort. I have had it all.

The anthologies in this work are about thought, or rather seeds that determine life. It is not an easy thing to harness our thoughts, it is like trying to herd cats. Nevertheless, as you will learn, much of life is a learnt behaviour, and you can learn how to harness your thoughts, to direct them to a better life.

What follows are many stories, where each will sow a seed of potential. There are seeds for abundance, for happiness, authenticity, seeds for confidence, seeds of compassion, seeds of trust, all of which you need if you are to have a good ride in this life. Take these seeds and plant them, nurture them, and like the acorn that has the potential to grow into something mighty that overlooks the forest beneath, these seeds can make you strong of mind and happy. Nevertheless, it is up to you.

There are thirty-three seeds in this book. There are stories set in Africa, in China, Australia, in unknown and ancient lands. There are animal stories, and folk tales — all designed to give an interesting reading experience, whilst imparting a seed.

Some are long and will take you an hour to read. Some will only take you a few minutes. Each seed is equally important. I suggest that you read one seed a day. Read it at night before you sleep. Let it mature in your mind as you sleep. Then think about it in the morning when you wake up. Take the seed with you to work. I suggest that you get a physical seed and put it in your pocket. Every time your hand goes to your pocket, the seed will remind you of last night's story.

Pat Grayson

THE SECOND SEED

What would you do if you knew you could not Fail?

The applause was deafening as he ambled to the podium. Although stooped, he carried an air of confidence and distinction that age could not disguise. Somehow, he seemed larger than his diminutive self. Shaggy white hair flopped over his wide forehead. Enormous eyebrows sheltered bright sparkling eyes, eyes that twinkled with intelligence. His clothes were those of a gentlemen who walks in the park. Not dapper, nor pretentious; comfortable perhaps? Most notable was his smile — wide and authentic, the smile of a man who has had a satisfying life.

Finally reaching the podium, he lent on it for support. As the attendant helped with placing the mike on Dr Jardine's lapel, he surveyed the audience. He did this with confidence and interest. He saw eager young faces, the faces of the graduates from America's premier university to whom the day belonged — the cream of the business students who were to be capped after his speech.

His first words were hardly audible, almost as if they were to himself. The students leaned forward, straining to hear. They did not want to miss a word from this captain of industry, whose modest beginnings had not prevented him from becoming a household name. With more focus and louder this time, he said, 'What would you do if you knew you could not fail?' Still, it was offered as if his mind were elsewhere, and as the students followed his speech, they could see that it was.

He reminisced about a time, sixty-eight years earlier, when he was fourteen. He talked about a dream he had had. A profound dream that had directed the course of his life, shaped him as an icon, not only in his own country but also around the world. In the dream, he saw himself determinedly striding up a mountain, higher and higher, short of breath, tired but driven. Onwards he continued, passing gnarled, stunted trees and ice-covered moss, until in mist and cold, he reached the summit. Immediately, he heard a friendly voice, 'So you finally made it?'

Peering into the swirling haze he saw an elfin man with a long white beard and bushy hair that seemed to merge with the fog. 'Sit down on this stone and rest, for I have a missive that I am to pass on to you.'

Some forty-five minutes later, zombie-like, he made his way back down the mountain with the words of the elfin man ringing in his ears, "Live your life as if you cannot fail." 'And so ladies and gentlemen, I did,' announced Dr Jardine. 'I had the mantra *I cannot fail* guiding me all these years. Consequently, I did not have the insecurities that seem to consume most of society. I recommend that you contemplate what you would do if you knew you could not fail.'

He became quiet, letting that last thought sink in. 'You would be dauntless, navigating life's impediments as if they did not exist. Knowing that you could not fail would give you the confidence to embark on any project, in any situation, knowing that you would win. With no thought of ridicule, your creativity would flow. With the outcome assured, you would work with zeal for the early fruition of all that you did. You would do more in your life and there would be no procrastination. Imagine the tasks you could accomplish in your allotted time if you knew that there was no risk?'

Other than his voice, there was not a sound; all eyes were trained on Dr Jardine, totally intent on gaining the wisdom that was offered.

'By knowing that you could not fail, and because of your positive, no-nonsense approach, you would attract a willing band of supporters, all carried along by your vision and unconquerable will. When you have thoughts of failure, there are barriers. By believing in yourself, there can be no obstacles or none that are insurmountable. You would not be paralysed as most of humanity is when confronted with dilemma. With the mantra, *I cannot fail*, you would always find solutions. Because you would experience no scarcity, you would have no greed. What you build would be for the good of all.'

He paused to let the magnitude of what he said sink in. Then resumed 'When you know that you cannot fail, you will not have self-esteem issues. There will be no space for them in your consciousness. Knowing that you cannot fail permits you to live without the necessity for a large ego.' Then lowering his voice for emphasis, he added, 'Life is so much simpler when there is no need for airs or graces, or to impress.'

He continued along these lines for some time, with the students clinging to every word. Then, by way of winding-up, with his assured smile, he said, 'The premium is probably in the relationships you'll form... I have been married for fifty-two years. They have been good years, very good years, and do you know why? I married because I knew I could not fail! I was not afraid to be myself – there was no pretence. Knowing that I could not fail granted me the freedom to allow my wife, Mary, to be who she was.'

When he finished, the ovation was long and thunderous. For a few moments he stood there, with that open smile, knowing that once again he had not failed and that the guidance he had received from the mystic would continue to guide others.

That was thirty-six years ago. Mine was one of those eager young faces, and I have never forgotten his message. He has long departed, but his legacy remains. I embraced his words "I cannot fail", and they have served me well.

THE THIRD SEED

A FOLK TALE

The Search for Happiness

Ancient China was feudal, where the wealthy owned the land, the people were peasants or vassals – who, for the privilege of being able live and work on a small piece of land, were expected to offer service or produce in return. Many of the Landowners were greedy and overly taxed their serfs. The Landowners literally owned the peasants and could do as they pleased with them.

There was however one young man, who was virtually starving, even though he had worked "like a dog" for his lord, who wondered, *what's the point?* This led him to ponder *what is the point of life*, perhaps much as you do. His conclusion was that life was what each made of it. That being the case, he determined to make his a happy life... but how to obtain happiness? In fact, it was this last question that preoccupied much of his mind but he could not find a satisfactory answer. His name was Gawa.

At first, he asked just about everybody he came across. Most got annoyed with him, saying, 'We have enough to worry about just trying to survive and please the landowner, let alone to worry about happiness... life is hard and we must bend our back and be submissive to the landowner.'

Nevertheless, Gawa, being a clever thinker, reasoned why they did not answer his question – because they were afraid to seek happiness, thinking that it was not to be has, or that it would always elude them. He kept wondering, how can we live a happy life?

One day, without saying a word to anyone in the village, he packed what little food he had and set off to ask the Immortal Princess Wencheng.

I need to tell you about Princess Wencheng. She was, and still is, a legendary figure who had watched over humanity for thousands of years. She was loved by everyone for her compassion, humility and wisdom. If she did not know the answer as to how to have happiness, then no one would.

It was mid-summer and hot as Gawa trudged in the direction he thought he needed to go to find the Princess Wencheng. He headed towards the Tibetan region in the Himalayas. He had been walking for days. One day, feeling thirsty under the fiery sun, he went into a farmhouse and asked for water. The man was kind and invited him to stay. He asked his daughter to bring tea. Seeing how thirsty the young man was, and his sweat soaked clothes, he asked, 'Where do you go?' Gawa told him of his quest to find happiness. The man stroked his chin, which only had a short beard, and with a smile of broken and missing teeth, complimented Gawa for his ambition.

The man was thoughtful for a moment considered his daughter. She was of good appearance and hardworking but had not spoken a word in all her eighteen years of life. Of, course she was not married. The man hesitated before asking the young fellow, 'If you see the Immortal

Princess Wencheng, ask her why my daughter does not speak?' Gawa nodded, finished his tea, and feeling refreshed, continued his journey.

In his search for the Immortal Princess Wencheng, and where happiness comes from, he tramped over many hills and valleys, where days turned to into weeks. One dark night, he deemed it unsafe, as there were wild animals that prowled the area. Finding a small village, he begged from household to household for a place to stay. As he was a stranger, and a scraggy looking one in his rags, the villagers were reluctant to put him up for a night – after all, they knew nothing of him. At last, a householder took pity on Gawa and treated him with hospitality, letting him sleep in the work shed. Hearing the young man's quest for happiness, the owner said, 'There is a peach tree in my garden, which blooms but no fruit grows. Ask Princess Wencheng why the fruit does not grow?' Again, Gawa said he would ask the Princess.

He walked not knowing how many days passed. One day, as he hoped he was getting closer to the Princess Wencheng, he came to a wide river. There was no ferry or bridge. Pausing to figuring out how to cross, when a large carp splashed out of the water and from its open mouth came the words, 'Where are you going?'

Amazed, but happy to answer the question, Gawa said, 'To see the Immortal Princess Wencheng but I need to cross this wide river.'

The carp cruised close to the bank, 'Why do you want to see her?' Gawa explained. Hearing this, the carp announced, 'Get on my back and I'll carry you to the other side.'

On the other side, the young man thanked the carp for the lift. The carp waved its tail, and after hesitating asked shyly, 'Ask the Princess Wencheng why can't I jump over the dragon gate (in Chinese mythology, a carp that jumps over the gate became a dragon, which is deemed auspicious) at such an old age.' The young man accepted the carp's question and bid it farewell.

A week later, he finally found the Immortal Princess Wencheng. He had never met an immortal before and was afraid that he did not pay her enough respect. Soon he relaxed as she was friendly and accommodating. He asked the three questions, 'Why does not the girl speak?... Why does the peach tree yield no fruit?... And why can't the carp jump over the dragon gate?

With a knowing smile, the Princess answered each question. When he was about to ask his question, and the reason for seeking her, she suddenly vanished – one minute she was there, the next she was gone.

Gawa, sitting under a tree, waited patiently for the Princess. He slept under the tree, and lived in its shade for a week. Realising that she was not to return, he decided to return home.

Even though his question had not been asked or answered, he thought, *since I had asked for others, and received satisfactory answers, it was worth the journey.* As he walked the long distance back, he realised he was happy.

When the young man returned to the river, the carp was impatiently waiting, anxiously swimming up and down the riverbank. The young man was greatly moved and gave Princess Wencheng's answer, 'You should pull off the two large whiskers on your chin if you want to jump over the dragon gate.' The carp was delighted. It leaped about and opened its mouth cheerfully as he carried Gawa back to the opposite bank.

The carp, so overjoyed gave the young man a gift; a blessing, 'Gawa, you will surely be happy since you have found happiness for others.' Then with a wave of a fin, the carp sunk under the water.

Feeling good, Gawa strode briskly and returned to the house where he had stayed for the night. Before the owner asked, Gawa, with a smile gave the answer, 'My friend, the Princess asked you to dig the mud from around the peach tree, and then it will bear fruit, and indeed, you will be well blessed.' The man laughed with joy, first, that there was an answer from the Princess Wencheng, and secondly, because it made sense as for some reason there was piled up mud against the tree, as if someone had dug it up and filled it in again. He immediately asked Gawa to dig out the mud at the base of the tree. He dug, and dug some more, until he felt something solid. He paused to look at the man... There was a box! Upon examining the contents, it was full of valuable coins. The man was poor and cried with joy. Being generous, he offered Gawa some of the coins.

Gawa did not accept the riches, no matter how much the man persuaded, for Gawa wanted to help the man, and not receive profit by doing so. The man was touched and blessed him with, 'Thank you for finding our happiness. By doing so I am sure that you will also be happy!'

The man and his family asked Gawa to stay with them, but the young man had one more message to deliver, so he only stayed for two days and said good-bye, before, once again heading off. A month later there were many peaches hanging on the tree, so many, the branches hung to the ground.

After Gawa walked for many days, he returned to the first man's farmhouse where he asked for tea. The daughter answered Gawa's knock. As she saw who it was, she smiled and shouted, 'Father, your son-in-law is back!' The old man was so excited that he ran to the door, delighted his daughter had spoken. Surely, this was a miracle? The farmer invited him in and offered tea.

His daughter welcomed him like an old friend, chatting endlessly. The man was delighted to see his daughter so lively in front of this young man. He asked the young man what Princess Wencheng said. Gawa became flustered, 'She… she… she said your daughter would only speak at the sight of her husband.' The man's eyes smiled, and so held their hands in a ceremony of marriage – they were husband and wife.

When the good news spread, all the folk came to bless them. The man who had the peach tree also came to bless them. He and his wife carried the bag of money and offered some as a wedding present. Gawa, and his new wife, walked throughout the community and handed everyone a coin until none were left. This made everyone happy as they could pay off the landlord.

The carp was correct; that by giving happiness to others, Gawa found happiness, and Gawa learnt that in giving there is receiving. The immortal Princess Wencheng, as always, displayed great wisdom by letting Gawa find his own answer to his question.

Gawa, became known as a man of wisdom and people came from far to seek him out for advice on all matters. He was known to be the happiest man in the region.

In his own time, Gawa became an immortal and was known as "The Happy Immortal".

The above story was loosely based on an ancient Chinese fairy tale.

Life – does it have to be Fair?

The wild dog cautiously led her five cubs. Having been out of the den for only two weeks, they were small and clumsy. Instinct had warned her of danger.

The young male lion had been prowling for three days and was hungry. He had been chased away from his pack, as it was time to fend for himself and create his own pride in another territory.

Coming over a rise, a movement caught his attention. Crouching, he scanned the lush, green bush. There... he saw the family of wild dogs, the male in the lead. The mother was constantly shepherding her young, who were full of play and excitement, thinking that the outing was a game. After a few short-tempered nips on the ear, they sensed her seriousness.

The lion had been well trained and was patient. If he rushed, he could lose the prey. Nor did he let out his fearsome roar, as this would have warned the dogs.

Watching them with close attention, he considered his strategy; going for the young would force the adults to attack him. However, if he ambushed the lead dog, the female would run with her cubs and leave the male to fend for himself as best as he could. Yes, that would be his plan.

Slinking, with stealth and tracking a parallel course, he wanted to meet the dog on open ground. He was not concerned about detection as there was adequate cover. Further along was the open ground he sought and increased his speed to arrive at the same time as his prey.

As hunter and hunted broke cover, the lion accelerated into a loping run. Thick armour-like shoulders powered the body, while his perfectly still head held deadly focus on the lead dog. With tail lowered and ears erect, he was beautiful, but devastating.

Simultaneously, the dog saw the lion, instinct and reflexes came to the fore in an attempt to survive. He knew that he had to direct the lion away from the pups but it was already too late.

The lion, with speed and power, leaped onto the terrified dog, its huge claws digging into his hide, while his weight pinned the dog to the ground.

At this point the dog's brain-chemical would have changed and it is unlikely that he would have felt the lion biting his windpipe, suffocating him. Death came swiftly.

We cannot judge the lion by our rules but must understand that many things in life do not seem fair. This meal was not just for the lion, it was for many creatures – jackals and vultures, ants and microscopic forms. Nothing is wasted. Even the herbivore eats from the plant kingdom!

The female dog was aware of the death of her mate. As humans, we cannot measure an animal's grief, but it is likely that there is an acceptance of life's harshness. She, in turn, must take the lives of other animals to feed herself and her cubs, and knows that one animal's tragedy is another's meal.

It is we humans who consider life to be unfair and let it affect us in negative ways. We retain the thought that life is tough, long after an event has passed, allowing it to reduce our power.

Although life can be harsh, it can also be beautiful, provided you get on with it. When you have been brutalised as you will be in one form or another, you must remain aware of your place in the universe. When you live in the, *life is not fair* camp you lose your balance.

You can moan, whine, and feel sorry for yourself or you can put it behind you, and, like the female dog, let it go and get on with life.

Winners know that life does not have to be fair in order to succeed and succeed you can with the right attitude!

THE FIFTH SEED

Authenticity

Actress, director, and activist, America Ferrera (TED 2018) said my identity is a superpower – not an obstacle.

Throughout this book, there are strong messages on happiness, and how to obtain happiness. The last seed in on authenticity.

There is no way known to man that a person can be happy if that person is not authentic. I would even go as far to say that it is a universal law that to be happy you must be authentic. It is authenticity that bring the other Seeds together – perhaps, it is fair to say that authenticity is the moisture that all the other messages need for germination.

Below are stories about a person called You. He or she is called You because this You could be you. The stories are on being authentic, as well as offering comment.

All our life we have been searching for something without knowing what it is, or why we are searching. Yet, we search nevertheless. Is it religion or spiritual sustenance? Is that what we are after – will that fill the hole? What about wealth, surely that is all we need? Will wealth buy our happiness? Often, when we find religion, or earn money – the hole is still unfilled. In fact, sometimes it is deeper. We keep searching… so we get deeper into our spiritual practices, and work harder to have more money, to buy more happiness. We keep searching, like a mole underground, where it is dark, not knowing where we are going.

Is it challenging not knowing what we are looking for? Yes, it is, and the reason is because we do not know who we are. As Lewis Carroll wrote in his profound story, *Alice in Wonderland;* "Who are you?' crooned the caterpillar. Alice replied rather shyly, 'I… I hardly know. I knew who I was when I got up this morning, but I think I must have changed since then."

Met You. This you is much the same as the many you's out there, in as much as she or he has authenticity issues. This You, is like you, the you who is reading this story. Below are many stories about You that you may identify with. To overcome these issues, this You hired a life coach, to help her feel better about herself.

The first instruction was for her to set goals and visualise better career achievements. She was to see herself, on the "other side", where the grass was surely greener.

You did this for a while but her authentic self emerged. She realised that by doing the instruction she was ignoring her deepest need – she needed to understand herself, not ignore her current inner needs, not visualising being "the success", whilst ignoring the need to learn about herself, and where she is emotionally at the moment.

She could see that it is through understanding and growth that we became fulfilled, not through setting goals, and willing herself to be on that so called, "other side".

Yet, thousands of life coaches earn a good living by getting their clients to step out of their authentic self, where what they need is to really know who on earth they are.

The things we most search for is our authentic self… who we are. Yet, not knowing who we are makes it even harder to know where to look. The elders and wise folk of the stories above would say, 'Look within, that's where you will find your authentic self – that is how to get to know thyself.'

This is like asking; are we seventy trillion cells or a human body? We are both.

The search for authenticity is the search for the self, and the knowing of one's self can lead to authenticity. I'll say it again in another way; we cannot find authenticity until we know ourselves. However, knowing ourselves does not mean we are our authentic selves. Moreover, knowing who you are, will identify if you are being the authentic you or avoiding the authentic you.

The great author, Joseph Heller, who wrote Catch-22, and numerous other books, was once at the lavish party of a multi-millionaire business person. Although Heller had done well out of his books (over ten million sold), he was not in the same financial league as the millionaire.

The millionaire was a bit drunk, and more arrogant than normal, when he announced loudly to the group, but specifically referring to Heller, 'If you listen to me, and do as I say, I can make you wealthier than your wildest dreams'. He then paused and followed up with, 'So what do you say?'

Heller said, 'No thanks.'

The millionaire was shocked and asked, 'Why on Earth not?'

Heller said, 'Because I have enough. I don't need any more.'

Heller remained true to his needs and wants. His authenticity saw him through. When he said, 'I do not need any more', I assume that he was referring to both money and self-esteem. It is self-esteem that is the relevant point here. He did not need more money for more posturing, or more power. That's authentic.

You was young and had a dream that he shared with all his work colleagues but none could see that vision. He went to many bankers but none gave him the financial support for his dream. This You approached business men and shared the idea – none were interested and laughed at him behind his back.

You though, being a feisty young man, did not give up on his vision. Nor did he listen when many called him a dreamer, a dreamer with no idea.

This You has a name, a famous name, one that just about every person in the world knows... Walt Disney. He was the Walt Disney who created Disney Land (and all the Disney movies), a place that almost everyone wants to go to at some stage in their life.

I love this quotation that Walt Disney used to say... "It's kinda fun creating the impossible". He created the impossible because he was authentic and worked his dream – never losing sight of it, and never taking no for an answer.

And whilst talking about dreaming, it was John Lennon, the former Beatle who sang, "I may only be a dreamer... but I am not the only one".

Authentic people follow their dreams and do not listen to the naysayers.

A small story to make a point; **Yogi finds his bravado or Yogi comes out of the Shadow.**

He's cunning, mean and ruthless. Dog of the world that he is, where he probably has all the dogs of the world within his genes. His sandy-coloured fur seems to propagate itself throughout the house, as it clings to everything he touches. He is below knee height and looks a bit like a feather duster with a shaggy tail attached at one end and a floppy-eared muzzle at the other, while four legs support the bushy undercarriage.

Let me tell you about the story of a boy named You. When little, You wanted to play with girls but his mother made him play with boys. You wanted to play with dolls, but his mother bought him guns and cars. At a fair, he was offered a balloon, and when You chose the pink one, his mother roused on him and gave him a blue one. As You grew up, he wanted to do ballet, so his father put him in the boys' soccer team.

All his young life his parents fought against You being gay. You was unhappy as he was being inauthentic to his natural inclination. As an adult though, he took firm control over his life, and accepted and acknowledged his being gay. He had a choice; to hide it or be open in his gayness. By hiding it, he would be inauthentic and living a lie. By being open and accepting his gayness, he would face the proposition of being ridiculed and insulted for much of his life.

What would you do?

Anyway, You adopted his authentic self and was happily fulfilled. You learnt that we can only be happy when we are authentic. You also learnt that those friends who loved him did so because of who he was – without pretence, accepting of himself, the good the bad and the indifferent, which we all have.

Based on Andrew Solomon's best selling book, *Far from the tree.*

Yogi believes that he is master of the house. On his canine evolutionary scale, cats are at the bottom of the chain. According to him, felines only have one brain cell and are creatures of little worth. Next are postmen and meter readers who have been put on Earth for canine sport. Female dogs are second from the top, and paramount are male dogs... Yes, you guessed it... Yogi is a male dog, and so all are subservient to him.

His house had four dogs, two males and two bitches and also two cats. Of course, there were some humans in the household, whose responsibility was to look after the animal kingdom, especially his royal highness, Yogi – the humans must always see that the food and water bowls are full, take the dogs for a walk at least once a day, provide tickles to the tummy and patting his back whenever requested.

Yogi was not always the Alpha dog of the house. There had been an elder dog, who was "Top Dog". Top Dog was allowed onto the family bed but chased Yogi away any time he tried to get up. It was Top Dog that ensured Yogi wait at the food bowl until Top Dog had his fill. Yogi was always second fiddle.

Top Dog passed on to Doggy Heaven. Before then, Yogi was just a mere shadow of who he was to become, not expressing his true character. Thereafter, Yogi "came into his own" and was far more dominant.

I think it was Mark Twain who said, 'The two most important moments in our life are when you are born, and the day you find out why you were born.'

The above is the way of the animal kingdom, where there is an Alpha male who dominates all below. But why was Yogi so timid before Top Dog left the realm? What if Top Dog never left, would Yogi ever have found his authentic self? Probably not.

Too many humans are like this, timid and only a shadow of their potential selves. But why? We don't have the Alpha hierarchy, but yet, we are subservient to much of life?

I know of two sisters in a household. They were two and a half years different in age. The elder sister was deemed to be better looking (that in itself is a travesty), and seemingly with more sporting ability. The younger one lived in the shadow of the elder. It was not that the elder tried to dominate the younger, but the younger seemed to let the elder absorb all the light, therefore the spotlight was on the elder, and the younger remained in the shadow.

Sadly, a car accident took the life of the elder. After a period of mourning, the younger sister started to step into her spotlight, or rather create her own light. She excelled at almost everything she did.

What would have happened if the elder sister did not pass away? Would the younger sister have expressed her true character and worth if the elder sister remained, to live until old age?

> You, a friend of mine, is smart, well-educated and has a senior executive position with a multi-national company. She is fourth down from the top of the internationally known company.
>
> A few years ago, she was offered the job of the person above her, as the man was to retire. This entailed more money, more responsibility, and greater status, as she would be the only woman on the board. This was a wonderful offer but You declined. Her reason; she would have less time for her family. You knows what is most important in her life, and she did not want to tip the balance – her authentic self was not swayed by the pressure the chairman put on her to accept the position. In fact, he hinted that if she did not take the job, she might lose her current position.
>
> You stuck to her needs. Finally, another man was bought in to take up that position – You remained in her current position and was happy. She knew that she would not sacrifice her family for her position with the company.

Back to Yogi; he is crazy for dog choccies and starts his manipulations at about six in the evening. However, if he gets them before eight, he forgets or pretends to forget, and commences the whining process all over again. The owner has a home office and so Yogi will wait at the entrance, doing the cute doggie thing – where a pooch lies tummy down on the floor with a dear little face resting on his two front paws that are extended in front of him, whilst button eyes follow his human's every move. This is a cunning ploy meant to melt the owner's heart. It melts his heart…

That is enough on Yogi, I could write more, but per normal, I digress. I used Yogi and the younger sister as role models to show that we all have to find our own strength of character. We cannot wait until another passes over to Doggy or Human Heaven. We must go out and get it, club it with a stick if we have to, drag it out of it hiding, for if you do not, you will always live in the shadow.

Most of you have seen this You, it might be your father, or a friend's father. As the self-designated head of the family – where, when things are not as good as they could be, they become tight lipped, and pretend they are not under pressure. It could be that they have lost their job, or because the economy is not as good as it could be and so their household finances are under pressure. Yet, they still put up a front that all is well.

The same could be said of an owner of a company or manager, where they isolate themselves, and have all the pressure on their shoulders, usually by choice. The manager and the father, because of the culture that they were raised in, cannot, or will not share the load and the worry (this is more often a man).

They think it is an admirable trait being at the top, weathering all the storms by themselves. But this too simplistic approach is inauthentic because they do not want to be seen, failing. There is the old saying, 'a problem shared is a problem halved.' The father or the manager are trying to be martyrs.

My description for authentic is: not false or copied; genuine; real; original, one's true nature. Some adjectives describing authentic: original, accurate legitimate, pure, true, actual factual, valid.

To be great, you need to be unique. To be authentic means you are being unique.

An Asian girl named You did not want to get married. Nor did she want children. She felt that there were too many horrible things in this cruel world, and to bring kids into it was just too much to bear for her. You's parents however, wanted a wedding, they wanted a grandchild as this was the culture. They put pressure onto You to accept a man, and quickly. You loved her parents and did not want to go against them, but to do as they wanted, she would not be authentic.

At the office where she worked did not help, as all the girls there were already married, had a child or were pregnant. Even the boss, a female, felt You was a threat as she was single. Society is geared to encourage young women to get married, and when they do not they are seen as outsiders, and misfits.

I will leave it up to you to decide if You was authentic to herself or inauthentic.

How does this relate to you as an individual? Have you ever asked the question; **Who are you – Really?**

If you have trillions of cells that die each day, only to be replaced with new ones,

then who are you – really? Certainly, you are not your body.

If you look in the mirror every month, you will see a changing face,

then who are you – really?

Who are you under the ever changing skin?

And, if your preferences and thought processes change over time,

then who are you – really? Obviously you cannot be your mind.

If you are fourty, can you relate to the person who you were when you were eight years old? Probably not – almost two different people.

Then who are you – really?

If 80% of the days that you have lived cannot be clearly remembered, and if you are not your memories,

then who are you – really?

Alternatively, if your entire memory bank were somehow wiped out, you would lose everything that forms your identity of yourself, if that happened.

Then who are you – really? Or are you your memories?

This morning you were grumpy with your wife, an hour later with your mates, you were happy, then agitated. So if, you are not your emotions,

And if your emotions jump around as just given,

then who are you – really?

If you were to look at yourself under a microscope (difficult to do, I admit), magnified a thousand to one, you would see that everything is moving and would look like those little bubbles in a saucepan when heating up, all bobbling every which way. So if your body is not solid matter, then who are you – really?

When you have conversations, you talk about me or I.

So who is your me or I?

To follow in someone else's steps, or mark your own path?
Which one leads to authenticity?

In most countries, there is a legal system. Of course, they have legal prosecutors. Some work for the government and some for companies. Most of the cases are civil, meaning that one person has a complaint about another. Therefore, both parties contract lawyers.

Most of these cases could be settled "out of court", thereby saving their client's hefty fees. However, the large law firms frown on any of their lawyers who resolve an issue out of court – they encourage a no settlement, as they want the courtroom time. Courtroom time fees command much higher billable fees than out of court settlements. This practice is worldwide, and I wonder how authentic it is. How authentic is it that the lawyer who represents both the client and the law firm that he works for as he tells the client that he will do the best he can for the client – yet, he could have closed it out early, but didn't? So both the lawyer and his firm are inauthentic. In fact; often the lawyer is not interested in guilt or not – their only concern is risk damage.

Whilst talking about lawyers, call me cynical, but I just cannot understand the inauthentic behaviour of lawyers who represent a client fully knowing that they are guilty. Of course, any lawyers reading this will suggest that even guilty people have the right to be represented. However, how often does the guilty party get off because the lawyer is smarter or a faster mover than the opposing lawyer? This is so disingenuous, yet, they are happy to make their fees, big fees, fully knowing that their client is a criminal and could hurt another or molest again. The fee is more important than the morality.

We just spoke about lawyers, and now onto politicians. Once again, so many are disingenuous. Usually, they join their party of choice, bright eyed and bushy tailed, wanting to do well for their constituents, especially the disadvantaged. However, once ensconced within the party system, many of the policies they wanted to bring to the cause are rejected by their own party, even before it gets to the political arena. The reason being is that all must tow "the party line", and if that policy, no matter how good it may be, does not fit the party agenda, it is squashed.

When this happens, these politicians become meek, take the pay cheque and does not push it. They give up, to fit in with the party. Therefore, his/her acceptance goes against his authentic need.

Worldwide, there is a suspicion of politicians, and for good reason, we just cannot trust what they say as too many times what they said, and what they did are totally different.

Then, there is our designer man; he was clever, and dissatisfied with much of the life that his parents offered, even saying, 'I'm not going to do it like you did Dad... I wanna be rich.' Nothing wrong with being clever or dissatisfied as that is how you grow. But the young man sets about to design his life.

He wanted to turn heads when he entered a room. To this end, he learnt deportment and how to carry himself. Of course, clothes were to be an important statement of, "his having made it", where each shirt and pants announced, loud and clear, 'Money, I have made it, and see just how stylish I am.' His car was chosen for the same reason as his clothes.

As part of his image and deportment, speech delivery was studied and perfected, as were the facial gestures. Soft modulating tones gave the message of, 'I'm wise, calm, and experienced, you should listen to me!'

He ensconced himself into a crowd of people who had the same ideals as he. These were the people who stood on the fingers of those they replaced and overtook on the ladder of business and success – they are the beautiful people.

So busy designing his life and image, he knew not who he was. If asked who the authentic he was, he would have said he was the image he had created. However, within, there would have been a little voice trying to be heard through the thick veneer that had been created – the searching that I mentioned above. The little voice was ignored.

Our young man earnt a lot of money, almost as much as he spent on financing his image. With a designer house and designer furniture, he fitted the image. So when he passed away suddenly in a car accident, there was no money left for his grieving wife (who was also a designed person and so she fitted the required image perfectly for him).

So who was he – really? Certainly he was not authentic. Nothing wrong with earning good money and setting out a nice comfortable life (remember the writing above about the evil of not having enough money?) but remember, who you really are – you are not the money or the image.

As mentioned above, the starting point in finding who your authentic self is; is to know yourself. Then identify what you like and what you do not like. What makes you comfortable and what does not? This is a necessary starting point, but these things may not be authentically you, they are the mask, to look good. For instance, you may have identified that a particular conversation makes you feel uncomfortable, and so you assess that this a natural part of who you are, and that is your authentic position. Yet, perhaps the reason why you feel uncomfortable with that discussion is that you need "to go there", to break through, and get to the other side, as the other side is your authentic position – we unconsciously avoid our authentic self.

But then like Alice, who said '*I may have changed since then*,' life flows, and things change all the time, and so for us to know our authenticity, we have to constantly evaluate. Authenticity is an active act, where you position yourself, irrespective of the fear you may have.

Listen to your body, to your gut because authenticity feels right. If it feels right, then it probably is. Inauthenticity does not feel right. Being authentic does not mean that you will achieve everything you set out to achieve, it is being real to yourself. Willing to make mistakes, willing to be vulnerable, but more willing to not be reduced by what people might say about you. You know that life is a wide canvas and you fill it in with what feels right, not what you should be doing. Know that you are ordinary, but do extraordinary things, not to look good, not just for money, but because you want to do those things. Make the choice to stand in your own power. It is not about intelligence or being blessed with creativity, you will have enough of both, if only you see it. It is your duty to yourself, not the duty to others. You know how to do this, and it starts when you trust yourself, and trust your place in the universe. Trust enough so you can say, I am going to be who I should be.

Remember, the very first story in this book, *What would you do if you knew you could not Fail?* Dr Jardine was being authentic. Being authentic is taking what you have and making the best of it… and do you know how you tell when you are being authentic? You are vibrant, alive, motivated, and full of enthusiasm. When authentic, you have better self-esteem, your confidence will be higher. You will have a greater sense of meaning and of course, happiness.

You was a young and idealistic shopkeeper. For years, he dreamt of running his own shop, instead of working in the one he did as an employee. You loved pets and had several dogs and three cats at home. One of his cats got diabetes, which appalled You. 'How could this happen?' he asked the vet when he was putting the cat down. The vet replied, 'It's the food colourant and preservatives in the "off the shelf" dog and cat food. It's really bad for them.' He went on to say; he makes all his own pet food, and his animals are healthy and live a long happy life.

This got You thinking, and it occurred to him that perhaps his love of animals and the wanting to start his own shop could be combined. He set about, and then finally opened his own pet store, selling preservative free animal food. He had done a lot of research and found suppliers who could supply good clean and healthy food. From the start the store attracted the type of customers he was after, that is, aware customers who want to ensure their pets got the healthiest food possible. You covered his overheads and even took a little money home in the first few months.

Then one day a supplier came in and offered a food that had a healthy sounding name, Eco-Green-Food. It was much cheaper, and so his profit would double. This food though, had preservatives and colourant. You thought about the product, and wanting the additional profit reasoned, just one product with preservatives should not do any harm.

Soon, more and more people came in and bought this product – you see, they were buying on price and turned a blind-eye to their animal's well-being.

It soon came about that 80% of his sales were from this product, and now he was making more money.

One day, You realised that he had traded his authenticity for profit. This realisation stunned him and he knew that sometime we all have to decide on being authentic, or not – now was his time.

To reclaim his authenticity he gradually cut back on the preserved food, and got rid of it entirely.

I love this story about this You. His real name is a household name. He ended up in Qufu in China's, Shandong Province. When I was there, I learnt all about this You.

This You was clever. Probably cleverer than anyone else alive at the time. So clever, all the wealthy land owners wanted him to work for them. He refused, as he had a desire to educate the poor. At that time in China, it was only the wealthy land owners and merchants who had education.

At first, the landowners took this You's refusal with grace. Then they offered him large sums of money to come and work for them – he still refused and continued to open up schools. Next, the landowners made it difficult for You to function, by pilfering his money, and putting pressure on merchants not to supply him, all with the idea of bringing this You to his knees. This You was of strong stuff and would not relinquish his dream of educating the masses. He begged, borrowed and scrimped to built a classroom. Children were educated in that classroom. Against the odds, more classrooms were produced.

> Many of the children who he educated, stayed on to help build more classrooms, and to help educate the waves of new students.
>
> This You, remained authentic to his want to educate. He made many enemies because he would not be swayed from the task.
>
> His name is Confucius.

Being authentic then is understanding that life constantly flows, and where you make a conscious decision, based on intelligent thought, and whether it feels right within. Above, I spoke about a life that flows, being authentic will encourage life to flow in a way that works. Authenticity sets you in the correct vocation that is you, not one that is expedient.

Remember though, that jobs are a part of today's system of commerce, which more often than not push us in an inauthentic direction, as the following shows; lawyers, doctors, dentists, and other professionals who work for large firms sign away their professional authenticity the minute they sign their employment contract. Part of the contract's terms are about "quotas". That is, how much money they are to bring into the firm each month, not how much good they are going to do to help their clients.

Doctors within those firms are known to cut down patient visit time (irrespective of the doctor not having given adequate time to treat the patient). This is done so the next patient is bought in on the conveyer belt of production, carrying their wallet.

The lawyers are happy to drag things out, to extend billing time.

These people probably embarked on their careers wanting to help people, but over time, and because of being weak, get swallowed by the system, and thereby accept this behaviour. As they do, their authenticity goes out the window. They justify the methods by saying, 'They all do it.' That is not an excuse, it's a copout.

And the reason why they become malleable by "the firm", is because most are married, have gone into debt for a biggish house, a nice car, education for their kids, and all the things that they are entitled to. However, because they have these debts, they are stuck in the system. Sure, they could leave the firm, but the next one is just as greedy and demanding. So they shrug their shoulders and fit in with the way of things. It is a trade-off; money for the debt, at the expense of authenticity!

The same with the building industry. It is common practice for builders to tender on a job and undercut to beat their competitors. When they get the job, the first thing they do is, "scope creep". And before the client knows it, the original quote is double – but hey, everyone does it!

An authentic person understands the bargains that are made to have a smooth life, and the trade-offs. They do not want the trade-offs, but they need the benefit that they can get from them. We all make trade-offs. We work for a big salary but the company owns us. We try to make peace with people who have different moral codes from ours so we do not rock the boat. By doing these things, we are not being authentic – we think we are being pragmatic. We use terminology that softens it for us, such as; instead of being bought, we have negotiated a salary, instead of standing up in a group and saying what really concerns us, we say nothing and remained quiet so as to be a "team player".

Being authentic does not mean being quiet, and not saying anything where the saying could cause trouble – if it needs to be said but you do not because of fear, you remain small, as the doctors do, and the lawyers. So authenticity often puts the cat amongst the pigeons.

This You is a girl. She was born in rural India, under the caste system. The caste system is not very good for anyone born within the lower ranks, but worse for girls. Their society thinks that women can never amount to much, only to… wash dishes, take care of the children, and of course, as sexual objects. They are told when to marry, and who to marry, without say in the matter. They are a product of their society, and in being so, lose their authenticity, and identity. That society is perpetuated by those within it, too scared to reject it.

As far as education is concerned, for girls, it is considered a waste of money and time, so most do not have it beyond the most elementary level.

> If this society is so biased by both its men and women, how can a young girl within its ranks break the pattern? Occasionally they do, but most do not as it is too difficult, things are too well entrenched.
>
> When such a girl does rebel, in an effort to have a more expansive life, one that she has a greater say in, she is usually regarded as a troublemaker. Troublemakers are chased away.
>
> However, the girls who do break away are not troublemakers – they are authentic. They stand in their power. They trust in their ability to make it in their own way. They accept and take the risk.

A Deloitte survey in 2013 revealed that 65% of people in the workplace reported changing some aspect of their character so they can fit in. Further to this, these people believed that conforming was imperative for their growth prospects. This report pointed out how much time-wasting and expense there is in trying to fit in; the clothes they wear, the decisions they make – moving from authenticity to inauthenticity.

At least if you need to make these bargains, know exactly what you are trading off. Too many times in our lives we become small to win praise, but know the cost? Buying a bigger house than you can afford in a suburb that is a notch above your salary will offer trade-offs where you cannot afford a holiday, always scrimping and saving. Where is the authenticity in that?

Another survey, this time AC Nielson, revealed that nearly three quarters of the respondents admitted to being influenced by peer pressure as generated by the media. We have become a society that is obsessed by image, where the pressure to conform is massive. Look at men and beauty products, where adverts show men in front of mirrors preening themselves, applying all sorts of "make up". They have even coined the term, "Metro Man" to make those men to feel good about this, and most are proud to belong to the Metro Man fraternity, as they feel that they are exclusively modern. Really though, the Metro Man was created by the agencies to sell more products. But even knowing this they still buy the products because they need to fit in.

Being inauthentic is normal within our society, as we are shaped by our parents, teachers and society. Society does not want us to be big, to live a big life. They want us to confirm, fit into the box and remain small – that way we are manageable. In Australia, there is a term, "the tall poppy syndrome". This is a term given by most Australians to anyone who dares to stand out. They think, *how dare you want to elevate yourself above me*. Let me give you an example.

A You worked as a bricklayer on a building site. He has lots of bricklaying friends. But there was a nagging within You's mind, *is this all that there is?* He knows that there is nothing wrong with bricklaying, but it just does not "feel" right for him.

So he decides to study and try another vocation. The other You's on the building site see this as a rejection, saying to each other, 'We must not be good enough for that You,' so they reject him and his friendship. This is an extreme case, but it reflects the mindset of a nationality. It also reflects why many live inauthentic lives, as they do not have the courage to withstand rejection by peers. I know about this first hand, as I was that bricklaying You, the so-called tall poppy.

I lived in South Africa for many years and saw many You's who had the opportunity to choose to be a racialists, or to use compassion. I saw this literally hundreds of times.

A child is born into a house where the white people thought that black people were inferior. The belief was usually perpetuated by the parents who with their prejudice (wanted to), believe that black people; had inferior intelligence because they were little more than monkeys; using the Bible treatise of them being choppers of wood and drawers of water. It was expedient for the white people to adhere to that biblical treatise. They took every opportunity to put black people down.

Most behaviour is a "learnt behaviour". Therefore, the child of these households had the opportunity for racialism or compassion. The choice was theirs.

I saw many who knew that racialism was a terrible thing, but they seldom said or did anything that would rock the boat within the household or the Apartheid system. They would keep the peace and say nothing. They were apathetic, too fearful to push an issue. This inauthentic attitude was one based of the fear of ridicule and segregation from their peers. They preferred to go with the flow as opposed to saying their true feelings.

There were many white people though, who were authentic, and had deep compassion for black people, irrespective of the ridicule of the government of the time.

You have to unlearn what you have learnt in terms of what society expects of you. Of course, you orchestrate your own smallness so you conform in the same way as your peers do. Fitting in is more important. Therefore, there is an anomaly in life, we want to fit in but we are unhappy doing so because the need to be authentic is a deep-seated thing. It has been said that it takes a long time to become yourself. Find out what you want to do, work out how to do it, and then get going on it. Often, to find ourselves, we become small. It is only when we stretch ourselves do we get to know who we really are, and what we can do, what we are capable of. Being inauthentic does not allow for this expansion of the self. It takes courage, and the work you have to do on the inside is greater than on the outside. Life is lived to be enjoyed but it cannot be enjoyed if we are not being our authentic selves.

Being authentic, will offer you friends who love you for who you are, not for the funny jokes you tell or the size of your bank balance. An unauthentic person is not likely to have many friends at their funeral – an authentic person will.

A boy named You loved painting. He wanted to become an artist. His father wanted him to do an apprenticeship. You wanted to paint portraiture, thinking there was joy in representing a face to a life lived. You was also attracted to Buddhism as he felt their philosophies suited him, but his girlfriend wanted him to be a Christian.

You never became a painter, did an apprenticeship to become a mechanic, and married the girl and followed her religion. No wonder he became depressed at the age of thirty.

What is normal? Society as a whole would say, 'Everyone to be like everyone'. Do not be afraid to be called a deviate if you don't want be like everyone. You can have everyone type of jobs; such as lawyers, politicians, accountants or dressmakers, and still be authentic, providing you know who you are, and it fits well with you – whilst understanding the trade-offs.

As you can see, being authentic is not always easy, but as I started this section, you cannot be happy if you are not authenticated, so we are stuck, and back to the trade-offs. Every day we get the opportunity to accept the authentic route, or the easier route. The easier route would normally seem sour to our honest-self. Sadly though, we have been conditioned to become immune to the smell of it, and with our tail tucked between our legs, we head down the easier route. Sometimes the authentic route is simply too risky or too hard.

We also skirt away from authenticity because of our partners. The girlfriend who becomes a wife says to the would-be painter, 'No, you are not going to reduce our income because you want to paint... If you are to marry me you must be a Christian.' The spouse of the doctor, dentist or lawyer as spoken about says, 'We need the money so we can live in that nice upmarket suburb where my brother lives.'

Because marriage is a partnership, we often make ourselves small, and that is not a bad thing. That is the way of life, and always has been. Know though, the trade-off. Do not fool yourself.

> I drink wine. Red wine is my favourite. I have heard several stories of so-called "wine connoisseurs" who have an empty wine bottle with a top-class label on it. They buy a mid-priced wine and pour the contents into the empty bottle with the upmarket label. They try to pass this off to their friends and associates as the more expensive wine.
>
> Not very authentic behaviour.

Being authentic is a life-long journey. You do not wake up today and say I am going to be authentic and expect it to happen. It is the very essence of our journey. The search for authenticity starts when we are toddlers and young children, where we sing, dress up, make things – this is the start, and a healthy start. Sadly, through life, our peers, parents and authoritive figures knock it out of us. We are scared to show our true selves and wear a mask, and so put on a persona.

Let me give you an example. I was about fourteen when I was to go to my first dance. I was both excited and nervous. I had never danced, but I did not think that mattered much as all you had to do was to jump around and have fun to the music. It was arranged that I meet three girls from my class at school. Anyway, we arrive and the four of us started to dance. My jumping and exuberance was too much for them, and they giggled, and jointly said, 'What on Earth are you doing… is that how you dance?' The giggling only stopped when I stopped. I was devastated, and for many years was afraid to dance. What should have been an energising expression of freedom became a nightmare. You know how I danced from then on? I carefully watched the others and did my best to emulate them, which curtailed natural exuberance.

The above event is such a good analogy for life; so often we trade the energising expression for what others are doing, or what we expect others to want from us. When things like this happen, it is like a switch is flipped in our minds, from freedom, to conforming… conforming to what the rest of the bunch are doing… fit in or fail. It is then that your "small-self" covers your true-self. Even companies have the crude saying FIFO, "Fit in or Fuck off", as they do not want unique people.

The authentic self is a true expression of your soul. The small-self is a mere shadow. When you allow the authentic expression of your soul to be, that is when you are at your most powerful. We are born to live with this power, this expression of our true selves. The ramifications of living with your true self are great, as you will be free of self-judgement, free of self-hatred.

Road rage is a common condition in this time of much hustle and bustle. The same with queue rage, a term I only recently heard.

I think that it is not the authentic self that is in either road or queue rage. What do you think?

For me to once again be a "free dancer", I had to say, 'Screw them,' and do it as I saw fit, but by doing so, I became vulnerable. So being authentic means a willingness to be vulnerable, or authenticity and potential vulnerability go hand in hand. However, what is the alternative – we all know the story of where the ugly duckling becomes a swan. Well, the ugly duckling could have, for all its life, thought of itself as an ugly duckling. What good is that? Where is the power in that? There is none, we only find our power in our expressed individuality.

Another story about myself; I am dyslexic. If you do not know the term please look it up as it is important to know what it means. Not only dyslexic, but badly so. I had to leave school at an early age because of it. In my school days of five decades ago, they knew nothing of this condition, and we dyslexics (of which one child in ten is dyslexic too a degree) were treated as stupid, as dunces, as a waste of the teacher's effort, as a disruption in the classroom, and usually consigned to the back of the classroom, where the teacher could ignore us. Once I was told to stand in the corner of the room, facing the corner, "because I was stupid". Therefore, I left school virtually illiterate, and became the bricklayer that I mentioned above.

As you read this, you think to yourself, *hang on, you are a writer, you have written this book… and many other books, in fact writing and knowledge is your entire life. So how can you be dyslexic and do this work?* The answer is because I found my authenticity through writing, through writing down my self-discovery. I am still dyslexic. I will always be dyslexic, but lucky enough I had the determination and foresight to write anyway, even with little writing ability. I must add that computers, replete with spell checkers and grammar police help smooth the way. If it was left to my hand writing, I would have been left for dead in the commercial jungle, like an old animal is left behind by the migrating herd.

Besides, if Beethoven could compose some of his best music whilst being deaf, surely I could help find my authenticity through writing? After all, it is the message that is important, not the appearance or delivery. When I started to write and find my authenticity, I started to find my core. I was not afraid to ask questions about myself. I did, thousands of them. I did not like all the answers, but I made sure I listened… that it was me listening. I learnt that it is only me that can define me. No one else, all the rest is noise. Sadly, most listen to the noise, are directed by the noise, and not bold enough to ignore the noise.

I remember a time when I submitted a piece of writing to a "so called" friend of mine who had been a writer for about thirty years. She scoffed at my work, 'What makes you think you can write on that topic' she asked. I ignored her, and continued with my dream to write.

Sometimes we have to use our authenticity with circumspect, for its expression could damage or hurt another. There is philosophy, that sometimes we do the wrong thing for the right reasons. Let me explain this doing the wrong thing for the right reasons. You may take a job that you hate, that seems menial. This would seem to be the wrong job, seemingly, the wrong thing. However, from the money you save you can afford to study so as to move on to the right thing. So sometimes we do the wrong thing, by not being authentic, but for the right reason, where perhaps your authenticity could be hurt or embarrassed. I know a girl, who by her own terms is "brutally honest", irrespective of how much it may hurt the other person. She would go on to say that this is being authentic. In that instance you have to weigh up the pros and cons and come out with what is right for you, what your gut says. One or two incidences of not being authentic will not make you an inauthentic person, but it may make you a nicer person. Many authentic episodes will make you an authentic person – remember, authenticity is a learnt behaviour. Being doggedly authentic at someone else's expense is not always a nice thing to do.

The point is, that being authentic is always a choice, a daily choice, as is positivity, or morality over immorality, being rational or irrational, happy or unhappy. Making excuses is debilitating…. This is about you, and you being happy.

The authentic person is aware of their vulnerabilities but does not stop them from acting in the most appropriate way. Your life is a demonstration of all the facets of the self and the authenticity you employ. In addition, following from this is the saying *that imitation is the best form of compliment*. I add, as long as they are imitating you and not you imitating them.

Meet You. She was invited to her friend's house to stay over for the weekend. When she left, she took some of her friend's fashion magazines without asking

On one hand, she acted as if the friend was her best friend. On the other, she treated her badly by stealing from her.
One aspect was pretending to be authentic, but her behaviour was inauthentic.

When you let go of the false belief that you are lacking or inadequate, in that moment, you arouse your potential. Who you are today results from your beliefs, thoughts and ideas of the world. Unless you challenge how things stand, you remain pulled by your desires and urges. We need only to look at mainstream culture to see how it seduces us into a false way of life. We are drawn into a fictitious existence at the expense of our sanity and hard-earned dollars. There is a better way, the progression of your authenticity of becoming who you were encoded to be.

To be yourself in a world that is constantly trying to make you something else is the greatest accomplishment. If you do not know who you truly are, you will never know what you really want. Or worse, others opinions of you does not change who you are or your potential.

For twenty years I have pondered this question on what it means to be authentic, and as you have read from the above, it is not easy. It is harder though, to live the inauthentic life, and I have a theory on this. Remember, I am not a doctor so these are only my thoughts, but the thoughts suggest that there are more inauthentic people with addictions than those who are authentic. I believe that there are more people who suffer all the various forms of depression who live an inauthentic life, than those who live an authentic life. Anger is another symptom of an inauthentic way of being, as is the pessimist, and the lethargic person. However, the biggest reason is that it is impossible to be a fully happy person if you are inauthentic more times than you are authentic.

What I have learnt over those many years is that authenticity is part of your birthright. The same as you have the right to as much air to breath or water to drink as you need. Your authentic self is there, but covered and hidden. You need to find what you have within... and that ladies and gentleman, is the source of the searching, the driving search, the cause of dissatisfaction. Many do not find it, and consequently have disruptive lives, lives without flow. Some find a bit of it but are too afraid to buck the system and so accept too many trade-offs to go against the grain, or stand out in the crowd. Then, there are a few who find it and understand its power and beauty. These few use it to the fullest, and it is these few who have the most empowered lives. Lives of great achievement and happiness. These are the people who when on their deathbeds will have a smile on their lips, knowing that they lived life to the fullest, and had a life of value. By doing so, they probably add value to the lives of others.

This story like most of the others, is true. The You in this story was born a dwarf. For her first eight years of life, it never occurred to her that she was different. Then she learnt, because; most people she came across told her, or stared, or laughed, or were embarrassed and pretended she was not there.

For the next eight years, she was confused as to why she was different, and why it was harder to make friends. However, as she become an adult she accepted her dwarfism, and so she should.

Her mother though, did not. You was quite happy and had friends. She had a good job as a secretary in a smallish company.

You was around nineteen, still living at home, when her mother told her about a new medical procedure that dwarfs were having. This entailed a surgeon operating and placing, either a titanium or bone insert into the femur of both legs. This was normally around 100mm long.

When the mother tried to encourage You to have the insert done, You flatly refused. The mother was adamant (clearly, she wanted what she thought would be a "normal" daughter). The exchange got heated, until, in her power of her authenticity You shouted, 'By having these inserts done, all that you will do is to make me a tall dwarf'.

You did not have the operation.

Based on Andrew Solomon's best selling book
Far from the tree

There are some of those, who realise in their authenticity that they do not want to blaze the trails of life but still live authentically, but quietly authentically, as that is who they are meant to be. They are not encoded to blaze trails. They are still empowered, and therefore living quietly is good. They still live their lives with confidence and joy, but on the quieter spectrum. They retain strong views, their views that come from within, not those taken from the general public, not from the media feed rubbish, and so they quietly express these.

So where is our authenticity situated in our mind or body that we have to search for? I cannot rightly tell, but I suspect it is in the same place where our intuition resides, of which most of humanity believes in. I think this must also be the same place as where our creativity sits. Creativity is another aspect of birthright that we all have but must find and develop as authenticity and creativity are bed-mates.

When you do find your authenticity, at first you are likely to use it fleetingly, like an electric current, not trusting it, nor knowing its power or value. That is OK. You start off slowly, and over the years you learn to use it wisely, to call on it on a daily basis to take you to a life of expansion and gratification. Yours is their waiting for you, right now, so make a start, take a stance, and look within, understand who you are (really), and start to express your power through expressing your authenticity.

Before we can utilise our authenticity, we must understand that first we, as humans, must meet our most basic fundamental requirements of the body. These are required for survival, such as: breathing, food, water, sleep, sex, homeostasis, and excretion. Once these needs are met, our next level of physiological needs are in support and attainment of safety and security for the body. These include personal security, family security, continuity of health and wellbeing due to illness or accidents. These needs are perceived to be the base fundamental requirements for the existence and continuity of the body.

However, it is usually these very needs that tend to bury our authenticity. It is through recognising and claiming your authenticity where you achieve Self Actualisation. It is the highest inner calling of that individual's inner need being realised. It is the completion of an individual's true potential. You have listened to that persistent and compelling voice, where, at last you are paying attention. Now, with your identity discovered, the world is at your feet. Now, because of the recognition of your authentic self, all the given abilities of the universe are yours to use, your imagination, wisdom, creativity, and genius are all employed, as you would employ a hammer to drive in a nail or a screw driver to insert a screw.

At the level of our conscious interaction with the world, our behaviour is underpinned by our unconscious beliefs. These beliefs are our image of who we are or what image we portray that is best suited to a particular situation. This image is a self-creation or construct that forms an image of the self that we play out to represent a certain role. An image may be a daughter to her parents or a mother to her children or a wife to the husband, etc. These are roles that are holistic personas with particular attributes, personalities and characters. The images that are created may only have small differences between each, or an almost completely different character mode, depending on which role is played out. For example, a person can be ruthless and dictatorial as the head of an organisation but gentle and tender to his children. Because of our unconscious changing of masks, we are often unaware that we carry these different images in our lives.

You was the Dispatch manager in this small company. Under him was a smart kid, just out of school with lots of ideas. After about six months the youngster knocked on You's door and said he had an idea which could speed up the loading of the trucks, and therefore streamline the dispatch operation.

You sat stunned whilst he heard the idea but kept his face bland. When the young man had finished, You gave a desultory laugh, stood up to indicate that the interview was over, and said, 'I'm glad you are thinking about our dispatch, but that idea would never work here.' He then indicated that the young man go back to his duties.

You let the idea rest for two months, then went and knocked on the door of the owner of the business and told him that he has an idea to streamline dispatch.

At the end of the discussion, the owner was excited, slapped You on the back as he congratulated him for his great idea on behalf of the company. The owner even suggested that You's annual bonus could be bigger this year.

> You left the office, pleased, but there was a feeling of guilt in the pit of his stomach. The feeling was his authentic self trying to be heard, to be expressed. However, You's need of recognition of the job well done, and also the extra bonus, was stronger than the need for authenticity, and so he never owner up.

Most people relate to themselves through their vocation. Are you really an accountant or dressmaker? Are you not human with your own unique personality? Remember, at the start of this chapter on authenticity, you read the "Who am I".

"Only the truth of who you are, if realized, will set you free," said Eckhart Tolle; surely, this is the authentic self? Beneath the façade that you have taken on, the authentic self must emerge to reveal the core self – the spiritual part of your nature.

Equally, we recognise inauthenticity in others by labelling them as "fake". We are less likely to detect the same flaws in ourselves.

The American mythologist Joseph Campbell wrote, *"The privilege of a lifetime is being who you are".* The authentic self is concealed beneath the formed image of the ego.

In the story that I wrote about Roger, is it fairly easy to identify the authentic self from the egoist self, from the fear self.

I wrote the following some years ago, and think it is appropriate here. Do you live as a verb or a noun?

For an authentic life, I like the verb or noun concept to describe our approach to life. A verb life is one of doing, whereas the noun life is of acceptance and static. An adverb in this concept is a life of seeking and experiencing.

Most people do live a verb life but for only short periods before slipping back into being a noun. Noun people like rules and safety but it is the verb aspect of life that gives meaning.

If you want to explore all the boundaries of life, and to break through the "glass ceiling" to be authentic, then be a verb person. A verb life is a well-lived life. I will take the verb life any time as the verb life is exhilarating and dynamic. It is animated and experiential, which is what life should really be about – this is the authentic way.

Authenticity; reflected in the palms of your hand. *The palms of my hands chart my life of events – of joy and sadness, success, failure, loves, hopes, hurts and fears. Resembling spider-webbed lines, with lumps and striations, blemishes, like a parched river pan – a biography of fornications and drunken exploits, of friends, compassion, children raised, of love, sweet romances, brutality, brawls, tranquillity, regrets, arguments, anger, attitudes and addictions, optimism and happiness and death – all are represented.*

Although my palms are cluttered and packed like an over-stocked graveyard, I revel in thoughts of lines to come and thrill in the prospect of new etchings. After all, an unblemished palm would indeed reveal a boring life.

The elusive more
They strive to gain, and strive for more
 the mind in pain, never to be poor
A time to go, the target set,
 a time to go, the target met
Yet more is craved
 pockets bulge
 health not saved
 and family sold
Positions call to satisfy lust
 no time to rest
 for more or bust
The years go by in just a flash
 a promotion is nigh
 as is the cash
Possession of joy
 not in your life
 tis just a ploy
 not worth the hype
The time has gone
 the death bed near
 to evaluate the passage
 to know what's dear
Like a knife the realisation struck
 that the joy of life is not another buck.

Being authentic means that you have consciously made choices on a moral code and integrity. A moral code and ethics is a path to authenticity. A moral code reflects your respect for humanity, your business associates and your family. In addition, a well-structured moral code mirrors your opinion of yourself. How can one really respect oneself if they have bad morals? They can't. Look at the lawyers' and the politicians' behaviours in the stories above, deep down, there must be a real feeling of dis-connect.

John Lovell wrote; *Living in "Integrity" is living by our own unique set of values and beliefs. When we live by someone else's values, we live in a state of internal conflict, a state of mental unease. This unease is the mind's moral compass trying to steer us back to our inner core that reflects our true beliefs.*

Meet the You Bus Company. I rode in one of their buses recently when travelling overseas. The marketing material on their website stated clearly, that each passenger has an on-board entertainment system. However, when I took my seat, there was no such thing. That is inauthentic advertising, the type that too many companies offer. In fact, so bad is most advertising, it is hard to believe any claims they make.

Well-developed ethics are a guiding light. It takes the uncertainty out of questionable decision-making and negates the likelihood of guilt. You are also likely to attract people into your life with a similar code of ethics as your own, so it makes sense to develop a meaningful code.

This is a big subject, one that requires total honesty and dedication, a subject that needs heart-rending assessment and continued application, and so your moral code could take years to become ingrained, as does your authenticity.

The Concise Oxford Dictionary on Morals defines morality/morals as: A concern with character or disposition, with the distinction between right and wrong. To select a strong morality and live by it reflects the authenticity that you place on your life.

If we are to be authentic in character there can be no grey areas. In order to eliminate the grey areas, we have to understand what the white and the black areas are. Those who have a deep sense of what is right and what is wrong are a lantern to guide others by.

When you define your moral code, look closely at issues of conformity. Do not decide what is white or black because culture suggests so. Know your own mind by setting your own standards. I love this saying from Eric Hoffer, "When people are free to do as they please, they usually imitate each other". Sadly, it is too true. Alternatively, "When all think alike, no one is thinking very much" (I don't know who said this). And my favourite, "Whoso would be a man must be a non-conformist", Ralph Waldo Emerson in his essay *Self-Reliance*.

I recently had a potential client. I gave him a quote to help him with his manuscript . This You said that the quote was fair and that he would give me the business, and so I allocated the time.

However, as I did not hear from him, I emailed him to see if he was soon to be ready with his work. His reply, when confronted, said that he had found a better price and so had given the work to another company.

There is nothing wrong with going for the best price, but for goodness sake be authentic, be honest, and tell the truth. Have the courage of your convictions.

Living in "Integrity" is living by our own unique set of values and beliefs. When we step away from being honest, we experience unease, uncertainty, regret and disquiet. However, when we are being true to ourselves and living to own beliefs, we are at peace, content, untroubled, relaxed and calm. Whereas, stepping out of integrity is similar to being in fear, where the mind is constantly juggling inner conflict. Stepping out of integrity is a stain on our authenticity.

Now meet You, a student at a university. He was doing a project but was running out of time. No problem, he went to the Internet, found the information, cut and pasted what he wanted, excluding the name of the people whose research it was. He then passed the work off as his own work.

There are so many students doing this that educational departments world wide employ software that they use to track plagiarism. Just too many people who are not in their integrity, wanting the pass mark at the expense of their authenticity. Such a shame.

Though life is short, it can be a long time to live in regret. Step upon a path to find your authenticity and you find your happiness. Live in "Integrity" and you will find your contentment and be at peace. Live by your values and beliefs and your life will demonstrate your purpose. Fulfill your purpose and you will find your inner delight, your joy and bliss. Your mind has been talking to you all these years, to stay true to you and say No to these others who would want you to live by their injected beliefs. In this way, you are saying Yes to yourself to follow your own path to inner peace and happiness.

This You that you are about to read about is forty-seven years old. His hair would be grey, except he dyes it. Botox reduces the wrinkles. He consumes buckets of protein weight gaining supplements and does weights to give muscles younger than his years. He wears the clothes of someone half his age. His car, of course, is red, and the music blares out, "Doof... doof... doof". The vibration shakes windows pains as he passes.

Do you think that he is being authentic?

Then this You, met a woman (oh, he was already married, but he did not care about his wife), who, he at first thought was lovely. He was attracted by her prominent breasts and slim stomach. Once enticing her into bed, he found that she had tiny breasts, once the massively padded bra was removed. Then when the girdles (two of) were removed, her stomach was fat (some fifteen years ago, she had a tummy tuck, but the results were even worse now, and she could not afford another). The beautiful long dark hair came off, as it was a wig, so did the false nails and eyelashes. Over the night of much exertion and perspiration, the layers of make-up wore off and her face was much more wrinkled than he first thought, and even a different colour. When they fell asleep, out came her teeth!

In their lovemaking, he could not have an orgasm, as all the rubbish that he was feeding his body had a negative effect on his lower "pipeworks". As she orgasmed, he pretended that he did as well, with much moaning, groaning, and shuddering (he had well practiced this over the years with other unsuspecting ladies), until collapsing on her.

He learnt, with dismay, that she was not at all as authentic as she made out to be. She in turn learnt the same.

Now, let me say here, before I am called a sexist, I have nothing against; small breasts, wigs, false eyelashes or fingernails. Nor am I against chubby tummies or thick makeup, after all, it is up to the individual, is it not? Or for men to dye their hair, build muscle, or the rest of that. However, what I am against is pretending to be one thing, when in fact they are another, all in an effort to fool.

So here we are with these two inauthentic people. Yes, he has a wife, and the girlfriend may also have a partner, but we do not know this. So, do two wrongs make a right? No, they do not. Do two inauthentic people make an authentic couple – not a hope in hell.

These people are fake!

IN SUMMARY OF BEING AUTHENTIC

Looking for hope outside of yourself is like looking for apples from a rock.

Authenticity and self-esteem are joined at the hip.

A joyful life is dependent on being authentic.

Being authentic means accepting your physical attributes, such as being too short or too tall, too fat or too thin, curly or straight hair....

Some are blessed with greater intelligence than others, and if you have not been blessed with high intelligence, who cares, as you have been blessed with enough to have a joyous life. After all, intelligence on its own does not guarantee anything for sure.

This next story could be about a thousand, or a million, or hundred million You's out there. Could be boy You's or girl You's. However, let us call this one a girl.

You, the girl, was married to with a man who she had stopped loving many years before. Actually, she was married to the inauthentic man in the last story – the man who tried to look and act years younger than his authentic self.

She stopped loving him because as the years passed, she could see that there was less and less of the real man, and more and more of the fake.

She was authentic, and wanted to live an authentic life, and find another partner, who was equally authentic. She was authentic enough to leave him.

You have read the above chapter on being authentic. You may ask how does Pat profess to know all of these things about authenticity? Or are they really true? This is a good question and the answer took me many years, in fact a lifetime to understand. You see, I lived an inauthentic life for a good part of my life. My self-esteem was so low, I did not want to be me, I wanted to be almost anyone other than myself. When I was young, many rotten things happened in my life, in fact so bad that many of my friends who know of these things have wondered how I have remained sane. However, I'll not tell you what those things were, you will have to read some of my other books. Know though, that in my search for survival I adopted inauthentic behaviours, and these behaviours became my way of being. Because of this inauthentic way, I had a life that did not work, there was no flow, a difficult and dysfunctional life – in fact, the life of a loser. I lived my "small self" and not my authentic birthright "big self".

For many years, I floundered in this life, like fighting to get out of a thick fog. At first, I did not know that there was another way of living. However, the most wonderful thing happened... I heard that voice that called, the one that I started this authenticity section with, and that was the searching...

My life incrementally improved with each step towards the authenticity that I took on. I have a good life now, a very good life. Oh yes, it has its ups and downs as all life does, but it is one that I can now look back on and be proud of and happy about.

These stories have explained many aspects and behaviours around authenticity. The character's called You, could be you because the scenarios could fit your life.

If you cannot identify your inadequacies, your fears or your limiting beliefs, life will push you around. It is required of you to take responsibility and the initiative.

From the stories of this section, you should now know that being authentic is based on choice. The choice is being real to yourself or collapsing to some hidden fear that may result if one tried to be authentic. Being authentic is standing up and announcing that you are unashamedly yourself – for better or worse, irrespective of the outcome, irrespective of friends disappearing from your life, irrespective of how much pressure others place on you.

I repeat my contention; that happiness and authenticity go hand in hand. An inauthentic person cannot be a happy person – how can they be when there is the feeling that things are not as they should be?

Questions

- How would you rate your level of authenticity?
- Where and when do you not display authenticity?
- How has that affected your life?
- Why have you held on to these behaviours?
- What do you want to do to correct these behaviours?

From the Buddha: **"Though he should conquer a thousand men in the battlefield a thousand times, yet he, indeed, who would conquer himself is the noblest."**

Authenticity is a collection of choices that we have to make every day. It's about the choice to show up and be real. The choice to be honest. The choice to let our true selves be seen. – Brené Brown

Henry David Thoreau said; **most people live lives of quiet desperation and go to the grave with their song within them.**

THE SIXTH SEED

The Weight of Fear, or the daily drinking from the cup of happiness

He was a simple farmer, and in that part of China he carried his produce to market on a bamboo pole – a basket at each end. His hat was conical and kept the heat and sun off his head. Yet, his dry face was wrinkled and pinched beyond his age. A cigarette dangled from his mouth, his eyes squinted from the smoke.

In his youth, he was tall and straight, and seemed to have no cares to weigh him down. Life though is a funny thing, and in seventh century China, there was much to worry about, and so his resolve diminished, and like water erodes rock, his health wore out. It is no different today.

When he was seventeen his father died. Being the only boy, the responsibility of the land was on his shoulders. Like the two heavy baskets on his poll, this responsibility weighed him down. Then there was Bai, the youngest daughter of the farmer next door, whom he fell in love with, and she with him. Bai means purity, and that is how he saw her, a girl of purity. It was not long before they married. As wonderful as it was, this increased his responsibility, as hers was an extra mouth to feed.

Soon, they were blessed with a beautiful baby girl. He loved his daughter but worried that as she grew, she would be an additional burden on the family. And so, like another stone in a bucket, more weight was placed on his shoulders.

Now at twenty-seven years of age, he was no longer straight and tall, but slightly bent and bowed, such was the weight on his shoulders. Every day he woke up before the sun and trudged to the fields to toil, not returning until the sun had disappeared. *What I do is not enough* was his constant thought.

Joy of joys, a little boy came into the family, and again, one more stone of worry was placed on his shoulder. That year was a bad year, as the rains did not come. The crop, which was only subsistence at the best of times, was meagre and so he was worried as to how he was going to feed his family. Setting off to market, he was more bent with the weight of his fear, more so than from the weight of the produce.

His life continued, fear piling upon fear.... one fearful day followed the next. It could have been different. He could have looked life directly in the face, and even with its hardships, looked at the good, and not focus on the difficult. Of course, he could not control the rains, but he could control how he thought when the rains did not come. He could also have been grateful when they did come. When fearful, life beats you, and he was beaten. His son was seventeen when he died.

The father's gloomy nature had been handed down to him, like one hands down a farm implement. He in turn passed the gloom to his son, and so it went on. There was however, a son many generations later, who, even though was born in the most difficult of times, refused to let life beat him. He realised early that life could be fashioned – that if left to run its own way, it will surely falter and withhold on what it can offer. He had stumbled on the idea of drinking a cup of happiness every day, and so he did.

When he went into the fields each morning, it was the same time in the morning as all the previous generations but he did not trudge, he had a spring to his step. Moreover, in lean years, he did not bemoan his lot; rather, he was grateful for what he had, as it was always enough. Over the years, because of his bright nature, the sun seemed to support him by shining more. Often the rain was on his lands, but not those of his neighbours, who were still drinking from the cup of gloom. Never wealthy, because the times were too forbidding, but his attitude towards a rewarding life blessed him with a rewarding life.

THE SEVENTH SEED

Journey to Self

It seemed that I was born into darkness, where images could just be discerned. Roots of trees as thick as a man's body lay strewn above the ground – slumbering serpents supporting trunks of massive height and girth. Thick humus carpeted the ground, debris from the solid canopy that hid the sky far above. It was soft to walk on, damp and mildewy. The grotto of my mind was a cold and a thriving place for all manner of creepy-crawly things, things that slithered in the near dark. Leaves constantly rustled as some creature scurried away from a predator or was the predator. Things growled and hissed as fights were often heard, while combatants struggled for survival.

In this cauldron of my early life, fear clutched at my gut and was a constant companion. Somehow, some way, I knew that to stay in this claustrophobic dungeon of my mind made me vulnerable. I had endured this tomb of mind from childhood to adulthood – but a sense niggled at my mind, pushing me to move and seek something better. I did not know where this sense came from, but I felt it could be trusted. Therefore, I determined to leave the relative security of the known for the unknown and set off to find myself.

At first, my progress was slow, and for a time it seemed to get darker, which scared me more. Nevertheless, as I grew and developed I learnt that to move from one mind space to another can incur darkness, as our fear takes over. I continued the journey, stumbling on, falling over life's impediments and overcoming difficulties. For this journey to self, I was alone. I had to be, as no one could share it with me. Nor did I have any idea of the direction to take – how could I? I did not know the destination, and if I did, how could I know if I had made it? Never having faced myself before, it felt awkward, like wearing a coat backwards.

It was difficult cutting through the thick bush that clung to me, like a thousand silent arms – like beggars, reaching out, restraining, clutching, all the time demanding. The terrain was always uphill so my and legs were exhausted from the pushing and pulling as I struggled higher and higher. At times, I would slip and plummet to a point where I had been some time before. I would lie there, feeling sorry for myself and wonder what lesson I was supposed to learn. It crossed my mind many times to give up as the journey was too arduous. Nevertheless, I struggled on.

After a while, I started to learn the ways of my inner realm. It became easier. I developed an assurance that things would keep improving and so I was able to cover more ground. The once formidable dark and dank depths of my inner self did not seem so hostile. It was the same, yet different. What had changed? I had, and, as if to support my evolution, I was given beams of light that radiated through the bush, showing the way. It illuminated the jungle of my mind, giving beauty and form to its interior. However, there was more journeying to be done, and so onwards and upwards I clambered.

Once, I came face to face with glowing eyes, menacing from a long dark shape. It snarled and spat, while its breath soured my nostrils. Had this creature confronted me in the past it would have devoured me but I held my nerve and it crawled away.

Although it seemed to be years that I had been on this journey, I sensed that I was making progress as the darkness gradually gave away to light. High above, through the trees, I could see blue. I could not understand what this was but felt it to be friendly. Continuing, somehow I knew that my direction was correct and that each step took me assuredly to a better place.

Suddenly, without warning, I was out of the jungle and on a stone ledge that jutted over the valley. The sun nurtured – The open space liberating.

I looked over the jungle that had previously owned me, and could see the rivers that I had forded, and the scrub that had cut my hands. At the time, I could not see any logic or plan to it, but now it was all so obvious and perfect. From my position of elevation, the wilds were beautiful. Yet to reach this point I had been obliged to travel through those wilds and endure the experience.

I'm now much stronger, forged in the knowledge of who I am, but I also know that the journey to self is never complete, as there will be new internal frontiers to conquer. For now though, I revel in the joy of knowing that I have won the victory of the journey to self.

THE EIGTHTH SEED

Luck and Positive Thinking

Driving the other day, listening to the radio, the talkback was about luck, and whether it exists. There were many views on this, including when you are prepared (as after many years of dedicated training) then luck is more likely to find you. Some simply said luck does not exist, and there were people, who, with a scientific mind-set, thought all things are chance based and ultimately a mathematical calculation. There were people who said they were lucky, and those who were not.

My take on luck is that it is linked to positivity. I categorically know that when I live with a positive mindset, things work better. Conversely, when negative, things invariably go pear-shaped. Therefore, luck is really a factor of being positive, and bad luck one of negativity.

Those who called in and said they were lucky, seemed luckier, and more uplifted than those who said they had bad luck, and seemed dogged with bad luck. So convinced of their bad luck, they strove to convince us listeners of all the unlucky things that happened to them. Their lists were long. There were even some who were convinced that bad things come in threes, and waited for bad luck two and three to arrive, with great expectation.

Irrespective, your belief in luck or no luck, will happen according to the positivity you hold.

In addition, did you hear the joke about the man, who on his death bed, said, 'Darling, you have been with me through thick and thin. You were with me when I had that car accident. Moreover, you supported me when I was fired from my job. And… remember, when I lost the winning lottery ticket? And now that I am dying from this unknown disease…" He paused, struggling with the effort of speech, and in a last breathless whisper, crooned, 'I have come to the conclusion that you bring me bad luck!'

THE NINETH SEED

From Fear to Love

Roger, newly born, is without blemish. No fear disturbs him, nor does guilt or hate. His slate is clean, with his main focus on food, warmth and being clean. When these are met and he is not asleep, he has an inquisitive mind and wants to take in all he can.

Also emerging in Roger are two energies. Sometimes these seem to oppose each other. One is soft and gentle and often resides in the background. The other is loud, aggressive and wants prominence. The first is called Soul, and the second, Ego.

The influence of Soul and Ego is impressed upon Roger's mind. The mind is passive in as much as it pretty much does as it is bid by Ego. Nevertheless, the mind does have a function, and that is to retain memory, offering learning and reasoning power, and supports the actions of the body. The mind is a bit like an old-fashioned switchboard, which directs all incoming communication to connect and redirected to where it needs to go, and as such, helps to build the personality. The mind though, is passive and easily influenced.

As a baby, the initial influence on Roger is not all that marked, and so the child is happy and without issues.

Ego starts his 'childcare' work early to influence the child.

Ego is ruthless and selfish in its desire to survive and will do anything to gain and retain control of Roger's mind. Its entire performance is to this end. It does this in many ways, such as trying to move the mind from *love to fear*, because when within fear, rationality goes haywire... when in fear, Ego has complete control. Another way Ego divides and rules is through convincing the mind that it is not good enough, that it has inadequacies and that things will always turn out badly, and so Roger, via the mind, has self-esteem issues. Ego is also good at having to justify himself to make himself look better. It does this so well that often Roger gets in a huff to express his self-perceived superiority in a discussion or an argument. When Roger was older, often he would have to be right and would say or do almost anything to prove that to the other person.

Soul, on the other hand, would try to teach the belief that he does not have to be right every time, and that there are times when it really does not matter at all. Ego is pushy and at the forefront, and because Soul is gentler, it comfortably waits in the background. Of course, it is Ego that has its way, ensuring Roger's mind feels that it must be right... and damn it, it will be right, irrespective of the consequences!

At the age of four, Roger is expressing his personality, which is a combination of his experiences, and the way that he remembers these experiences that he has had, plus the results of Ego and Soul's influence. So Roger is a mixture of Ego and Soul, where one minute he is loving and gentle, stroking the cat, and in another, he is shouting for more ice cream.

At ten, the influence on Roger is greater. His knowledge had increased, and he is seemingly more confident with the way that he is growing into the world. Nevertheless, underneath, there are self-esteem issues that he has difficulty coping with. Ego has done a strong job of instilling fear to make Roger feel uncertain in many aspects of his life, such as playing soccer or even being nice to his sister because he has allowed himself to be jealous of her, thinking that she is more loved by their parents than he is.

It was at this age that Soul said to Ego, 'You know, as we are both in this body of Roger's, perhaps we should work together to make Roger a happier person – are you willing to work together?'

'Why would I want to work with you? 'As far as I'm concerned you can go to Hell. Like this human, I have been given free will and I choose to do exactly as I please. You have no control or influence over me….'

Soul replied, 'You may think that now, but you know that I have infinitely more power than you and that my power comes from a greater connection. You know that my power has come from the connection that created everything, and that when this body of Roger's terminates, I will be reabsorbed back into that power. Your time here is limited.'

'Listen to that rubbish. I have control of Roger, and as he gets older, my control will be even greater. I will play him better than Mozart played the piano. I will play him at each stage of his life… and at this young age it is easy to play him. All I do is suggest to his mind that he does not have as many toys as his friend Peter and he becomes angry. Alternatively, I could suggest that his sister is given things when Roger is in another room. He listens and takes it all in.'

Soul reasoned, 'There is one big difference between you and I, and that is you are fear, where I am love. Moreover, you know that for this person to have the ultimate growth, which is his reason for being here, is to learn and understand that he must move from fear to love. And this will certainly happen and you know that it will happen.'

Roger is now a young man trying to make his way in life. He currently has a desire to have a big car and flashy clothes. In quieter moments, he knows that he cannot afford these, and sometimes can't understand why he craves them. If one could look into Roger's body at that time, Ego could be seen slouching against a wall with a smug grin on his face. Ego knew where this unreasonable desire stems from.

Although he cannot afford it, Roger goes to the bank and borrows the money. He even almost convinced himself, as he did the bank manager, as to how he will be able to pay off the car.

Also, in those quiet moments, Roger felt that something was missing. He did not know what this was but felt a strong pull in another direction. It felt like he was a leaf on a stream and that the stream was ever flowing in a specific direction. This unknown feeling kept suggesting to him that all he had to do was to let go and float away with the current and all would be right. However, Ego explicitly would not allow that to happen and so the leaf would get caught on logs and rocks and get stuck in eddies.

There were times in drunken conversations at bars and parties when people spoke about a better way, a spiritual way, one that is softer and gentler. Where fear was put aside and love embraced. In these conversations he instinctively knew this was correct. Nevertheless, none, it seemed, knew how to attain it, and of course the feeling would go when someone shouted out, 'Whose round is it?' Once again, it was Ego lurking in the background, ever vigilant to stamp out insurrection.

Soul asked Ego, 'What do you get from keeping Roger in fear?'

'Control... I get control.'

'But why do you need control, what are you scared of losing?'

There was silence from Ego.

At thirty, Roger has two children, a beautiful girl and a lovely little boy. He loves them but no longer loves their mother. It is Ego, who in the background pulls the strings to ensure that the dislike of his wife grows. It seems that they have a massive fight once a week, where doors slam, voices are raised, and insults thrown. If only I could get out of debt thinks Roger, it would not be so hard on either of us. We would not have to work as hard and perhaps we could get a nanny to help with the children. Damn it, life is just too hard.

Ego calls to Soul and says, 'Hey you… see how easy it is for me to manipulate Roger? I have said it before and I will say it again, that I have the power to do as I choose with this human.'

Soul smiles a gentle smile but says nothing.

'Cat got your tongue?' asked Ego. 'Nothing to say? You claim that you come from a superior energy, how does that energy support you and Roger when I have complete control?'

Soul, in a gentle voice said, 'It is true that you control Roger. He is fearful, in debt, and has low self-confidence. He is argumentative because you have made him of low self-worth. He and you have free will, and so he will grow or decline according to his own will. I will not interfere. But I will always be here as a soft and supportive influence, one where, as he likens in his own mind, as being a leaf on an ever flowing current moving towards a life of deeper meaning. You know that what he is referring to, as the leaf is where he moves from a state of fear to one of love. At any time in his life he can move from the fear that you effect on him, the love that is his birthright.

From fear to love is a spiritual journey offering the choices that he makes throughout his life to become the person who he should be. Offering understanding about the fear that blocks his path to inner peace and denies him his love. It opens a spiritual path, encouraging him to follow a journey that gives freedom from the tyranny of the fear that you spread.'

Ego did not bother to answer and wandered off as if he hadn't a care in the world. But Soul called out after him, 'You have kept this man small for long enough. It's time you release your grip on him.' Ego just kept walking away.

Because of his difficult situation, or perhaps to try and get some sense back into his life, Roger started to allow himself to float down the stream with the leaf. It felt good. In fact, it felt better than good – it felt natural and how it should be. To do this he aligned himself with friends who were following this path. They recommended books, and so with the guidance, and what he learned from the books, he started to get a better understanding as to how he was in fear and not love. All he had to do was to compare those friends with himself, and he could see that they had lives that flowed better, and that seemed to work in a way that gave them a satisfying life. They seemed calmer and more compassionate.

His life was hard with the debt and long hours at work, and then the coming home to his wife, who seemed to hate him. His only value were his children, so natural and unencumbered – was I ever like that he wondered?

At forty, Roger was sleeping on the couch and not in the main bedroom.

What's that noise? Whatever it was, it awoke him.

Seems to be getting closer.

There it is again, even closer.

It was a dark night and with the thick curtains, there was virtually no light.

Peering into the dark he made out a blob of grey.

'Thought you could escape me, didn't you Roger?' This was followed by a shrill laugh. 'I am always with you, you know that.'

Roger panicked, 'Who are you and what do you mean? Lucy, is that you? Is this a joke?'

Roger knew this was not his wife playing tricks on him.

The grey blob was big and close. He could hear its breath. It emitted a revolting smell. Roger pushed back into the couch to put space between him and it.

More high-pitched laughing sent shivers through him. 'No sense running Roger, you can't get away from me.'

'Who are you?'

'I represent your fears, Roger, the fears that rule you.'

'My fears, what do you mean?'

'I'm your friend, after all you would not let me live in you if you did not let me.'

This was followed by more laughing.

Roger felt he was going mad. Frantically his hands went to his ears to try to block the thoughts.

'You allowed me to come to you when you were little. We have an agreement... remember?' 'What agreement?' asked Roger.

'It's easy, you allow me to live in you and I take care of your self-esteem, and for all of these years this has worked just fine.'

Roger asked, 'How do you take care of my self-esteem?'

'I took it away so you don't have any. No self-esteem, no fuss, I am in complete control. I send you messages, just like I am doing now... messages of inadequacy, rage, resentment and childish tantrums to hide the fact that you have no self-esteem. You remained angry and full of hate. This was good and works well, especially in your case with your childish tantrums. You don't have to worry about achieving goals or silly things like challenging yourself to get ahead.'

'Rubbish, I would never allow this to happen.'

'Roger, don't talk nonsense, you know as well as I do that the deal was that you hand over your power, and up until now you have been good and meek.'

'If I have been good and meek as you say, why did you come to me now?'

'So you know you are not going to get rid of me so easily. I represent your fears and I am here to stay. Don't think just because you are reading those silly books and attending those discussions that I will leave... No, you can't get rid of me.'

Roger tried again, 'I wouldn't have let you stay in me if I knew you were there.'

'You, and just about the rest of humanity have no choice. You also know the feelings that we send as a constant reminder of my dominion.'

'What feelings?'

'Animosity, nervousness, shame, and the best is self-contempt. When you are confronted with issues that needs a decision, I send timid emotions, such as doom and gloom, the feelings that you call butterflies in your stomach, I increase your heart rate and make you sweat... you know, all the normal fear things.'

Roger burst out in frustration, 'This can't be true.'

It replied, 'Then why are you sleeping on the couch, you loser?'

Finally, it moved away.

Ego was pleased.

Soul watched with concern but let 'free-will' reign.

Roger realised that all he had heard was true. He had given his power to his fears. He could see that he had been living to his fears, not allowing his potential to come through. The thought depressed him.

It suddenly struck him that right now, in this sad state how insidious fear is. *I have these feelings and do not even notice. I need to be able to change this and be more positive – at all times.*

Ego laughed in the background, 'Loser.'

It was then that Soul said to Ego, 'In time he will wake up and you will not have a hold on him. When we embrace love, we see a mind content and in harmony with its world and the greater Universe. This mind reflects an inner journey of the self, where the mind found what we have all searched and longed for all our lives; a mind content with inner peace.'

At Roger's fiftieth birthday party, holding a glass of wine in his hand, Roger took a minute to leave the party and to go outside for reflection, trying to make sense of his life. He was just starting to get out of debt when his wife finally left him, and bitterly he thought of the 50% of their assets that went with her. His children were now grown up. They both loved him and treated him with respect. Even better, soon they both had children and so these grandchildren gave him a different perspective on life. He did not care how much time he missed, he would never sacrifice his time away from them.

Although his life was still difficult, he pursued the leaf as it pulled towards a calming influence. He was not as panicked and was calmer, and happier. Moreover, although he did not really understand it, he was moving from fear to love. Still, he had a long way to go.

Ego doubled its efforts to retain control. Recently he was able to nip in the bud an insurrection that Roger was planning, whereby he was to spend more time in quietness, listening to Soul. Ego reminded Roger of the debt that he was in, and of that payment that he had to make in two weeks'. Of course, Roger panicked and stayed longer at work to try and earn that extra commission.

Fifteen years later Roger was a happier person. He knew that the floating leaf showed the way, and since he had spent more time pursuing it, his life was much better. Behind the scenes, and unbeknownst to Roger's mind, Soul and Ego had another conversation. It was Ego who was saying, 'You, with your love may have gained ground over Roger but I still have ultimate control. My control is not as strong as it was, but I still have control. For instance, Roger is scared to trust his new girlfriend, even though it is obvious that she loves him and wants only the best for him. It is easy for me to suggest to Roger's mind... just remember what happened with Lucy... and that they are all like that... and that you will never satisfy any of them… and that they are all going to end up taking your assets, that she's only there whilst it suits her.'

Soul in its gentle voice said to Ego, 'I am with love, I am calm, I give compassion to the mind. You create the opposite, you disrupt, unsettle and create nervousness. You know that it would be in your interest to back off a bit, as the mind will be happier and the body healthier, meaning the body will live longer, and give you a longer life.'

'Fool you,' said Ego. 'Do you think I worry about the peace of mind of this person? I have one desire, and that is to be prominent in all that this person thinks and does.'

Not ruffled, Soul continued, 'I also allow the mind free will to choose who or what it listens to, and so it is up to mind if it lets you influence it. By nature, I am more powerful than you, and therefore have no fear of you, but the human does.'

'You think that I am evil…'

Soul said, 'No, you are not evil, just misguided.'

'Look here Soul, his body must have clothes, food, drink, and sleep; and be led. I do the leading him. What's wrong with that?'

'Ego, perhaps one day you will understand that when a human is at the point of love, as opposed to that of fear, that they have achieved their specific purpose for their life. This is the divine instinct, which all humans naturally respond to.'

'Who cares?' replied Ego.

'In addition, when I talk of fear, you Ego, are a classic example. Your whole purpose is to retain control because otherwise you fear that without the control you will be diminished. This is true, but you cannot see otherwise. In fact, you are more fearful than the human.'

'I am not in fear,' said Ego angrily, and quickly removed himself from this conversation.

In the last days of Roger's life, he was the happiest he has ever been. His children were with him, as well as his grandchildren, and he felt nothing but love for them. He is glad that his life is ending this way and knows that this is how it should be.

Soul interrupted Ego's worries, 'I thank you Ego for the role that you played in Roger's life. You have taught him what love is through knowing what fear is, and thereby you have inadvertently taught him to move from fear to love.

Do you remember when Roger was ten years of age, you and I had a conversation, where I said that I have the energy of a greater power than you do? You laughed at what I said. But do you not understand now that I allowed you to continue with your role of disruption and sowing fear so that the human could understand what love really was, as a result of having lived in fear? And you have seen it in this last quarter of his life where he lived mostly in love and moved from fear. So I have much to thank you for the role that you played, even if unwittingly.'

Ego was frantic, knewing that Roger's body was about to expire, and with it would be his end. Ego was afraid because it did not know what would happen to him once Roger lost consciousness as a result of death. He panicked at the thought of not having an existence – of not being able to have an influence within a life. At times, Ego wondered what the purpose of his existence was for. In fact, he had wondered this for most of his life but because he did not have an answer that satisfied his worry, he focused even harder on maintaining control within Roger's mind. He had to, he had no choice as it could only be through control that he felt he could cling to something. Now, at this late juncture of his existence he wonders if he has been foolish with that belief. He sighs and knows that he has lived an entire life and still does not have the answer. *Perhaps that soft fool Soul knows better. What if he is right? How would Roger's life have been if I did not exert such negative influences? What if I allow Roger's mind to move more from fear to love earlier?... Oh... this is idiotic. I'm just scared because I'm about to expire and I don't know what that really means.*

Roger knows he is about to go. He pities some of those other people in the aged care facility who are bitter about life. Being full of love as Roger is, he does not let this affect him, and so is to pass over with a heart that is warm with love and gratitude.

He knew that his move from fear to love, at the age of around fifty, where he had to step upon a path to find what eluded him all his life. At that time he yearned for the feeling of calm and serenity, the feeling that he felt he deserve to honour himself and step outside his self-imposed darkness, believing that he was unlovable.

Finally, he walked in the sunshine of his freedom. To truly know what it is like to feel like a free man, worthy of his own belief and love.

With him, at his bedside were his children, and his wife Helen. Almost his last words to them were, 'Our reality is a by-product of our thoughts, or more particularly, an effect created by our thoughts, where our thoughts are the cause of this effect. This conforms to the most fundamental law in nature, that is cause and effect. We can see the effects of our thoughts throughout our life, and when we change the cause, we create a different effect.

Our journey is to search for the essence of our self. To look inside our heart and find the inner passage that holds our potential, by moving from fear to love... I did this through listening within. You, my children can also listen within.'

Roger had to stop and rest a while. His family urged him to remain quiet and rest. He but he would have none of it, and in what seemed to be his last breath continued, 'The Ego is a mental construct that we self-create. We identify with this image as who we are. This image of self is a substitute image of the loving self that we are unable to wholly identify with as we live in fear. It is important that you move out of your fear and into love, and by doing so you will find ...'

It was at this moment that Roger's love merged into the greater energies, Ego became dust and was scattered in the winds.

For the umpteenth time Soul smiled at the successful conclusion of another life. It could have been easier on Roger if he followed the leaf earlier. With free will, what will be will be.

THE TENTH SEED

Noooooooooooooooo!

The child was born into a loving home

but the first word it learnt was No!

It should have been Yes.

Through repetition, No's became ingrained, like an army marching through the land subduing all in its way.

No, don't touch this, No don't do that, No, don't pull this. No, stop it now. No, that's a dangerous thing to do. No, don't eat that.

As the child grew so did her reasoning, which felt that something was not right. But the Nooooo's outweighed the reasoning, and even said Noooooooo is correct.

No, don't be that. No, you can't try that.

No. By being different, you will be different, and that is a No thing to be. A No, No.

In the child's mind the No's were building, No, No, No, No, No, No, No, No, No, No. Ten trillion Noooooooooooos, only a few Yes's, until the Noooos seemed to strangle him.

No, No, and with each new No he moved further from Yes.

With each new No was an added weight, a weight that slowly stifled the life out of him.

No, No, No, No, No, No, No, No, until Noooooooooooooooooooo, he shouted, my will is gone, it's Noooooooed out of me, my hope is gone, it's Noooooooed out of me, as is my joy.

I sleep with No. I walk with No. I think with No holding me back.

No, I can't do this…

No, I am not good enough.

No, No, No I can't win the race, or pass the exam, Nooooooooooo more, will I hear No!

Stop it… do you hear? … No more No's… ever.

I cannot be happy with a No mind, a No attitude, a No confidence,

Nooooooooooooooooooo more, will I think No, Nooooo more will No hold me back.

To you my parents I say No more No's… … and you my teachers, I only want Yes's,

Yes, to happy, Yes, to power, my innate power,

Yes, to compassion,

Yes, to success,

Yes, life is great,

Yes, I am good enough… of that I am certain.

THE ELEVENTH SEED

What's the hurry?

Today people are living longer. With the right mindset, a good wholesome diet, exercise, and with a belief in your active longevity, there is no reason why you cannot live well into your nineties. There have been many technical advances in things like nutrition and movement, and with all the information out there, living to the nineties is well within the reach of all of you. However, you do have to work on it. It will be worth it, but only if you have quality of life, meaningful health, and enough assets.

The reason why I give you this, is that many people have a kind of inbuilt panic that they need to secure X amount of assets and lifestyle by certain timeframes. This puts pressure on you, and when you hunt too hard for things, you chase them away. Why not look at life differently, and instead of saying that I need to have X number of assets by the time I'm forty, why not extend it into your fifties, as after all, you should have many years in front of you? This gives you a completely new perspective on how you manage your life. It gives you freedom and removes the pressure.

It is not the trying to do the things within a timeframe that is the problem, it is the not achieving those things within the timeframe that that is a problem. That is when you set yourself up for the fall, bruise your self-esteem, and panic that you will not have enough assets to sustain you in your old age. The resulting negativity will take your goals even further away.

Why not look at your life and think, *I can live a good healthy life until I'm ninety. That being the case, twenty years could be a good long retirement?* This means you can work until you are seventy – yes seventy, if you want to. However, the trick here is to do the work that you love. For me it is writing (I'm nearly sixty-eight), for you it might be painting, running a landscape gardening company or looking after children. So perhaps with this new perspective you can work at your current job until you are say forty, as by that time you should have accumulated some assets (perhaps not all of the assets that you would like) but enough to get you by. Slowly, and after hours, you work the wanted vocation and finally move into this full time, and you have thirty years to do it, and another thirty years to create those assets.

I suggest you take out a piece of paper and play around with the time frames and ideas as given above. When you do, you will remove an element of tension from your life and set the intent for a better and happier life.

THE TWELFETH SEED

Painting your Life

Our thoughts are the energy that manifest on the canvas of our lives. We are born with a clean slate but as we take control of our existence, we paint it dark, paint it light, paint it grim, paint it happy.

Our thoughts are the hands that direct the brush, the eyes that give direction, the voice that shouts the way. Gleeful feelings with trust and faith will produce a vibrant and glorious picture. Gloomy thoughts direct the brush to produce decay.

The wonderful thing about life is that at any time we have the ability to paint over our work, to create those palettes of happiness and forests full of joy. Stand back, look at the painting of yourself and see it for what it is. Having done so, take the time to visualise vibrant petals of love and joy. As you are your own artist, start painting now!

To cover dark with light may take a few coats, so start in one corner of your life and gradually move over your entire composition to draw in happiness, sketch wealth, mould love, and sculpt health.

THE THIRTEEN SEED

In the land of Zelta

In the land of Zelta, there was a tribe that lived in the desert regions. For as long as living memory, they had no rain and forgot what rain was. Zelta is believed to be in the Mongolian Plain, at the foot of Mt. Tianshan – but it could be somewhere else.

Although it was a difficult existence, the inhabitants were content just to survive and have each other. Drinking water was collected from the sleepy snake-like river that was fed by the far-off mountains. It was a pleasant life, with a silver sun in the deep blue sky that watched over them. It was also a life of consistency, where day after day was much the same without cause for concern.

Nevertheless, the day came when far away, on an unknown seaboard, clouds gathered. At first only a few, but like villagers coming to a market, they became many until the sky was dark. Rising from the sea, they were blown far inland...

On this particular morning, Cuiyun rose, and set out for his day's foraging and greeted the villagers with a pleasant laugh, and a 'How do you do?' He and his friends headed off towards the hills where food was still to be found. They could not understand why it was getting harder to find the succulent roots and bulbs from which they survived.

Later, when Cuiyun and his friends straightened up to stretch their stiff backs and take a breather, with a sharp intake of breath, they exclaimed, 'What's that?' They were looking towards the horizon and saw a dark line that seemed like a large, dark, fat lizard stretching across the land. 'What an odd thing,' they agreed and watched it for a time. It got bigger, menacingly sneaking closer, and as it did the mood became solemn. 'I wonder if this is as the prophet said, 'the end of all things?' said one.

As it grew, massive blue-purple clouds hunched over them, angry Gods to fall and crush them. They swirled menacingly whilst racing across the sky to devour, and as they did, day became night. Dropping their implements, the men ran towards the village and their loved ones. As they rushed, panic was everywhere. People shouted, 'It's the end of the world... It's the end of the world.' Frantic mothers hurried to protect their children.

It was at this time, when the blue-purple Gods cracked with anger and threw a jagged light that blinded eyes and assaulted the ears – their skin tingled, as if covered in ants. 'To the cave,' they yelled, 'quickly' but most of the yelling was lost to the wind.

To their horror, the Gods grabbed the snake-river and plucked it high up into the sky – then with wrath, hurled the water onto the frightened villagers. They had never seen water coming from the sky, so it must be the river up in the air.

The rain came in sheets, so thick that they could not see five paces in front of them. 'The river... we are in the river... quickly, into the cave.' They went deep into the cave hoping to hide, but the howling wind followed with arms that reached in, bringing the snake-river with it.

For hours, the villagers cowered while the Gods savagely attacked. Finally, after a time, the Gods tired and relented, the wind stilled, and the river was placed where it belonged.

They woke up to a normal sunny day, the fierceness gone to terrorise others. Slowly, they left the cave, in ones and twos, only to see the damage to the land... trees lay on their sides and their huts were scattered across the land.

The next day, still shocked, they went out to forage. To their delight they saw green shoots emerging from the land, that would mean the bulbs would grow and become abundant. 'How?' they wondered.

There are times in our life when we look at what we consider to be "negatives". But for every negative, there is a corresponding positive. Look for the positive in all instances. It is in recognising your fear that opens you to growth. You can let your fear go. To do so you must trust, as I learnt to.

THE FOURTEENTH SEED

Body-verse

PART ONE
THE HORDES

It started with just a blemish… so small it would need to be magnified 10,000 times to be seen. An imperfection on one tiny cell within Body-verse. On its own it was meaningless. However, it was not long until it multiplied and enmeshed the entire cell. That imperfection consumed, leaving all in its wake lifeless, and of no use to the human body.

Three days later it had infiltrated all the cells around it. In that short time, those beautiful cells, that once looked like sweets, now looked like they had been slashed and burnt. They were now dead.

At this time, the immune system of the body would not have registered the destruction of a handful of cells. After all, the human body has roughly 70 trillion of them. However, the menace multiplied quickly, and a handful became hundreds… Then thousands… Soon hundreds of thousands… It was only when several million had been destroyed that the immune system started to raise the alarm. Perhaps bureaucratically, so its response was slow – like a defending army sending out a small patrol against a barrage of attackers. Therefore, the hordes multiplied and kept consuming more cells in exponential gluttony.

Body cells have an important function. They are the powerhouse for the body, where each one is a mini battery that generates electrical energy for the welfare of the collective. As the hordes consumed, the carnage started to show with devastating effect on the body's energy system until it started to shut down. There seemed to be no stopping these hordes.

Body-verse

PART TWO
DEVASTATION

'Brigadier, how many casualties are there?' the Commander asked.

'Millions Sir; the enemy has killed many of our cells in Gall Bladder, which is now partially dysfunctional. Opposing troops are infiltrating via the Hepatic Ducts towards Pancreas and outwards from there. Not only are we under attack from the inside, the Epidermis is also being ravaged. Large areas of epithelial cells are dead, and as the foe captures new tissue, it destroys with a scorched earth policy.'

The Brigadier waited for her superior to respond.

'How is Body-verse taking it? Will it survive?'

'I'm not sure, Sir. It's reeling, passing in and out of consciousness; the energy is failing and biochemical function is in disarray. But worse Sir, fatigue has set in.'

With a quivering voice the superior asked, 'Where have you deployed the forces?'

'Well, Sir, we have the Haemoglobin Brigade infiltrating Bloodstream to boost the Red Cell Regiment. The enemy is using the Lymphatic and Vascular Systems to advance rapidly throughout Body-verse. We've detected malignant opposition as far as Left Foot... At this rate of advance, it will only be a matter of weeks before they have destroyed all the main organs of Body-verse. Protein Force is in capitulation and Body-verse is losing weight.'

The Commander continued, 'Are we having any success with Blood Defences?'

'Although it is early days, it takes time for the Immune Battalions to spring into action to combat infection. It seems that we are holding our own on further advances. But with the lightning speed of this unknown adversary, much ground is already lost.... Sir, do I have permission to speak freely?'

'Yes, Brigadier, go ahead.'

She was quiet, gathering her thoughts, 'Sir, if we do not rally, and soon, it won't be long before Body-verse's systems will start shutting down. Engine Heart will slow and Blood Units carrying much needed oxygen will diminish. That means supplies required by the Enzyme Brigade will not get through, and if they are hampered in their operations, infection will advance and conquer new territory. Body-verse's temperature will initially rise and billions of cells will combust... and more organs will be slaughtered. If that happens, the mysterious energy that enlivens Body-verse will diminish. Body-verse's ambient temperature will reduce and become cold...' At this stage, the Brigadier's voice trailed off but the unspoken horror of genocide was evident.

'Brigadier, your assessment is correct. Indeed, things are grim.'

'Sir, our army of Joint Protective Forces has been securing Body-verse against invasions for eons but never have we faced such a powerful foe. Sir, is this the scourge that they call cancer?'

'I'm afraid so, Brigadier. To be precise, we that work in Brain have confirmed it is called Cancer. Its method is to destroy the Lymphatic Units, multiplying millions of its own white cells, thereby disposing of our White Blood Cells. Once those defences are gone, Body-verse, as we know it will be in total decline, and, as you said, once our Body-verse is cold, no life can be sustained and we will all be wiped out.'

'Sir, you are more knowledgeable about these things than I, a woman dedicated to the defences. I've heard tell that there are other Body-verses out there. Is that correct?'

The Superior spoke with reverence as this was a subject close to his heart. 'Our intelligence has indicated that there are other Body-verses out there with ecosystems similar to ours. They are collectively called, Mankind and they form part of what is known as a Universe. This is much the same as we form part of the Body-verse. We first deduced this from studying newly generated cells. There are unknown strands of DNA that are alien to us and our needs. Body-verse is perfect... there are no coincidences. This suggests that we have had contact with external influences, which supports the belief of other Body-verses. Cell Memory gives glimpses of things beyond us and that there is more to life than just our Body-verse, much more... Who knows, there may be Body-verses beyond Body-verses. It would be egotistical to assume that we are alone.'

As the Commander grew silent, the Brigadier asked, 'Sir, some of the Capillaries and I were having a drink in the barrack's canteen and we postulated that if something created our Body-verse, and our many cultures of Cells, Enzymes, Bacteria, Hormones, Mucus, and all the others, then that creative force could have fashioned much more than us and that it is likely that we are a very small component in a wonderful scheme of things... Sir, has Mind tried to make contact with that something that is beyond us?'

The commander was quiet for a time, wondering how much to share with his junior colleague. 'Yes, for some time we have reached out to the so-called Intelligence and some claim to have made contact. But, sadly, most don't believe... if they can't see it, it does not exist.'

The Commander, after pausing in reflective thought, said, 'Sorry, Brigadier, but there's a briefing at Mind. I have to be on my way but, before I go, I will tell you in confidence of a strategy that we are devising to eradicate the invasive force that consumes us. Some of the wiser ones suggest that if we believe in that Creative Intelligence you just spoke of, and if we embrace it with trust, positively believing, then we can win this war. We will propagate the message that if we all align ourselves with faith, whilst thinking in a positive way, then against all odds we can win this war.'

'Sir, do you mean to say that there is power in trust, and do you really suggest that this will help to destroy this cancerous fiend?'

'Yes, Brigadier, we have had evidence to suggest this. For instance, do you remember when Body-verse broke Right Leg? Perhaps you were too young? Well, we worked feverishly to heal bone but it was beyond our capacity. Yet it mysteriously mended. What intelligence fused bone to bone in such a perfect way?... Anyway, we were stunned at how fast it healed. Cell Memory talks about this Intelligence that seems to rule all things... But I must get going.'

'How are you getting back to the top, to Mind, Sir? It's dangerous out there.'

'I am to travel via Cerebral-Spinal Fluid as that path is most direct.' Putting out his hand to shake that of the Brigadier, the Commander said, 'Go well, Brigadier. Times are tough but we have to forge ahead with confidence and believe that the creative force is on our side.' Then he was gone.

The Brigadier, although being aware of the need to get back to her regiment, for a time sat and thought over the mystical things the Commander had spoken about. Thinking of this Intelligent creative force made her feel small. She wondered what the name of this force was. Then, briskly, got up, put on her helmet whilst thinking, *can't ponder the imponderable* and went back to war.

Body-verse

PART THREE
FLASHBACK

The human body is a marvellous creation. However, for it to remain functional, the owner must be positive in nature, and respect it. In our story, the owner was a person who always looked at the negative side of things, and not the good that was on hand. Further to this, there was no respect for the body. The person would think or say, 'I don't care what

I feed my body, my body *must handle it. Besides, I just love junk food.'* This ignores the body's innate intelligence that occupies every cell.

It has been proven scientifically that the body is affected by the mind, so if the mind is negative, or emotional in a negative way, the body (can) respond accordingly. This particular Body-verse had had many years of a negative thought supply, as well as a lack of respect for her body. The body listened and it heard, *You don't care what you put in me, or what thoughts your live with, therefore, why should I look after you?* So slowly, over many years the body's resources depleted, until such time as it was overrun, as the story tells.

I do not suggest for one minute that every cancer is caused by negative thinking, and a lack of respect for the body, as there are other influences, such as environment, genes, perhaps tragic events in the life of the person, and of course, the extent that the person worries. Also, there is no doubt that with a bad diet, the immune systems are compromised, thereby, reducing, and in some cases offering no resistance. What I am suggesting is that negative thinking, coupled with a lack of respect for the body is a contributing factor, exacerbating the situation. I suggest that with a turnaround from negative thinking, to positive thinking and a respect for the body, then the body is given a greater chance of health.

Let us see how it ends up.

Body-verse

PART FOUR
SLAUGHTER

Ten days later, the Commander was heading up a senior staff meeting in Mind. In attendance were politicians and top military people.

Standing up he said, 'We are here in a last-ditch attempt to find a way to control this menace that is destroying us. Our information throughout Body-verse has revealed a grim and worrying affair. You have all read the report, and so I shall not elaborate. You have also had time to think of a strategy and so I open the floor to you.' He sat down.

The long table held no less than fifty people – yet there was a palpable silence. No one looked at the Commander or at anyone else. Most looked gloomily at the table surface, as if it held the secrets of warfare.

'Well,' the Commander said, 'Are there no suggestions?'

'Commander,' said a voice from the other end of the table. It belonged to Governor Jones, head of Synapse Energy Systems, a lady of considerable intelligence and expertise. She stood to address the gathering, took off her glasses to clean them but this gave the impression that this was done in an absentminded way while she composed herself for what she was about to say.

'As the report states, we have been overrun. I don't mean to be a pessimist. In fact, through the years most of you have considered me to be overly optimistic. Our forces are almost beyond hope. The cancer grows stronger each day while our troops, as brave as they are, have nothing left to fight with. It is only a matter of time until every single cell, each organ, the Arterial System, Lymph and all the other systems of Body-verse will all ...' She did not finish the sentence, but let the silence communicate the inevitable.

'There is however, hope. Perhaps it may be just a glimmer of hope.' Her voice had developed confidence and excitement. 'Some of you will scoff at the idea, others may be willing. I shall let the Commander elaborate, but I will tell you, here and now, we have no choice but to adopt the suggestion. I am all for it.'

As Jones sat down, there was a buzz of discussion as all were anxious to know what was to follow.

The Commander let it run for a while, and as it did he surveyed the audience as if to gauge its readiness.

'We have an ally, one that we have always ignored, even though it has supported us many times. Within this room we have the most advanced thinkers of Body-verse, and for many years we have pondered the question as to who we are and why we are here. Yes, collectively we serve Body-verse, but whom does Body-verse serve? I personally have had conversations with many of you about this very subject. And in most cases we agreed that there is "an Intelligence" that knows the logic of it all but is beyond our comprehension.'

Not a sound could be heard. All attention was focused on the face of the Commander and the words that he offered. 'After the miracle of the healing of Broken Leg, a group of us, consisting of Wentworth from Mucus, Colonel Ying from the Marrow Corps, Costa and Skolly from Casualty, worked as a group. We would silence ourselves to shut out all thoughts and noise and try, in some way to connect with that mysterious force.' This was said with a sweeping arm, indicating that all could see and understand.

'We learnt that our voice is a small voice, but when we went into the silent background we heard the "big voice"'.

Upon hearing this, the audience stirred and a flurry of questions rang out. 'Did it speak to you?' 'What is it like?' 'Is it friendly... will it help us?'

Waving for silence, he continued. 'Of course we did not see it, but certainly there was a presence, a benevolent presence.' He lowered his voice as he said this and there was a gentleness that suggested that the Commander had indeed experienced some mystical force. 'Gentlemen and ladies, we are convinced there is an Intelligence that created us. And that if we believe in it, it *will* support us.' The Commander's voice increased in speed from an excitement that he could not, nor perhaps wanted to control. With luminous eyes his enthusiasm was infectious.

'We have called this Mysterious Force, The Intelligence... and it will come to our aid, if we acknowledge it.'

He slowed down and cautioned, 'But we must do our bit, and that is to fight with a strong mind and heart... People of Body-verse, we can beat this scourge.'

The atmosphere in the room was transformed; where before it had been thick and lifeless, there was now a resurgence. The commander knew that he had given hope. *After all*, he reasoned with himself, *a life without something larger than us to believe in is a life without value. To feel as if we are a part of that Intelligence, is to feel at home.* 'Yes!' he shouted, 'With belief and with The Intelligence on our side, there is hope!'

It was Michelle, the ever hopeful head of Epidermis, who shouted, 'I knew it! There is no way that we are an accident! I have always felt that we are a part of something profound. I say we adopt these principles of positive thinking and believe in The Intelligence – after all, if it made us, then it must be willing to support us.'

'You've gotta be kidding!' shouted Pulmonary's representative, Lee. 'Our heart function has all but stopped. Don't you realise that we have lost many of our best fighters? My people are exhausted beyond belief… and with at least forty trillion cancerous cells that have converged over much of Body-verse, you say put trust into something external to us, to lessen our own control and responsibility?… Are you crazy?'

'Perhaps,' said Jones. 'But I remember having a discussion with you in your office in Valve and it was you who said that it amazed you how all of the parts of Body-verse work with such apparent ease and synchronisation. At the time you were in awe, and you even said it was inexplicable that there seems to be a universal cooperation of cells, such as a toe working in sync with the brain at the other end of Body-verse. The same with all the other seventy trillion cells, all acting as if we were really just one of us. Well, I can't explain it, but I know that whatever The Intelligence is, it is there for us. Besides, what else are you offering?'

Body-verse

PART FIVE
FAITH OR DEATH?

The meeting continued for many hours. A resolution of the acceptance of The Intelligence and of its powerful support was drafted. It spoke of The Intelligence and its support but stressed the need to be of strong mind and heart. It went on to say that life within Body-verse could flourish again if all trusted and believed.

There was no time to waste and the message was sent via the Electrical Circuits of the Neural System. It was headed *Urgent – Communication from Mind.*

The next morning the Brigadier was down behind Stomach, in Pancreas, trying to encourage the girls to continue with insulin production, when the directive arrived. Since that discussion with the Commander, she had had a sense of support, of comfort, but was not sure how to express it.

She tore open the envelope and read the contents. It took her some time to digest the full implication but she sensed that this was the way, and the only way for the survival of Body-verse.

In shifts, she explained the new orders to all in Pancreas. At first she was worried, but realised that most of the troops had already accepted that there was a hidden governing force, and if used with positivity there was a chance. It gave them strength that this force was supportive and benevolent. But what amazed her the most was that they were galvanised with new purpose and belief. Slowly at first and then gathering momentum, insulin production increased.

The ground fighting started from Pancreas, it was fierce as the cancer was well entrenched and seemed invincible. There was slaughter on both sides and for a time, neither side advanced. After a week of carnage, the Pancreas forces broke through the centre of the cancerous lines and started to control the battle.

The Brigadier's next duty call was to Inflammation, where after discussing the directive, the army went into battle, with sleeves rolled up, wooden clubs brandished, and a newfound confidence. For the first time in months they started to hold ground against the determined cancer forces.

That success gave confidence to the Spleen Brigade where they took up the challenge and with their colours flying, rushed the enemy with bloodcurdling screams in a do or die effort. The Small Intestine was liberated, followed by Bladder and Duodenum. After each successive victory, gratitude towards The Intelligence grew.

Body-verse

PART SIX
POWER IN TRUST

It was several months later. In a small room inside a well-functioning Right Kidney, and in a far more relaxed meeting, the Commander informed the Brigadier, 'Over the months, one by one, each organ, each cell, each duct has been won over and, although tired, Body-verse has started to heal and new cells are developing. Scorched and blackened organs are returning to a healthy pink. Haemoglobin function is almost normal, and the Energy Systems have improved. Waste materials are excreted, blood pressure is returning to normal, and lucid thought has returned to Mind.' With a smile he concluded, 'Body-verse's lights are starting to shine.'

'Yes, it's a miracle,' said the Brigadier. 'A miracle beyond bravery, one of quantum proportions. In our last meeting you said if we all align ourselves with belief, then against all odds we can win this war, and that there is power in trust. Fortunately for Body-verse, you were right!'

The End

THE FIFTEENTH SEED

Your roar is within you!

Little Lion was only two years old and wanted to roar like her daddy, Shumba. But her roar seemed not to be there and only came out as a squeak.

Worried, Little Lion said to her daddy, 'Daddy I am sad, I can't roar. I have tried and tried.'

Shumba was wise and said in a soft loving way, 'Your roar is inside you; you don't have to try and force it out. It will come when needed.'

Little Lion said in a rush, 'Where inside me, I can't see it, I can't feel it, what do you mean, inside of me?'

'Well, it's hard to explain,' said Shumba 'but when we are born we are given what we need to survive. We are given muscle to fight with. We are given speed and cunning, which allow us to catch our prey. Our roar is the power that puts it all together. Without the roar, our speed, strength and cunning would not work as well.'

Timidly, Little Lion said, 'But roar is only sound.'

'No, it is much more than that. Our roar is an expression of our strength, our will to fight, our determination. Our roar is our knowing that we are king of the jungle! But as I said, it is inside of us. It is inside of you.'

'Oh,' is all Little Lion could say as she wandered off through the scrubby bush. *What does he mean, it is inside of me?*

I know, I will ask Elephant. He is smart with such a good memory, I am sure that he will know, and so Little Lion hurried off towards the river, where the trees grow tall and strong. 'Good morning Elephant. Please may I ask you a question?'

Elephant stretched his wrinkled trunk high to grab a branch. With elegant, slow but determined strength, Elephant pulled the branch until there was a sharp crack, like a gunshot. As it broke, the branch fell to the ground. Elephant placed one big foot on the branch to hold it firm, whilst his trunk broke it into a short length that fitted comfortably into his mouth.

Little Lion was grateful that the foot that was on the branch was not on her body.

Elephant paused his graceful rhythm of reach, pull, break and eat, and with small smiling eyes looked at Little Lion and said, 'How can I help?'

'Elephant, Shumba, my daddy, said that my roar is my power and that it is inside of me, but I am afraid that I will not find it.'

Elephant said in a voice that was strong and forceful, 'If you can face your fear, as you face your reflection in the lake, you will find your roar. Yes, it is within you.'

With that, as if all that needed to be said had been said, Elephant resumed the rhythm of reach, pull, break and eat.

Feeling just as confused, Little Lion moped along until she saw Owl sitting regally in a tree. Little Lion thought, *perhaps she will know where my roar is. After all, Owl sits and sees the goings on all night.*

As Little Lion approached, Owl said, 'Who who, goes there?'

'It's me, Little Lion'.

'Owl, I have a terrible problem. I am a lion and I am supposed to roar, but I can't. My daddy Shumba said that my roar is an expression of my power, and Elephant said that if I can face my fear as I face my reflection in the river then I will find my roar.'

With that, she looked into the wise face of Owl and waited for an answer.

'So, you have not found your voice yet?'

'No, I don't know where it could be.'

'Do you not know that you must change the way you think about yourself, after all, if you think of yourself only as Little Lion that's all you will be. You must see yourself, powerful and strong, like you see Shumba – now there's a lion,' said Owl with a hint of a shudder.

With that, Owl flew off to investigate another area of her domain, but as she went she hooted, 'Remember, your roar is inside of you!'

Despondent, and with her head hanging down, Little Lion continued along the path. 'Haa, what on Earth is wrong with you?' spat Cobra. 'You could have stood on me and I would have been forced to bite you.'

'Oh, I'm sorry Cobra. I have looked for my roar everywhere and just can't find it. My Daddy Shumba says that my roar is an expression of my power. Elephant said that if I can face my fear as I face my reflection in the river, then I will find my roar. Owl said that I must see myself, not as Little Lion, but more like my powerful daddy. Still, I don't understand. In fact, I don't even know what to look for, let alone what to find.'

Cobra raised vertically, to the same height as Little Lion's face and simply said, 'What they are all talking about is "your spirit".'

'My spirit, what do you mean?'

'Your spirit is within you, waiting to be released. That's what they mean by your roar.'

'Released, huh?

Cobra thought of himself as an intellectual and launched into what was likely to be a long explanation, 'Well, it is all a question of understanding that we animals, not just you felines, have the creative power of the Universe within us. Some would call it strength of character, whilst others refer to it as positivity. We of the reptile kingdom refer to it as spirit. Now, if you take the left and right hemispheres of the brain ...' At this stage a dejected Little Lion continued her way back towards her home, but some thirty seconds later Little Lion could hear Cobra shout, 'Hey, where are you going? Oh well, it does not matter, but remember your roar is within you!'

Oh great, everyone tells me how easy 'it' is, and that 'it', whatever 'it' means, is within us all, and all I have to do is to know that 'it' is there, and 'it' will be released. It's easy for them.

These were the thoughts that filled Little Lion as she crested the next hill. They were quickly dispelled when she saw her younger brother, Prince, cowering. A pack of wild dogs had surrounded him, their menace obvious. Without thinking, Little Lion charged down the hill, and as she did she let out a deep-chested roooaaar, so loud that the entire valley shook. Birds shrieked out of trees, and rocks tumbled off cliff faces. A minute later, the distant hills returned the thunderous roooaaar.

The terrified dogs ran in all directions and were far away long before the roar finely settled and the valley returned to normal.

As they walked home, Little Lion was proud that she had saved Prince and finally understood what the wise folk of the bush had told her. She knew her roar was an expression of her power, and realised that even though she was scared of so many wild dogs, she ran towards them anyway, and so she had faced her fear as she faced her reflection in the lake, just like Elephant said.

Owl was right when she said, 'See yourself not as a Little Lion, but powerful like Shumba,' and although Cobra drove her nuts, she also knew what she was talking about when she said 'Your spirit is inside you and you don't have to go looking for it, it is already there.'

And so now Little Lion knew her roar – it was her strength, her potential and her determination, but most of all, she knew it was within her. She was no longer called Little Lion, but Lioness The Brave!

THE SIXTEENTH SEED

Return to Joy

CHAPTERS

A C T **1**
T H E   S C H O O L

The children waited quietly, not knowing what to expect. The only noise was the hum of his wheelchair as it slowly crept along the front of the hall.

There were 300 children in the school hall and twelve teachers. All waited in silent anticipation. They knew little of Anthony Montgomery, other than that at some stage in his life he had an accident and was now a paraplegic, and that this man had come to talk to them about happiness.

As they watched the wheelchair negotiate the ramp that had been created to take him up to the top of the stage, the thought went through every single mind... *what if that was me in that wheelchair... how could I be happy?*

He was wearing a cowboy hat and checked shirt, jeans and cowboy boots. The kids thought that his clothes looked funny for someone in a wheelchair.

The progress up the ramp was painfully slow as clearly Anthony was being cautious but then his voice rung out, 'Speed kills yah know.' At first only one or two students laughed at the irony of his wheelchair going at snail's pace and the occupant talking about going too fast. Then the rest caught the joke and there was sporadic laughing. Finally getting to the top of the ramp and onto the stage, he accelerated quickly and raced towards a back wall. Just before all thought he would hit it, he swerved and raced forward towards the front edge of the stage, where half a meter before the drop he skidded to a halt. He sat there in his wheelchair and laughed. The laugh was more of a cackle as he enjoyed his little prank.

He fell silent as he looked at the audience. He marvelled, as he always does when in front of a new school... Such potential, such hope, all waiting expectantly to hear what he had to say.

The headmistress, Mrs Wentworth, had met Anthony out at the school gates and accompanied him into the hall and up the ramp. She now fiddled with the microphone, and when satisfied said to the children and teachers in attendance, 'Please welcome Mr Montgomery.'

The obligatory 'Hull…ow Mr Mont…gom…ery,' sounded out in a bored monologue.

When quiet, she continued, 'Thank you Mr Montgomery for coming to our school. It is kind of you to come and talk to us.' Anthony acknowledged what she said with a little happy cackle. The children were to hear that cackle many times over the course of the morning. It was given spontaneously and came from the heart.

Upon receiving the microphone, he looked at the audience and cackled again in delight. Already the children were softening to this odd but fun man, and many laughed.

He started with, 'Electric powered wheelchairs for an independent lifestyle! That's what the ads says. Indoors or out, a Zippy electric wheelchair has the performance and manoeuvrability to get yah where yah wanna go.

I'm a country boy, coming from outside of Broken Hill in NSW… … No, no, I didn't drive this all the way from there to get here.'

Many were not listening to what he said but were listening to the tone of his voice, and most came to the conclusion that his voice smiled – the cackle infiltrating his vocal cords. Others were laughing at the words about the wheelchair and the vision of him travelling 1400 kilometres from Broken Hill. This was unexpected, but then they did not know what they expected. This man, who could only work the top half of his body was laughing and chatting like he was a thirteen-year-old.

'Yep, highly powered for an independent life, and available with a host of drive bases, reliability and luxury for a fantastic driving experience. Make yar day-to-day a thrill with the Zippy…

Enough wheel chair talk, we gunna get down to business, happy business, joy business…. But hang on,' he cackled again, 'let's not be so serious so soon… Me time here with youse is too short to be serious…

This thing was crash tested before I bought it. Just as well as I've been told that I'm not the best driver.' This time the laugh from the children was loud and spontaneous. Even some of the teachers giggles.

'But if I'm not, probably because I was taught by me mum…' More laughter … 'And did yah know you can even get a 4-wheel drive wheel chair…? Gawd, can yah imagine me tearing up and down mountains in that thing?' The crowd laughed. 'But maybe I will someday.'

With a cackle he continues, 'One of me favourite TV shows, Dr Who, The Doctor says there's no point in being grown up if yah can't be childlike sometimes.

Really, these things are like magic for a paraplegic. And look here, it even has me lunch in it. I got bickies and a small bottle of milk. … It goes up and down kerbs without getting stuck… don't wanna get stuck do I? And do yah like this sporty red colour. I could have got classic silver or boring blue…'

Again, he took time to scan the audience. Again, he cackled.

'Now we gunna talk about being happy… You kids, you look at me, and shake yah head and wonder how the hell can he be happy living like that… Well, I tell you I'm happy, and in many ways probably happier than most of you. I know that happiness is like a muscle… yah can grow it or shrink it according to your thinking. It is about the way you allow yourself to see your life and the world around you. Some think that by being successful they'll be happy. That's nonsense. And some think that they'll find happiness like you find a gold nugget. That's also not true. Yah manufacture happiness, yah don't find it. Think about that for a minute. Imagine if you had to search for happiness, like some search for the Holy Grail. Jees, I can't even find me wheelchair keys, how on Earth am I gunna find the Holy Grail? So, most won't find happiness. But that's the point, as most of humanity have not found happiness because it's not like a nugget you find on the street. But you can learn how to manufacture happiness, and that's why I'm here today, to tell yah how…'

He continued his gaze and was silent for a moment, as if considering… 'Okay, let's get this out of the way… yah all wanna know how I ended up like this, in this wheelchair.... Well, my Mini Minor had a punch-up with a truck... That was bad enough... but I was in it at the time, which of course made it worse for me.

Was pretty gruesome, and for a while they didn't know if I'd survive... but takes more than a bust up with a truck to stop me... The coma lasted about three months... best sleep I ever had... they kept saying after I woke up, "Did you have a pleasant nap?" That's a good one.

I was in hospital for over a year. Then they thought I was completely paralysed but I showed them... I was also blind but my beautiful sister Mary insisted they sew the eyes together, and it worked. I can see pretty good now.

That's me sis over there, against the wall. She's the quiet one... I'm the noisy one... always was.'

All heads turned, and Mary gave a shy smile as she moved her cheek towards her shoulder.

'Was it fate that me accident happened? Nope... I believe that handing your life over to fate is a cop out and shirking yah responsibility. It's allowing something to happen at a time when perhaps, with a right approach and right action the final result could be different, better different. By taking control, yah more likely to have a better outcome. So my mind said, not to let an accident rule me life. I was gunna enjoy life anyway.

Believing in fate indicates that yah think that all situations are pre-ordained, and that yah have no control over circumstances. With this belief yah must think there's someone upstairs orchestrating yah every move... like some giant chess match, plotting yah downfall or success... let's give this bugger a hard time! ...No, no one person is more important than another... no grain of sand on a beach is more important than another.

Nah... me accident wasn't fate... just happened... Yah see, how could I be happy if I thought it was fate that smashed me up? I would of kept thinking, why me, why not that other bloke?...

Fate is a myth... one that reduces yah ability to happily produce the life that yah seek... Yah in control of yah own destiny... Yes, there may be external influences... like a punch-up with a truck... but the direction yah travel is the direction yah set for yourself. Yah born into certain circumstances, but it's up to you and yah thought processes that determines whether yah remain stuck in yah circumstances or move on...

... Just hang on, I need to take me tablets. I'll only be a jiffy...'

A C T 2
M A R Y

When Mrs Wentworth sat down, she made sure it was next to Mary, *after all, we could not have a guest sitting on her own.*

Whilst Anthony was taking his medication, she asked Mary, 'So how is life for you Mary... must be difficult on occasions?'

'It ain't so bad,' was all Mary said.

Mrs Wentworth tried again. 'It is wonderful that you help him so much. Clearly he appreciates all that you do?'

Mary was thoughtful... 'When Anthony was little, even then we knew there was something special about him. Oh... it was not just motherly or sisterly love... there was more... We knew that there was something profound about him... We could never put our fingers on it... that was until after the accident... such a horrible time...'

'It must have been, and it must have changed all your lives.'

'Sure did... At first, we didn't know how it was gunna turnout, but then Anthony got this bee in his bonnet that he could help people... We thought he was nuts, but he wouldn't give up, and when he said, well if you're not gunna help, I'll do it on me own...

He was smarter than me and he was right... now we have been to 319 schools over the last nine years. I know because I keep the records.'

'That sure is a lot of helping children.'

Mary was silent... as if not sure to say what she was thinking. She took a deep breath and said, 'You know one of the things that makes me happy... That's helping people. Happiness comes from serving and helping people... When you have done something for someone you feel good after... well the more you do for people, the better you feel... I'm sure you know what I mean... You see, we all have challenges, some you can see, like when you look at Anthony. But others you can't, like if you look at me. Or, if I look at you, I can't see your challenges. Even if we did, we couldn't really understand the difficulties of the other... I mean, even seeing Anthony in his wheelchair can't give you any idea what his challenges are. We can see his shoes but we can't walk in them. But in some ways it's a good thing, me not really seeing your issues... and you not seeing mine. But we must reach out, and help each other.

We travel a lot, where we have to fly. Well... it's awkward... you know, getting him on the plane, toilets, and things. But when people get over their initial embarrassment of their having to interact with someone like Anthony, they love to help... it makes them feel good...'

Mrs Wentworth was thoughtful before she asked, 'Why do you think people are embarrassed when they first encounter Anthony and his condition?'

'Dunno... it's like they think they are the reason he's in the wheelchair... kind of guilty that they are able-bodied and Anthony isn't... Once they decide to help, such as putting his bag in the top compartment they love to do it... It's natural to wanna help people. And it's natural to feel good after.

At first, Anthony was embarrassed, having to ask for help, but I told him that it takes more guts to ask for help than shutting up. Now that he has seen how much people like to help, he sometimes asks for help, even if he don't need it, just to make them feel good about themselves. Society can only thrive when we help each other, when we walk side-by-side, giving more than we get.

If you treat others with love and respect, your outer life will reflect that love and respect...and yes, it's been hard, but I couldn't be more fulfilled. Every time I help Anthony, and see him help the kids, it makes me all warm inside... can't explain it.'

Mrs Wentworth, was quiet, and with a side smile she considered what Mary had said, and wondered, *sometimes it is the shy and quiet ones that have such great but unannounced wisdom.*

A C T 3
T H E S C H O O L A N D A S T O R Y O N H A P P I N E S S

'Some may think that life ain't fair?' Anthony continued. "Was it fair to me? Yep, on balance it was. It took on the one hand, but provided with the other. Life is never gunna try and be fair… if it did then there wouldn't be any crooks, typhoons, nor would there be accidents, like mine… is it fair that babies die, or people are born with deformities?… There's no justice in the world. I had to accept life's harshness and get on with it. Too many bemoan the fact that something did not work out. Yah moan, 'It ain't fair'… Don't use a lack of justice as justification for unhappiness. It is all part of life's process, and if yah accept this, then yah'll be better equipped to take responsibility for yah life.

I'm gunna read yah a story written by a fella called Pat Grayson." As he said this, he started hunting around in his bag for a book… Yes here it is. It's called Happiness, Could it be so Simple? Now, I'm gunna read this in me best voice.

Hundreds of years ago, too many to remember, there was a discussion about a simpleton – "Well he must be," said the King to his Queen.

"Why?" she asked.

"The fool is happy," said the King, "yet he's poor. Only we of nobility hast riches, and therefore hast the right to happiness."

"Are we happy my King?" enquired the Queen, "there hast not been much laughter within the realm for *some* time."

"Of course we are wife. It's only that we are not laughing much at the moment because we hast so much to worry about, with the wars and famine."

"Dost thou not think the simpleton hast nought to worry about?" Asked the Queen.

"How can he ye stupid woman. He hast nought to worry because he hast nil." "Perhaps that is all the more reason to be worried. But yet, thou are correct, he dost seem happy. In fact, he is positively filled with joy," said the Queen.

"And that is why he is a simpleton. To be happy you must have wealth, you must have power, otherwise life would not be worth living," said the King with superiority.

The Queen raised an eyebrow but thought it prudent to say nothing. But after a time said, "I suspect that if thou hast wealth and power... thou worry about its loss, but if thou hast no wealth and power thou hast to worry as to where thou next meal comes from!"

"Thou raving woman... But ... hmmm... I wonder if he's really so happy or the lunatic that I suspect him to be?"

The Queen put down her embroidery and then said, partly in jest, "Well, why don't thou go forth and dwell at his abode and see fore self."

"Splendid idea" he said. "Perhaps he hast some coinage hidden." He then shouted, "Servant. Mount thee horses. Her Highness and I are to go forth. Haste with thou."

Clipperty-clopp, clipperty-clop, as they rounded the last bend and into the village. Upon doing so, there was the very person they came to see. He was dressed in rags, like rotten seaweed. Yet he smiled at all the villagers he passed. The two royals stopped to observe him as he paused and stroked a dog. The Queen, who was most astute, observed the face. It was smooth, unblemished and radiant, like the sun with a boisterous smile. Being her subject, as he was, she knew him to be about her father's age, and that is three score and five years – but he looked so young!

It was the King's shout of, "You there. Thou with the dog" that interrupted her thoughts. The King continued, "cometh here." The man did as he was bid.

"Highness, what an honour." He said this with a deep bow. He then waited to see why he was summoned, all the while his face radiated. Although a large man, he seemed to float with lightness.

The King blurted, "Why art thou so happy? Dost thou hast coinage or prosper hidden?"

"Nay my Lord."

"Then art thou stupid to be so happy, when thou has so little?"

Surprised, the man hesitated but then said, "Stupid I ... I don't fink so ... But would that matter?"

The children in the area watching the spectacle laughed at this comment.

The King was not sure if the peasant was being honest or mocking him, so ignored the comment. The Queen had a trace of a smile on her face but quickly hid it.

The King grunted, "Take us to your abode. We shalt see it."

"Yes Yar Highness. Taint far, just around the barn."

Upon arriving, the King looked for a room but there was none to be seen, only twenty or so timbers leaning up against an internal corner of the wall covered with hay. The peasant asked, "Do thee want to go within Me Lord?"

"What. In there... thou dwells in there?"

"Yes, Me Lord. Oh, taint much yaar Highness but I dinee need much Me Lord to be happy."

"Are thou truly happy?" Asked the Queen.

"Yes, Me Lady. One don't need much to be happy."

"Folly," shouted the King, "how can'st thou be happy, look at the rags thou wears?"

"It ta be nice to hast new clothes Me Lord, but it ain't me clothes that make me joyous."

The King, irritated, even more so than normal, barked, "Well what dost make thou happy?"

"It just is, Me Lord. Happiness just is ... it's not carriage science Me Lord ... It just is."

They ignored the humour and the Queen encouraged him to continue.

"Well... I guess it comes down as to how yaa fink about life. I mean ... yaa godda fink happy uva wise yaa fink grim, so I fink happy. I always finked happy, maybe because I is happy. Me muver was happy and she finked happy, and she showed to be happy. And now me kids is happy – we's all happy."

For the second time that day the Queen raised an eyebrow at the King but this time with the obvious question, "Could it be so simple?"

"Blah, thee a fool," he said to the man as he stormed back to his horse.

The Queen with a sparkle in her eye said, "He calls thee a fool because thou are happy but thinks of himself clever when he is unhappy."

The man just continued smiling.

Anthony looked at the kids before saying, 'Good story ain't it? Yah see, this is what I keep saying, it's simpler than yah think it to be happy...

Happiness is a process, it ain't a thing... To be happy is a technique... it is the way yah talk to yahself... that process... That happy thoughts make yah happy. That telling good things about yahself makes yah happy... believing yah doing well makes yah happy...

We gunna have a two minute break while I just give me voice a break. I'm sure the teachers won't mind if yah talk among yahselfs, but no running or shouting.'

There was a hum as the kids started to talk about this weird man, but they thought him funny and liked him.

A C T **4**

T H E   S C H O O L

'Yah cannot be in a situation that you don't accept and be happy… not over the long-term. If yah allow the situation to squash yah happiness, yah a prisoner of yah own thoughts. It's better to accept the situation for what it is, and do the best yah can to change it or get out of it. But remain positive and happy.

If yah let yah life push yah around because yah believe the thought that what will be will be, then you'll never be happy… How can yah if yah let life work against yah?… Yah just can't… If yah believe in fate then yah belief will become yah fate, usually with the wrong ending…

Yah think I have come here to talk to yah about happiness. Not really. Happiness is short lived. People think they want to be happy, when really they need to be joyful. When yah live with the deep seated joy, yah'll always be happy.

Happiness is linked to things that happen to yah, such as being noticed by a boy in yah class. But in life there's always balance, and I can bet that there will be just as many boys who don't notice yah.

Happiness is a choice. Choose to be happy today or choose to be sad today, it is up to you. Yah know, most people are about as happy as they make up their minds to be… yet they say they wanna be happy, and that it must somehow descend upon them.

To have joy, yah got to have the intention… Let me give an example. Suppose yah were lining up to play a game of soccer. Yah likely to have the intention of, first playing well, and also for yah team to win… Yah wouldn't even think of playing without that intention. The same applies with joy and happiness … if yah don't have the intention of being joyful, then it's probable yah won't be. Yah got to want to be happy… don't just happen.

Be grateful for what yah have. Happiness is not in having or achieving, happiness just is…. The grass may seem greener on the other side, but unless yah internally happy, yah will not be any happier for going there.

Let me tell you another story... There's this guy on the athletic track, his name is Happy. His opponent's name is Joy, and they're about to have a race. When the gun goes off, Happy sprints down the track like it's burning up behind him. Joy starts off slowly, enjoying the audience, waving at everyone... he's having a grand old time... And after a while he caches Happy who's sitting on the ground, puffing like crazy... Nah, don't worry, this ain't that hare and tortoise story... this one's better... Anyway, Joy smiles encouragement as he passes Happy, and continues down the track. Later... when the race's over, the coach took them into the locker room and beat the hell out of Happy...'

Many in the audience could not help but let their shock be known at this last statement.

'No he didn't... just wanted to see if yah were listening... in the locker-room he sat them down and said, '"Fellas, well done, but neither won"'. Yah see, Happy is what we call a sprinter, and so he has short bursts. These are really needed. Joy is a marathon runner, and so can run all day. Yah see kids, Happy is short lived, ... things like laughing at yah buddies when the teacher ain't looking. It's also for things like getting a new hairdo. Joy is a life-long feeling of overriding joyousness. It's deep seated, and don't shift easy. Whereas, happy is here today, and gone tomorra.

It's Joy that I've come here to tell yah about, not happy... but I use the word happy all the time.'

He let what he said sink in before continuing.

'Joy can never come from an external event, if it did we could never have control over it. It comes from within... mustn't it? Yah see, we are born happy... it's in our nature to be happy... but through thinking we move away from happiness... We kind of forget it's there. We got to move back to happiness... that's why me little talk is called *Return to Joy*...

Research shows that after a few months, people who win a lottery ain't no happier or sadder than they were before. And research has also shown that people, who like me, had terrible accidents, after a period of settling down are also about as happy or as sad as they were before the ordeal. Of course, there's an adjustment period... and boy, I can tell yah that mine was difficult, in fact it was downright horrible. But I adjusted. Yah got to understand that I'm the same as everyone else... I just sit down a lot...'

More laughter...

'Some people ask me if I suffer. I say to them, only when my mind lets me...

Dale Carnegie, the author of *How to Win Friends and Influence People* said, "One of the most tragic things I know about human nature is that all of us tend to put off living. We are all dreaming of some magical rose garden over the horizon – instead of enjoying the roses that are blooming outside our window today."

Let's now talk about laughter. Yah know that laughter is a defence against the universe... sure is... And did you know that yah can't laugh and be angry at the same time?...

Years ago, a university in the States, called the Clark University did research which indicated that smiling creates mood changes for the better. Always try to be happy and feel like laughing all the times... Apparently, it takes sixty-five muscles to frown and only five to smile... so that tells yah something.

I hope yah are getting it now? ...

And how da yah know if yah joyous? ... Yah can feel it... Yah heart's warm... Yah always feel like singing... not much worries yah... but most of all, when yah feel joyful yah smile inside. When yah smile it's best to smile from within, from yah toes up to the top of yah head. Yah know what I mean...'

He paused and then asked, 'Yah all having a good time' he cackled into the microphone.

'Yes, sir,' some shouted back.

'Good...'

ACT **5**
G R O W I N G   U P

'Mum, I don't want all these dolls and things you keep giving me,' pouted young Mary. 'I want boy's things, I want guns and cowboy clothes like Dad has.'

'But Mary, I gave you those things last month and you said you want dolls... Sometimes I despair with you.'

'Yah can please me by giving me some chocolate!' Mary tried.

'At 9 o'clock in the morning, not likely, you're going to eat a proper breakfast young lady.'

'I don't want a proper breakfast, I want chocolate,' she shouted.

Her father Barry tried to ignore the commotion and focused on the stock control for the farm as it had to be ready for the morning's meeting with the accountant. There always was a stock sheet that had to be ready.

Mary was four years old and a difficult child. It would seem that she was born with the "otherwise" gene.

Her mother Johanna bit her lower lip and was perplexed, not sure how to handle Mary as she was so difficult. The paediatrician told her that Mary would improve as she got older. But she did not, not until she was six when Johanna bought a baby sibling into the household. It was a little boy, Anthony. Johanna had problems with the birth of Mary and could not have a natural birth again, and so Anthony had been adopted. Johanna was worried as to how Mary would take to her little brother but she need not have worried as she was besotted by the little thing.

'Mummy, I wanna pick up Anthony. Why don't you feed him with your titties like other mothers... can I have titties to feed him? ... Mummy I wanna have titties. I don't want to feed him with a bottle.'

So determined to be with Anthony, Mary would tell her mother to wake her up when she was doing a night feed. She couldn't do enough to help her mother care for her baby brother, especially on weekends when there was no school work to do.

Mary wanted a part in everything that Anthony was doing. For his part, Anthony was delighted as it was like having two loving mothers.

Later, when Mary was about seventeen, she often said, 'I seem to have been born to help Anthony.' At the time she did not know what was in store for them both. At that young age, the family of four were a happy and content unit. Both Mary and Anthony did well at school and were good students.

Anthony's fighting spirit soon became evident with all that he did. It was especially obvious on the athletics field, and always represented his school at inter school galas. He usually won, but when he did not he got angry.

The two siblings, although six years apart, were inseparable, and shared many jokes and laughs together. As they grew, Anthony was intrigued to see the physical changes in Mary's body. And later, was even more intrigued when Mary started talking to boys. Although jealous, he never said anything, but wished he was old enough to thump them. He did not realise that he himself was going to be particularly good-looking, becoming tall, wide shouldered, with a tanned complexion, which was offset by jet-black hair. Johanna knew that she would have to keep an eye on her young son.

Anthony believed in living life to the full and wanted to dazzle the world. He was ambitious, with much talent. At one stage, Johanna received a letter from the school secretary saying, 'Mrs Montgomery, please will you explain to Anthony that he cannot sign up for all seventeen extra after hours activities…' Anthony was despondent, but in his normal way, continued unabated.

After high school and before university, he took a gap year. He thought he wanted to be a councillor, to help people but was not sure. For a time he worked in a volunteer programme in Zambia, where for three months he worked in a private game park 100 kilometres from the Zimbabwe boarder. He loved every minute of it. At first, he was used as a groundsman, and shelter cleaner, but later was given the task of looking after the warthog enclosure. In that short time he became fond of the little wire-furred tusked male named Lightening as he could run as fast as a bolt of lightning, or so they thought. He had been found as a young wart hog and had been traumatised in some way, so he was bought back to the shelter. Later though, he never allowed himself to be assimilated back into the bush, as all the other animals did.

It was also the friends Anthony made when over there, many parties, and daytrips secured friendships for life.

A C T **6**

T H E   S C H O O L

'There are many who have life situations that are not good... But they are still joyful. And there's many who have good life situations but have no joy. Whatever the situation yah have, yah have to accept that situation. If yah don't then happiness is going to be overshadowed by longing for something yah don't have. Don't become trapped in yah own ideas, in yah imaginings about how the world should be. That don't mean that yah have to accept every situation as being permanent, but what it does mean is that whilst in the situation yah make the best of it whilst plotting another way.

To be joyful yah need to make and prepare for the right life that suits yah.

Perhaps the desire to experience life, instead of searching for a meaning was primed in me by me biological mother... who I never knew. Because yah can't control many of the things that happen to yah in life... Many of yah will try and control yah life because when yah do, yah think yah more likely to be happy. As sure as the sun comes up every day, yah'll never be able to totally control life. You will be able to control aspects of life but yah'll never have total control as there'll always be things that'll interfere...

Just after me accident, I had no control over anything... that annoyed me. I realised that the only thing that we can really control is our mind and how we see things. So if yah unhappy, it is yah fault. But if yah joyous it's also yah fault...

Gunna change tack a bit now... Don't become bewitched by the media. It'll have yah believing that yah can never be happy if you are chubby, especially if yah a girl. Rubbish... course yah can! And yah boys, yah don't have to be muscular and wearing the latest trend in clothing to be liked... If there is only one thing that yah can get from this little chat today, it is that yah recognise who yah are, and love yah individuality. Because even if yah did have the muscles and the clothes, or... the girls with stick figures... with uplifted breasts...' The boys interrupted his words with sniggering. Some of the younger girls were red-faced. 'Then yah gunna be unhappy if yah don't have them, like in the advert... Learn to love who you are.

It's the same with thirty-year-olds, only thinking they'll be happy when they have that shiny new car, and travel here and there, whilst takin lots of selfies to prove how cool they is... to put on Facebook... and show the world that they are in Cambodia, or on the Great Wall of China...

Yep, they's good things to do, but don't do them because the media suggested that yah a loser if yah don't. When yah see those adverts on telly, or hear them on the radio, they are really secretly asking a question, do yah have this because if yah don't yah a loser. Or do yah look like that because if yah don't yah a loser, and so when we hear this hundreds of times a week, we need it, because we don't wanna be a loser... ...Our entire self-esteem is wrapped up by the need to have it...

On the other side of the coin, is that they tell us that to be happy we must be winners, and so if you buy this model phone, then yah gunna be seen as a winner. Bull... It's all bull. Yah are a winner when yah see yourself without judgement and without regret... That yah recognise yah faults but yah don't let them define who yah are. Yah see, yah can't be happy if there is more negative talk inside of yah than positive talk... See yourself as a unique and beautiful contributor to this planet. That will make you happy... Don't compete with yourself... What I mean by that is that yah don't challenge everything that yah do as being bad or useless.

When I was yah age... Before me accident... oh did I have dreams... I was gunna conquer the world, and be the best rodeo cowboy in Australia... and the world was gunna love me because of it. That thinking was wrong. The world wouldn't love me for what I did... The world would love me for who I am ... and only if I first loved myself...

So don't listen to all of that media junk as it's very reason is to make yah dissatisfied with yah lot so yah cajoled into buying their product. Yah can't avoid modern life, but yah can avoid many of the messages that it gives or sends. How can yah be happy if you just buy x-brand computer, and when yah show it with pride to yah mates, one of the buggers says, "it may be new from the shop, but it is really last year's model."

Yah have to raise above all of that nonsense. Yah have to know who yah really are, otherwise yah get lost in yourself.

The brain... no... the mind really is the control of yah. The way I see it is that the mind has the subconscious and the conscious parts... I'm not very scientific with me explanations, but I know what I'm talking about. The subconscious mind is like a recorder... where it records all that it hears. Then it replays it back to yah all the time. So the subconscious mind is where the mental habits live. Most of the recording that the subconscious mind has, went in when you was just a little thing... yah could call it programming. It plays this stuff back to yah, behind the scenes, thousands of times a day. And so when yah learnt no, don't do that yah bad boy... yah naughty girl... yah dirty thing... that's what gets programmed into yah... and it reminds yah all the time... yah bad boy... yah naughty girl... yah dirty thing. And, because it rules us, we don't live to our potential, we live to our programming... Yah get that... Yah understanding what I'm saying?... Yah live to yah programming.'

There was a chorus of 'Yes Sir.'

'And the only time it's not playing in our subconscious mind is when yah thinking with the conscious mind... the conscious mind always overrides the subconscious mind, when yah use it. But listen,... scientists, those clever people, they tell us that we only use our conscious mind about five percent of the time when we is awake, and the rest of the time the subconscious mind does its own thing, of; yah bad boy... yah naughty girl... yah dirty thing. So how on hell can yah be happy if yah got this negative stuff playing all day telling yah, yah a bad boy... yah a naughty girl... yah a dirty thing... ...Yah can't can yah? So to be with joy, yah got to tell yourself a different story. And yah got to do it all the time.

So what I mean when I say yah got to prepare yourself a different life... to be joyful, yah have to see yourself as joyful. For every second where yah tell yourself yah gunna get the big job, gunna earn millions, then yah not telling yourself just how grand yah are. And remember, as yah only use yah conscious mind five percent of the time, yah godda make the most of it...'

Another cackle came... then another... He watched the kids, and even looked directly, seemingly on purpose, at some of the teachers. Some squirmed a bit and looked at the floor, not taking in his gaze. He cackled again as they did.

As if giving them a break in focus, Anthony busied himself, first by taking off his cowboy hat, and wiping his brow, as if a hot day on the lands. Taking out a water bottle, he took a drink. The 'Aaaaaaarrr' of pleasure came through the mic. 'I love me water... the nectar of the Gods they say... and I believe them...

...But even now yah still programme yah sub conscious. As yah go about yah day, yah taken in impressions... but the impressions are really yah perceptions. They are the way yah think yah see a thing'... As he said this, he pressed a button on his consul and moved the wheelchair to the other side of the stage. You...' he pointed to a student of African heritage, who was towards the right side of the hall... He then moved to the other side of the stage, 'And you,' pointing to another child, 'yah both see things differently... Yah perception is different. So it may be A, but yah perception tells yah it's B, and so it goes into yah subconscious as B. Now yah believe it was B, when really it's A. So yah godda look closely at how yah see things...

When I came in here, and up that ramp slowly... I did that on purpose... slowly... cause I knew all of yah was gunna think, jeese, this's a pathetic old fart.'

The kids burst out laughting, but he shut it down quickly by raising his voice, 'Perhaps I am an old fart, but I am other things as well... But yah perception didn't see that... yah saw an old fart...' He cackled long and hard at his own words. 'Careful what yah think of things... how yah see things... because if yah wanna live with joy in yah heart, yah godda take in the right perception...'

He continued moving the wheelchair up and down the stage, as if walking, as he talked.

'I love coming to schools and talking to young people. I never have a set plan as to what I'm gunna say... It just all kinda comes out in the way that it wants to. I do come here with one main thing to tell yah... and that is that there is a technique for livin' life, and by getting yah young, I can show yah that yah can change yah life in the twinkling of an eye... Sometimes the twinkling may take longer. But that's okay... To think joyous is simple, but most make it hard, when really it's simple. If yah have more good feeling thoughts, then yah feel better. So you have to watch yah thoughts. Or perhaps yah don't have to watch yah thoughts as such, because there's millions of them every day... and to try to monitor them all would make us batty. Rather, watch how yah feeling... at this point... right now... And it would be right now for the rest of yah day... are you feeling good right now?'

The children were silent, and so this time he asked louder, 'Are yah feeling good... Right now? A few children put up their hands to say yes.

'That's sad, only a few of out of so many of you... Okay, as yah mind can be influenced by the media as I just spoke about, it can also be influenced by yah actively telling it that yah a nice person, that yah a happy person, that life is really good to yah. If yah tell yourself that often enough, I guarantee yah that yah will feel better about yourself...

...As yah take time to study, or exercise, to improve yah performance, yah need to take the time to tell yourself that yah happy and have much to be happy about. Yah need to do this every day. Yah don't have to spend hours doing this… just a minute or so here… or a minute or so there… Or when yah catch yourself doing something good, tell yourself how wonderful yah are. If yah realise that yah have just said, or thought something negative, replace it with a positive…

… When I was growing up there was a movie, can't remember the name of it, but there was a saying… smile, and the whole world smiles with yah, cry and yah cry alone… Yep, that's true, but the deeper meaning is that when yah smile you feel better. That smiling helps with the good feeling thoughts that I mentioned earlier. Stock yah mind with good feeling thoughts.

Now living yah life properly is a technique. The technique is not to overcomplicate yah life. Sure, it's good to have goals and aspirations… Don't have too many and don't think too far ahead into the future. Think just a few goals. The mind needs to be stocked with happy. The mind don't care what goes into it… A bit like a cupboard at home – it's an open space waiting to be filled. Yah could fill it with tins of baked beans, or cleaning material… It don't care. It will take in whatever yah put in there… So if yah put in more thoughts that are not good feeling, then yah are not gunna feel good…

It's the same with life in general. Your life will be determined by the thoughts that yah think the most. So your thoughts may be consumed with success in life, and in some ways that's not a bad thing, but while yar focusing on the success, where are the good feeling thoughts? Yah have to take the time for the good feeling thoughts… For the happy thoughts… …for the joyous thoughts… to be grateful for who you are, and yah time of being alive.

Another way of looking at how the mind works… You've all heard of 3-D printing?" Almost every hand in the audience shot up. 'Yep, of course yah have. So how do yah know what's gunner print at the end?'

Not so many hands were raised this time, Anthony pointed to a boy towards the back and said, 'So, what's the answer?'

The boy, clearly pleased to have been selected shouted out, 'It depends on what you put into it… What I mean Sir… it is the material and design you put into it that gives you what comes out of it.'

'Absolutely... brilliant young man!' continued Anthony. 'What you put into that 3-D printer governs what comes out the other end... So what you put into your mind governs what comes out of the other end. So I will tell yah again for the hundredth time, maybe even the thousandth time... if yah want to be happy, yah have to put happy into yah head. When yah forget, because your busy... other thoughts, not so good feeling thoughts walk into yah mind... And guess what... You ain't so happy no more...That new shirt that yah mother brought you will only make yah happy for a little while. And once you've worn it three times it's just another shirt... One like the others hanging in yah cupboard. Things don't make yah happy... You will make you happy with your happy thoughts.

Am I starting to make meself clear?...

... I got a buddy. Poor bugga has Spinal Dysraphism. The big word means that there's a road-block between the brain and the spinal cord. I say poor bugga as he's worse than me. But he says, "You have to find personal meaning in life..." What happens to the human heart when the opportunity to participate is removed? When yah tongue no longa makes the sounds properly to talk with other people? When words remain stuck somewhere between yah mouth and yah head? When physical circumstances remove yah from people? The pain and fear of isolation... when people look at yah funny like...? He says, yah got to look only at the good... your mum and dad for helping yah. Look at your buddies that come and visit. The fact that yah still here, and able to read, or think or laugh... yeah... you got to laugh, even at all the things that make it hard. Yah got to look at your life and know that there is still meaning in it. That it's made yah mum stronger... or that like yourself, referring to me ... traveling all over helpin' youngens before they get too stuck in their ways. But there's more... I'm valuable, even if me body is failing... I still have value... I can still help people. I can think and advise them, and tell them a funny story when they're down. Some just get motivated just seeing me in me wheel chair, with me head flopping around, trying to have a go... yeah, it's hard, but there's still meaning... sometimes yah have to search a bit harder than others... but it's there... and it can give yah value and self-respect. When yah find meaning, yah get joy.

Me buddy reckons that there's no dis in his ability, there is only ability. If there is dis-ability when the mind puts it in the dis. Yah got to laugh at that.

That's what me buddy says and he's right. All of you there, and you teachers, you all got so much meaning in life, but if yah don't look for it, yah won't see it. Uncover what lies beneath yah, there's more to yah than what yah think...

Did yah know I was adopted... yep... special... was hand-picked out of all the other crying bubbas. Me... me... me... me... take me, we was all saying in bubba talk. I must have been the loudest cause they picked me. And wasn't I lucky it was them who picked me. Me Mum, God rest her soul, and me sis... over there... they were the ones that bought me back from the dead... really... The doctors had given up on me... I was a gonner as far they as they was concerned. But me sis Mary... now don't be shy Mary... she use to sing to me. She sang songs she knew I loved... for hours she'd sing. The nurses thought she was batty, singing to the soon to be dead one. Anyway, she bought me back with songs. And me Mum, she also. Then when I was out of the coma, still the quacks reckoned I was gunna be brain dead... Well some of yah may think I am... but at that time me mum and me sister didn't give up on me. They nursed me, and gave me a life. So if I was picked by other parents, then I could be brain dead, or dead dead. So on the one hand, I'm in this chair, but I have these wonderful loving people looking after me. Well Mums' gone now... God bless her.

We all need things to get us off our backsides... well you kids do... I can't no more... But there's students who beat themselves up for getting only ninety-nine percent. How did I make that one mistake they cry?...

The point is, yah still got to work on yah happiness. I bet Federer, the great tennis player was happy with all his wins, but when he finally hangs up his racket, all of those wins won't sustain his happiness. They'll please him but not give the deep seated joy. He'll have to get that from somewhere else, and he will...'

A crying child could be heard, and a hush descended in the hall. One of the teachers started to go to the child, but Anthony whispered,

'Leave him... let him cry a bit...' as he spoke he put a finger to his lips and indicated for all to be quiet.

All waited until the child started to compose himself. Realising that they were quiet for him, the boy became embarrassed and quickly tried to wipe the tears and snot away with the back of his hand.

Anthony engaged the wheelchair, reversed a bit and headed down the ramp. Turning right, he parked opposite the boy before pressing the hooter twice, "bip bip..." The stunned and embarrassed boy looked up with big round eyes to see this strange wheel-chaired cowboy only half a meter in front of him offering him a wad of tissues. The boy took them and did a better job of cleaning up his face.

Without the mic, and in a soft gentle voice that only those close by could hear, Anthony said, 'What's yah name mate?'

'J...JJ... Joshua Sir.'

'Wanna come for a ride Josh?'

Joshua's eyes became even bigger 'Me... on that thing?'

'Yep. Come on... get up here, and sit behind me... ...That's it, make yourself comfy, an hang onnnnnnnnnnn,' as they took off down the corridor and out the door on to the quadrangle. Joshua shrieked in delight. The quiet in the hall was broken with laughter... as if they were on the wheelchair. Many ran to the door to watch. Teacher control was ineffective as they themselves tried to see... all had big smiles on their faces.

Round and round they went in big figure of eights. Joshua giggling with glee... and Anthony cackling loudly. Finally, Anthony aimed for a clump of trees in the playground and came to a halt in the shade.

As Joshua was getting off, 'What do you think of that?' cackled Anthony.

'Fantastic sir,' Joshua giggled.

'Well yah can't have one, not unless yah break yah back or something...'

Joshua laughed again.

'How old are you Josh?'

'Fourteen Sir.'

'Jeese… yah got the world at yah feet…'

He let the silence do its work for a moment, before asking, 'Josh… what did I say back there that made yah feel bad?'

A sniffle started, he took the tissues out of his pocket and cleaned his nose, 'Sir… you didn't mean to make me cry… wasn't your fault… …It's just that my little sister Jeanie has been diagnosed with the same or one called Spina Bifida'.

Sniff, sniff, more tears.

Anthony waited. Joshua continued, 'It's horrible, she's only eleven and already it's bad…' Sniff… sniff… sniff. 'But Sir, what makes me sad is that I don't know how to treat her…'

He became silent, pretending to focus on the tissues in his hand as he folded and unfolded them.

Gently, Anthony said, 'Yah love Jeanie don't yah?'

Joshua nodded yes, his focus still on the tissues.

'So how did yah treat her before?'

'I… I played games with her. Sometimes silly games… and I let her dress me up like a mother… she'd come and hang out in my room before I did my homework… You know… stuff like that…'

'Well, why not do the same?… Sure, yah may have to be a bit inventive… she's still the same girl inside… she won't break. Be straight with her… tell her it makes yah sad that she is like that now. Don't pretend it's all sunshine and roses… it ain't… but you can still have good fun…'

He was silent and Joshua nodded his head in understanding. 'But yah know something else Josh?… Jeanie wants to help yah as well. Girls are smart… smarter than us blokes… tell her yah own problems… like…

when yah have problems with a teacher or bully at school. Let her hold yah hand when yah sad... she needs this more than anything... And yah know what yah call it?... it's called love Josh... it's love... and when yah share yours, yah'll make her the happiest girl in world, even in a wheelchair.... And you'll also be happy'.

For the first time Joshua looked up and had a small smile, as he handed back the rest of the tissues.

'Thanks mate', Anthony said, 'never know when I'm gunna need these... this work uses lots of tissue...'

A giggle from Joshua, and a cackle from Anthony, as Anthony pointed to the back, 'Get on mate, got to go back before those teachers have a fit.'

'Wheeeeeeeeeee,' as they headed back.

'Come now children,' one of the teachers said. 'Back into your seats'.

'Wheeeeeeeeee' as they headed down the corridor just missing fleeing children. 'Wheeee' up the ramp, until the wheelchair came to a sudden stop. Both still giggling and cackling as Joshua headed back to his seat.

The rest of the school were shouting out things like, 'Way to go Josh... Sir... can I have a turn...'

After more cackling, he waited until it quietened down.

'So where was we before Josh demanded a free ride?'

More laughter.

'Can't remember, but don't matter as I'll start anywhere...

The technique is not to overcomplicate yah life. Over achieving... Some reckon they must be the best at everything they do. And while they are so busy improving their skill or ability, there's no time for looking for happiness. Nothing wrong with wanting to be good at yah job or sport, but remember, when yah go overboard, there's less time to work on or be happy...

... Even now you are all striving for academic success... it's not gunna make you joyful. It will be a relief, the happiness that you get from yah high mark is really only a fleeting happiness. And that's not the deep seated joy that I talk of. Equally so, if yah fail, yah'll be miserable for a time, but within time the joy will return as there's more to life than just academic success. So if yah can hear between the lines of what I'm saying, it's no one individual event that'll give yah joy. It's a mindset that knows that it can manufacture joy, but there must be the right balance in life.

Don't mix with unhappy...

Now, about money. Many of the children that I visit ask me about the importance of money, and will money make them happy.

Yah got to have money. But yah don't need much to be happy. There are some that don't care about getting happiness. All they care about is money... It's their bank balance... that's all that counts. They think seeing their investment portfolio grow will make them happy...

I keep talking about living life with technique. There's nothing wrong with money and earning money, by goodness we need it. But when it rules yah, yah not living within the technique.

Part of the technique is that if yah spend just a few minutes a morning just thinking of the good things in yah life then yah will go through yah day happier and more positive. Do it all the time and it will be that recording that'll play in the background... Think of it... yah got to be happier if all yah thoughts are happy thoughts... And yah all got a lot to be grateful for.

Yeah, bring to yah mind gratitude... Gratitude means seeing the good. Remember I said, the subconscious mind is a recording, and once recorded, it plays the stuff back to yah all the time... now, what would yah rather have playing... sad... I can't do this... I'm not good enough? Or, would yah do betta if it came... I'm smart enough... people like me, I can do this... I may not know it, yet, but I will... and so on...

...And to be happy, don't listen to the news... I care little for the news, as it's rigged to make us negative and pessimistic. Yah laugh at that, but it's true. Did yah know that the news broadcasters work on a specific ratio?... In a half hour news bulletin there are around thirty separate items. The ratio goes something like this; there are twenty negative things, such as people being murdered or killed in a car accident. They always focus on a war or two, with soldiers, bombs and people killed. Then they'll have about seven neutral things, that don't make us feel good or sad, of which sport and the weather are included. At the end they give a nice touchy-feeling thing to fool yah into thinking they are well balanced... And somewhere there may have been one or two other nice things. So we get bombarded with twenty bad things, and only a couple of good things. I don't know why the news is given like that but it's hard to be happy if yah listen too much to the news...

In yah life of working yah technique for happiness, peace plays a big part. How on Earth can yah be happy if yah ain't peaceful... if yah listen to the news yah won't have peace of mind.

ACT 7
THE ACCIDENT

Anthony had been out on a new date, wining and dining in Broken Hill. He did not drink, nor did she, but they had fun. He loved that she laughed at his jokes. At one stage she put on his cowboy hat... and looked kind of cute.

After driving her home, he was heading towards his place when it started raining heavily, a rare occurrence in outback Australia. Anthony drove in his beloved Mini-Minor, which he called Chug-Along. It was fifteen years old but he did not care, it was his first car, and he was eighteen years old... his life in front of him. He slowed down and drove with caution as he went through a traffic light that was green in his direction... the horn blared into his ear, directly into his brain. He never saw the truck that slammed into his driver's door, his body receiving the full impact of the four ton delivery truck. For a time, the truck and his Mini-Minor, skidded down the road until finally slamming into a tree. The time was 11.15 pm.

At 11.18 an ambulance was returning to the hospital after a false alarm, when it saw the aftermath of the accident. Anthony was in the Emergency Department within eight minutes ... Within two hours he was flown to Sydney, where he went to the Royal North Shore Hospital ICU. This saved his life, but not his body, the paramedic thought.

A day later, Mary and Joanna arrived at the hospital in Sydney. They both knew their world had changed. In the dark hours and days that followed they sat vigil over Anthony. Although he was in a coma, they spoke to him, heart to heart, soul to soul, encouraging him to return. But at the same time they gave him permission to let go and pass over if he had to. The most used word was love... we love you Anthony, and we are here for you... always here for you.

Even though there was no conscious communication, they could feel that Anthony was fighting, his spirit courageous. With each passing day hope increased.

In consultation with the doctors, they were told of the spinal cord injury that was so bad that if Anthony survived he would most likely be mentally incapacitated, and probably a paraplegic – a gruesome prospect. They explained that a quadriplegic loses the use of all four limbs. They also explained that they would not be able to bring him out of the coma, only Anthony could do that.

Black and silent. They were the first thoughts Anthony had upon regaining awareness. Kind of nice... comfortable... In pitch dark he lay without trying to move, and somehow knew he could not. He became aware that he was only mind, nothing more, no body, no shell to house the mind in – just mind. No external sounds, nor any other thing or person – just him, his mind in the cocoon. He had no idea how long he floated in this state, until, with shock, someone moved his arm, as if a rag doll. He heard the voice, and knew it belonged to Mary. She seemed to be talking to herself... 'Anthony, you gunner be okay you just wait and see. You gunner come out of this coma and be good as new. Screw the doctors, we know better... we know that if you decide to live, and have a life, then that is what'll happen...' She continued this way for some time, but Anthony was in no hurry to be released from this cocoon. Things started to come back to him... the horn blaring, then nothing... floating out of his body, looking at the scene below, at his mangled body, whilst a paramedic attended to him... At one stage, he saw the paramedic shake his head to his partner, indicating that this kid was not going to make it...

No, he was not ready to face the world, and so he allowed the cocoon to keep its embrace. He did not know why the darkness and the floating state was comforting. Later, he would think that he was preparing himself, psyching himself for what lay in front of him. But more so, he was fascinated with this new reality. It gave him time to consider who he was. From the conversations around him, and from what he saw when he was floating out of his body, he knew his body was broken. After listening to the doctor's talk, he questioned himself... okay, what does this mean to me? I'm alive, but broken... At one time he heard a male voice, a doctor say to his family, 'I'm sorry, but I give him absolutely no hope of any reasonable life quality... the damage he received from that truck was just too brutal for a human body to withstand. Humans are incredibly resourceful at adapting, but I think it would be too much to ask for in this case. Anthony has severe brain injuries... Not to mention the snapped spine.... We also have reason to believe that he would be blind as his optic nerves have been severed.'

Anthony was fully aware as to what had been said, but sank back into the cocoon, knowing that he would deal with it later. He had more important things to deal with, such as, why are we given life in the first place.

The doctors were perplexed as a CT scan showed a higher state of consciousness from both breathing and brain wave activity, but Anthony still appeared comatose. Anthony had emerged from the coma some four hours earlier. His pupil size was consistent to that of a conscious person. Yet, he was unresponsive to the standard alert, vocal, painful stimuli.

The doctors knew of the current opinion that suggests that humans who retreat into a comatose state as a result of an accident do so because of the need for complete deep rest and recuperation. This is a "shutting or slowing down" of as many body functions as possible as a survival reflex. And although this is unprecedented, it could be something to do with that.

Every forty-five minutes the doctor on duty personally went and checked the monitors and to give the standard alert, vocal, painful stimuli and to check pupil dilation.

But Anthony knew differently. The coma offered the person's soul the space to evaluate if they want to remain or go.

The time, or rather the process that Anthony was going through made him know that despite the damage, he made the choice for life. More importantly, irrespective of the damage, to enjoy life. Then hearing his sister Mary singing to him, he knew that he was going to fight like hell for a quality life.

Once reaching those conclusions, only then did he start to show signs of consciousness.

He tried to move but his body did not respond. As far as he knew, his family were there. With his attempted movement, they all stared at the bed. It was Mary who shouted, 'Look... Anthony's moving his head... I knew it... I knew Anthony would fight and come back... Oh thank you God... we have a miracle.'

Each day bought its own problems and heartache, but also a positive in as much as each day was a gift.

Anthony had mental trauma because of the injuries, and the brain numbing drugs that he was on. He did remember the pain he was in. It came in waves through the entire body. At this period he was too busy fighting for survival to consider anything. Somehow, there was on a ledge of his conscious the need to live. The determination was a force that he knew from not where it came.

At times Anthony wondered if he was angry with God... to allow this to happen to him... all his plans... his life and talent, all wasted in this ruined cadaver that was more dead than alive. Trapped inside, sightless and unable to move, his mind worked overtime – getting past depression and anger... It snarled and snapped within. Somehow, he kept it to himself and showed it to no one as it was all too hard for them all. There was no laughter, just grim days and worse nights when all was quiet. Nights were the worst, where inside he wept in silence.

It was with the realisation that it was not his destroyed body that caused so much anguish, it was with shock that he realised it was his loss of identity... who was he? Now a freak, not being able to fit in... He was mourning. Mourning for his lost body. Mourning for his lost potential... for his place in society. He cried for all his little losses, and for the big obvious ones, like his independence. In his mourning the questions kept coming. What will it be like in the future? What will being completely incapacitated feel like? He did not realise that this feeling of loss of identity would later give him the brilliant platform from which to teach others about difficulty and identity.

Later he would think that watching his life drift by was intolerable. He did not know how but somehow he would help people through their crises. He learnt that the inner core can be stronger than most think. He would teach that when an issue in a person's life was so dominant, where normal reasoning departed, that they can come through it. He somehow knew he could guide people through it to a happier life.

This is hard, really hard, but somehow his strength of character will prevail. And that every day there must be some successes over the hardship. He knew that it could only be his mindset that would allow him to expand every single one of those successes. By not doing so, he would be at the mercy of a runaway mind that would create a sad, disruptive disappointing life. Every time he smiled he won. Every time he tried he won, and with each small improvement he won and he would keep on winning. It was not beating the body as such, it was winning over the mind. Though his body may have been broken, his mind and spirit were not. There was a choice – to be ruled by fear or to live with hope.

What had helped to bring this positive change about was a remembrance, which had a strong effect on him... He was about eleven. On the way home from school every day he had to pass the farm where a thirteen-year-old lived. For weeks, that thirteen-year-old boy would wait on his veranda for Anthony to come past and bully him. He would pull Anthony's ear or hair; or put his arm up behind his back in a painful way. The bully would sit on Andrew's chest and drool spit over his face. After weeks of this, something in Anthony snapped, and in his rage, he grabbed the top of the bully's shirt and yanked. Buttons and shirt ripped, and in a parody of slow motion, the bully looked down and saw the rip and started crying. As he did, he pushed off Anthony and ran back into his house. Anthony was never worried by the bully again.

He learnt that you cannot stop fear, but it was not going to stop him; and that like emotions, fear can't be conquered by suggesting that it is not there, but it can be mitigated with a determination that what you want to achieve is stronger than the fear. Will and desire can take you over, around, under or through fear.

Thinking about the episode, he realised that his condition and the way that his mind responded to it was never going to bully him again.

ACT **8**

THE SCHOOL

He was quiet for a moment, letting the children catch up.

'There was a wise lady who said, "It's only possible to live happily ever after on a day-to-day basis".

Purpose in life can help with finding joy. No purpose leads to a lack of joy. When yah have a fulfilling life, yah more likely to have a happy one... and when yah happy yah are more likely to feel fulfilled. To achieve yah purpose, yah need optimism...'

And then he cackled, 'Do yah know any happy pessimists? I don't...

Aristotle... I'm sure you've heard of him. Well I read about him, and he put a lot of time into trying to figure out the root of happiness. He said, h*appiness is the meaning and purpose of life, the whole aim and end of human existence...* yep that's wot Aristotle declared... And he also reckoned that true happiness comes from independence and stability... He's right, but it's more than that. He said nothing about having to work on happiness.

Now in terms of yah success... the want for success can make yah very unhappy... There is nothing wrong with wanting the best out of life but make sure that yah don't live a cockeyed life as a result. So it's all about how yah think success is and the balance yah bring to it. So how yah think of success will either support or take yah joy away.

What vision of yah future do yah focus on? If it is all about get, get and get more? Then yah won't be happy. If yah focus on achieving what yah love, a balance between work, study, family, and social life, then that's a better recipe for happiness. I'm not saying yah won't be happy if yah successful, I'm saying you'll be happy because yah set the right life balance and attitude to make yahself happy, and yah success is just a contributor. The right technique...

When yah consider yah success, don't listen to what society suggests as the standard. Yah must understand what's important to you. I consider success a state of mind. Even at yah young age, does yah success or state of mind make yah happy? If yah not fulfilled, how can yah be happy? Being famous or living in a big house has nothing to do with success. In forming yah own opinions of success, ask the questions: Do yah enjoy life? Will yah continue to enjoy life?

Identifying with money or power is not nearly as precious as identifying with happiness, love and contentment. When yah create yah own understanding of success, be true to yourself, not what society expects. Flattery is an ego issue, as are the labels that go around. Be careful of yah illusions, cravings and ambitions. When yah plan yah success, keep these thoughts in mind.

To achieve success, yah have to work for it. Whereas, failure is usually brought on by a lack of effort, either mental or physical. Success takes risk and guts. It takes character... failure is being less responsive. Yah get failure by being meek.

Yah must identify what's important ta yah. This includes family life, how hard yah wanna work, yah health and dozens of other things. To be successful, yah need to take time to evaluate. By doing so, yah begin the process that will take yah to that fulfilment... and therefore happiness. As there are likely to be many different topics, set goals and time frames for each.

Know that these aspirations may take time, and don't attempt to make too many changes at once.

And then, what's yah potential? How do yah plot yah potential?... But before answering this to yourselves, I want yah ta take into consideration... that to my knowledge, which is sometimes scanty... (cackle) but no scientist has yet discovered the limits of our potential. So back to the question... what's yah potential? The sky's the limit I'd say. So don't ever give up. Failure is giving up... Failure's temporary... unless yah let yah mind say otherwise. Failure's not fatal unless yah believe it is. ...What yah consistently think about yourself and yah abilities is what yah become.

Sometimes yah have to work on your optimism. The same as yah work on yah bank balance. If yah don't, it'll shrink. Yah must take responsibility for yah happiness, as there will always be times when life's against yah.'

He stopped talking, took out a biscuit and ate it... in silence for a full two minutes. After finishing it, he cleaned his teeth with his tongue and sucked his teeth for a while, which was heard through the microphone. When satisfied his mouth hygiene had been complete, he continued.

'We now gunna talk about love... But it won't be the type of love yah all thinking about'. As he said this he did a loud and exaggerated kiss on the back of his hand so that the microphone could pick it up. The children laughed and some made the same sound using their hands...

'Love... the big one... not romantic love. I'm talking of just being love and with love to others and humankind...

Love describes an attitude... or a state of mind. Love is also a verb as in 'I love yah'. Love is also a noun (his love of music), that's why the meaning of love gets confused and over used. And so love has become a part of everyday speech... I'd love a cold drink... I love that TV show and so on. And because it is such a big topic, I won't talk much about it now other than to say that yah don't get yah heart banging with love... fear does that. Love don't give yah sweaty palms... fear does that. Love don't give yah butterflies in the stomach, guilt or anxiety does that. So if yah can bring genuine love into yah life, where yah do what yah love... cultivate a loving way then yah get joy, and the intensity of it is governed by how deep the love is. As more love comes, there is less fear, less guilt, less anxiety.

Rumi... that olden Persian Mystic said this about love... "Your task is not to seek love, but merely to seek and find all the barriers within yourself that you have built against it". And yah can't be happy without love... it's impossible."

Love ain't external to us. It's inside us when we are born.... Just like joy... We don't have to go looking for love as we already have it. It's like the air we breathe, we cannot see it but it's there for us to use. To release love all we need is an awareness and a willingness. When we call for it, it will erupt... I'm getting philosophical... but love is a deeply spiritual energy... one that allows us to find peace, and internal power... even if yah life is not great at that time.

If it is to not find the love within, to share with others, then what's our reason for being here? When there's love – there is God. When one knows God – there's love. When there is no love – there's hate. When there is hate – there can be no love... Or simplifying it... when there's love there's joy...

Who likes looking cool? Go on, put your hands up.'

Many of the kids by now knew that some of his questions were tricky, so most did not put their hands up. But he continued anyway.

When I was recovering from the accident, I lost me identity. But later, I realised that identity is an ego driven thing... Did I need the identity I longed for?... No longer did I need to be cool... spend money on cool... yah know how much freedom I gained from not caring about being cool? ... At the same time, I couldn't care if I was popular. And yah may have noticed I don't drive the Mercedes Benz of wheelchairs... I don't give a hoot about prestige... Why do I need prestige? ... I don't. By not needing to be cool, popular or having the need to be with the latest devices... it's like removing a strait jacket... And you think I worry about other's opinions of me, not at all... I heard somewhere ...when yah follow what everyone else is doing, yah lose yourself... but when yah follow yah soul-voice, yah lose the crowd. Later, the crowd will find yah... and flock around yah...

In today's age, Facebook is the ultimate popularity contest. Sure, I use Facebook. I use it to keep in contact with me friends. But most want to show the world how popular they are... Look at how many friends I have on Facebook... They are not friends... not proper friends, they don't even talk to them... how could they as they don't know them. Taking photos of the food they eat, the places they visit... and the clothes they wear... all with poses that a model would do.

It's all show. All this is to tell themselves inside that they're cool and popular and this'll make them happy inside. The reality is, when night comes, and they are laying in their bed, they be wondering why's they are not happy.

People wanna be seen wearing the right labels... Gucci for instance. I thought that's what you said to babies, Gucci... Gucci... Guchi goo... perhaps that's what brain washed them to having to use that stuff. Or Armani... even Versaci... do those things make yah a better person? If yah had a choice, Armani or happiness... what would it be because Armani ain't happiness...?

Prestige's a limitation because yah focus is on the wrong thing... Focus on simple and happy. Yah can survive very nicely without all of that stuff.

To get these things is the wrong investment... invest in yahself, yah can't buy self-esteem. Envy is also a limitation, a debilitating one because it makes yah feel shit... Oh sorry... forgot that I'm in a school.

Begrudging someone else's luck, ability or possessions just creates discontent... Feeling envious is not living with happy... It's negativity 101, resulting from yah belief that yah not capable of doing something that someone else can. When yah envious, yah focus is on what yah don't have, not what yah have... Look at all the good things yah have. Can't be happy if yah always wanting something yah don't or can't have.

...Yah may ask the question how do yah change from being a sad person to a happy one? The first thing is to acknowledge that yah predominantly unhappy, and from that base set about to actively improve yah mental outlook. Yah can't chase happiness, yah must be happiness. Yah don't have to search far and wide for it, it's there already. Yah cannot buy happiness as it is within yah, a state of mind... Are yah happy now? If not, choose to move towards happiness. If yah don't choose to be happy, fine, stay sad, stay angry, remain unforgiving, be a complainer and continue a life that don't work! ... Man's the only creature on earth that can be perpetually miserable.'

ACT **9**

RECOVERY

Despite his dire condition, the family searched for improvements and as a family rejoiced in each tiny improvement. Never did they concern themselves with the doctors prognosis. It was when the bandages were removed from his head that Anthony realised what being blind really meant. 'Will deal with this later… I'm alive… I have a body… I have me family.'

It took weeks for Anthony's speech to form. At first it was like a voice that belonged to another… a wild thing that did as it wanted. Finally, cohesion came. The family and the hospital staff wept or laughed with relief. This was the first meaningful sign of cognitive improvement.

Rehabilitation was going to take several years, but so be it. They would rearrange their lives accordingly, nothing was more important than Anthony's fight for recovery, and as he had so much fortitude, the least they could do was to support him in every way possible.

By this time, Anthony had been transferred to the general hospital in Broken Hill.

For months, Anthony's progress was painfully slow, but Anthony seemed not to care. *Each day I will be a bit better than the last* was the prevailing thought he woke up with. The hospital staff had never seen a patient as determined as this one, not only for health but for a positive statement of life.

Occupational therapy, physiotherapy and speech therapy all continued, and within a year, Anthony was allowed to go home for short periods.

Mary had made a decision to dedicate her immediate future to Anthony's care. She instinctively knew that she had been born for this moment, and so released herself from her job to became Anthony's full-time carer. Nothing else mattered but Anthony and his comfort and rehabilitation.

Anthony spent hours visualising his arms working. Celebrations were held when for the first time he wiggled a finger. This indicated that nerve damage to that arm was starting to heal and respond. Two months later, with more rehab, and determination, there was limited control over both arms. Then there was feeling in his torso, and soon the ability for movement. Nevertheless, unable to move from the waist down, Anthony settled with this, and was satisfied with his progress. Being without sight was difficult, another thing to adapt to.

After eighteen months, Anthony finally went home for good. Mary had not wasted the time and had converted the house to suit her paraplegic brother. The insurance, thank goodness for the insurance, paid a private physiotherapist to come in daily for rehab. The progress was often so slow that it seemed non-existent, but all remained positive and committed to a fuller recovery.

There was one day, his dad Barry was out in the paddocks, and Joanna had her own doctor's appointment in town. Mary said to Anthony, 'I need to go to the shop, do yah think yah will be OK for an hour on yah own?' This was the first time that Anthony was to be left alone.... His coming out so to speak. This moment had been planned, and all three waited to see how Anthony would respond. As they predicted, he was fine and grabbed his first moment of independence with the same determination that he won rodeo events as a child.

As it turned out there was no need to worry, because when Mary returned, she was greeted with a happy, 'Yah get everything yah needed?'

At dinner that night, they told Anthony of the deception, and why, so they could evaluate how he would cope. He, as in days of old joked, 'Bull, yah snuck off to see some bloke. Didn't want yah little brother to hear yah kisses did yah?'

Left alone more now, Anthony always considered his luck… if that emergency vehicle had not been called out on that false call… *Why was I saved, is there something that I'm meant to do…* he realised just how precious life is. *And how bloody lucky was I to have me Mum and Mary to look after me…*

This was the time Mary had been waiting for and broached the question of an operation to re attach his retina. Not hiding the truth, she told Anthony that the possibility of success was likely to be less than twenty-five percent. 'And yah also have to go back to Sydney.' But surely the risk was worth it…. Although Anthony was tired of operations, hospitals and invasive practices, it was still worth the chance.

'It'll be okay,' said Anthony softly. 'We got nothing to lose.'

'Yep,' said Mary, 'it will be okay.'

And so they made the arrangements. Anthony worked his mind with visualisations of being able to see. The operation was for the right eye. When the bandages came off, at first there was only light, then blurry vision. But like mud dropping to the bottom of a pond, the blurring cleared. The entire family was there, and all laughed with relief. Three weeks later the left eye was done. He had gained eighty percent vision in the left, and seventy percent in the right. 'Just enough to allow me to be a menace in me wheelchair,' he would often say.

In time, his mates would come around and take him out somewhere, on a drive or to see a show. One day friends, William and Jessica, phoned and said they were going to listen to a talk on Buddhism and offered to take him. *Yeah, why not?* He thought. *Might learn something.*

He was to learn that it was a form of Western Buddhism that was easier to fit in with Western ways, and he enjoyed the talk. He did not become a Buddhist, but there was one concept that made him think about his life. He realised that he never really knew how to live – that he always attached himself to things, and by doing so, more often than not, he was unhappy when things did not come, or came slowly. For instance, when he could not continue his rodeo life, it showed him just how much he invested his mind into it, and how hopeless he felt. He realised that when we attach too closely, we set up ourselves for disappointment. We do it with money and lifestyle. Every day we are wanting things to happen, to come, to get here. And later, he had the profound thought, *now that I have given up the need to need, I feel much happier, have become content.* And with contentment, joy started to settle.

With determination, a new identity started to emerge; one neither based on achievement nor need. This one was based on who he was, not who he should be. It felt so much better, more natural. Not having to look good to the rest of the world gave Anthony a freedom he had never known. A strength of purpose grew in proportion.

Now that he could see, it was with a shock to see the response of his condition on his friends when they came to visit. They would be saddened and could not hide that fact. But after a time, they would invariably be inspired by Anthony's good cheer and determination. When they came in, Anthony would ask them about their life, as if it was the most important thing in the world, and that his issues were trivial in comparison, he always had a reassuring word for them.

A C T 10
S C H O O L,
T H E F I N A L W O R D

'We gunna start to wind up now and so there are only a few other things that I wanna say to yah. One is, yah'll not be happy if you don't follow the career that you wanna do... not what yah parents want you to do. If yah wanna be an artist, but yah dad wans yah to be a computer whiz ... be the artist. Respectfully, tell him yah why yah want to be an artist... Or why yah don't wanna be a computer whiz. Yah must do what yah love, don't do something because yah feel yah have to. There will always be regret, and regrets are not good feeling thoughts...

You must like the life that yah've created for yourself. It may not be perfect, but you can work on changing or improving it. If yah don't like the life that yah have you will never be happy. Live towards a fun life, not a life with too much obligation.

Another thing... don't look backwards at the issues of yah life... only look forward. Be happy now... right now... Not tomorrow or when yah graduate. When yah look back yah carry baggage... Baggage is a wonderful word that means gathering up all yah negative issues from yah recent or distant past and putting them into an imaginary bag that never leaves yah side. If the bag left yah body, yah couldn't extract each hurt or pain to live with its agony afresh... Baggage carriers allow themselves to wallow in their remorse, reliving the bad episodes whenever they feel like pressing the replay button.

To make the baggage easier to carry, and so they can stuff it with more of their miseries, they attach stainless steel castor wheels to the bag. You'll recognise the baggage people the minute yah say, "G'day, how are yah?" Then yah wish yah had kept yah mouth shut as they just don't know how to be happy. And yah can't be even a tiny bit happy if yah carry yah baggage...

Yah don't see me with a trailer on this buggy carrying me past with me. Yah got to feed the soul with happiness. Because if yah don't it'll feed on negativity. It's up to you what yah feed it...

A friend of mine felt that she needed a new beginning. She got divorced, moved into a new house, got new furnishings, bought new clothes, had a change of hair style, and guess what? Same old rubbish, just a new day, because her sadness and negativity came with her... towed behind the removal truck on those shiny stainless steel castors...'

The kids thought this hysterical.

'...I wanna tell yah about the happiness report that measures the happiness of people in all the different countries of the world. And can yah believe it, it's those countries that are not high in technology, or what we would call sophistication… They don't have all the gadgets and gismos. They tend to be family units that have lived the same way for hundreds or thousands of years… Even when they are hungry or cold, yah still see them laughing and having a great time of it…

Do yah genes dictate if yah gunna be happy or not happy? They only have about a 15% effect on yah ability to be happy or not happy for yah first few years… say till yah about nineteen.

But the biggest influence is from yah family, teachers and society… that's external influence. This clearly shows that yah happiness is moulded by the life you have around you. Yah can override that with yah own thoughts.

How do yah know if yah've had a good day, it's by the number of smiles or laughs yah had…

Second last thing I'm gunna say… the people with the big words would say, and the penultimate thing I'm gunna say. I wanna promise yah that if yah spend just five minutes a day thinking happy thoughts, within about twenty days, yah'll feel happier. But yah mustn't sabotage yah efforts with doom and gloom for the rest of the day. Yah must have more happy thoughts than unhappy thoughts… Got that, more nice felling thoughts than bad feeling ones.

I reckon it's best to spend five minutes just after yah wake up. When yah do it, stand up proud and tall, think happy… think gratitude… positive. A great way to start the day…

I wanna finish off with one last saying… if yah happy… you did it. …If yah sad… you did it. Happiness is manufactured by you… It's learning the technique… it's up to yah if yah have it or don't. Happiness is a process… an ongoing process.'

And on that note he passed the microphone back to Mrs Wentworth. She in turn said, 'Please give Mr Montgomery a big thank you and a round of applause.'

'Thank you Mr Mont…gom…ery…' they all said in unison, followed by much clapping. After a suitable period, only known by Mrs Wentworth, she said, 'Thank you children, that will be enough.'

And Mr Montgomery, on behalf of the school, the teachers, and the children, I would like to present you with this small gift of our appreciation.'

'Why thank you Mrs. Wentworth,' he cackled... 'this is most unexpected.' Meanwhile he had received literally hundreds of these tokens of appreciation. He then raised the wrapped present and shouted to the children, 'Thanks a lot.'

Then, after putting the present into his bag on the floor of the wheelchair, he waved to the children. He gave a special thumbs-up wave directed at Joshua.

'Godda go,' he shouted. 'Mary... give yah a race to the van.' And with that he engaged the motor and scooted down the ramp, along the corridor, holding the steering wheel in his right hand and waving in his cowboy hat with his left – cackling louder than ever.

Mary, could be seen dashing out the door ... she was not going to let him beat her again.

THE SEVENTEENTH SEED

In Action there is Hope

Many people seem to do nothing with their lives. They prefer to squander their time and leave potential talents untouched – precious lives wasted, really wasted.

Man has achieved his place in the world through evolution. If he had not adapted and evolved, he would have disappeared from the Earth thousands of years ago. Evolution of methods, tools, etc., are methods of creativity. Humanity is made up of individuals, and each individual must also evolve in his or her own way, to be as creative as possible. It is a natural urge to better ourselves and our lot in life. We do this through creation.

Look at the amazing architecture that shapes the horizons of our cities or beautiful art, computer systems and thousands of other inventions and creations. There are many people though, who sit on the sideline with their talent while watching the world and time go by.

I do not suggest that you have to go out and develop a new medicine or build a nuclear reactor. I do think though, that there is a built-in need to become the best we can with the tools given to us. With that comes fulfilment. Conversely, those who do not use their talents or creativity feel that they have somehow been left out of life. These are the fringe people, who have regrets and resentment, because they missed out.

I have not yet met a person without any abilities; all have something that they can do and do well. Perhaps yours is looking after children, working in construction, or growing things – but whatever it is, your job is to find your talent and to apply faith and enthusiasm to take it as far as it can go.

Life is about choice. We can choose action and hope or inaction and pessimism. *In action, there is hope – in endeavour freedom.*

It would seem to me that those who choose inaction are people of a negative nature. They would mutter, 'Oh, there's no point in doing that.' They may not be aware of their dissatisfaction but it will be there.

The Australians have a wonderful saying: 'Life, be in it,' – if we are not creating, we are not in it.

We grow as individuals by applying ourselves, irrespective of how often circumstances knock us down. Our universe is a curious place as it truly rewards those who try. Sometimes it does this in subtle ways, and at other times in a more grandiose fashion. Ultimately, doers are rewarded.

I have heard those people, to whom I refer as inactive, say that they are happy. I doubt that they are happy as their inactivity contravenes the in-built capacity to evolve and create. They are likely to be dissatisfied because of an underlying nag to accomplish. There also tends to be resentment to those who do use their creativity to get ahead.

So, how does action resolve negativity? Well, by an action, you move towards taking your power back – power that you gave away when you gave up hope.

The Australians have another saying, which is half sung; 'Come on Aussie, come on,' and I urge you to come on, and remember that *in action there is hope.*

Calling Your Will

Buffalo strips ripped skin, blood seeped out of wounds that had stretched and festered. With pain tugging at his consciousness, White Feather did not know reality from dream. Still, he did not yield to the tiredness.

It seemed like years ago that he had arrived from the city to the flat expanse of the reservation. Stepping out of his jeans and windbreaker, he had merged into a world that was far removed from stress and noise, a world of ancestors and truth, where culture and spirit are one. This was his ancestral home, and at thirty-six, he came to meet himself and to learn lessons.

White Feather was a Tsalagi or as the white people call them, a Cherokee. He was undertaking a ritual to call his will... Life had knocked it out of him.

Leapfrogging time dragged and raced with flashing images enmeshed in delirium and mixed emotions: sad, euphoric, puzzled, regretful, loving, hating; all to be worked through, continually searching for wisdom and, in doing so, the hope of finding his determination.

The blood-stained leather thong was embedded into slits in his skin. The other end attached to the top of a world tree. This tether was not long enough to allow him to seek the comfort of the ground, and so forced him to stand or rotate around the pole in endless circles. There was no respite; if he slumped, the weight of his body stretched the leather and tore the skin. In years to come, his scars would bear testimony to his search for himself.

The different bands of Tsalagi are endowed with different teachings. White Feather's were entrusted with the duty of rekindling the fire of clear mind. The Etowah's had been handed down this responsibility for generations.

The Tsalagi do not use helucigens to go into trance. They use fasting, chanting, drumming and fatigue. The first day is usually with vigour and intent. On the second day, exhaustion sets in and the mind starts to float into a place where truth is possible.

'Experience is what you get on the way to death, so use it and gain from it. You can't buy it, yet there is a cost as re-learning is expensive. Nor can you swap experience or receive it on a platter.'

This seemed to be the theme that came from White Feather's higher self. It spoke of embracing the teaching of experience. Into the future he saw that he was to be a leader and that wisdom was to be within his mind, and so over the days and nights that followed, understanding and clear thinking came.

Deep into the second night, with bitterly cold rain pounding his bent back and bowed head, White Feather remembered a time when a child – euphoric and feeling warrior-like after shooting a buffalo. He experienced the joy of young speeding legs to the kill. Then abruptly, tears flooded his eyes and rolled down his cheeks as he saw what he had done. His heart exploded in his chest with a grief that has never left him.

He was guided to know the sadness – 'feel it,' he was told. It was two years before he held a gun again.

The ancestors said, 'We are born to undergo experience. Every day is an experience, each minute a time to explore and extend boundaries. Your experiences become your library, always on hand and ready, provided you remember them. All are lessons, pieces in our jigsaw puzzle life. They are processes that must be retained and drawn upon. Sometimes in the process we lose our will. Our strength of mind deserts us and hibernates. White Feather, all your life you have been running away from who you could be. It is time to call back your will – call your happiness back to its place in your heart. If you do not take responsibility for feeling angry and sad, the anger will sit in you and reduce you to being less than who you are. Take the time to look deep within. To forgive the past and let go of what might have been, what could have been, and what should have been. Your will is never far away and wants to be reunited with you. Your season of spring is upon you, so call your strength from its hibernation. It is there to serve you but it will only serve you if you consciously call it.

You have surrendered your will and your grief gives you a heavy heart. An excess of grief in people can sadden the Earth. The Earth depends upon us to return the energy, to keep the cycle flowing. If we hold grief to ourselves we break the flow to Earth. We can return that grief to the Earth by tree-touch or sit on a rock and tell it your fears. When angry, let the river wash it away. By doing these things we acknowledge our remorse and let the flow continue. When a medicine man heals, he does so by clearing illusion. So, White Feather, let nature be your medicine man, to help with clear thinking.'

Aching and dizzy, an expansion of the senses, normal colours became iridescent; he was cold in the heat of the day, and hot in the cold nights, but the messages continued. Like an ox working a stone mill, round and round the pole plodded his bare feet – shuffling in the dirt, red dust plastered his sweaty frame. Grit caked the corners of his eyes. Later, in retrospect, the hardest part of the initiation was the loneliness. Although always attended by caring elders, he was on his own; no one shared the suffering or filled in the dreary periods when his mind was not visiting the other world.

White Feather knows his ancestors. They have shown themselves to him all his life. His main guide is his grandmother, during life and afterwards, who taught him good from evil. Then there is Tall Tree, who, true to his name stands tall and straight. It was Tall Tree who taught him patience, telling him that when snow falls on branches and weighs them down, they do not complain. They know that in time it will melt and the sun will shine again. It was Tall Tree and Grandmother who encouraged him to call his will.

His ancestors continued – a necessary requirement of experience is for it to come in various forms – the so-called bad experience is a blessing that few understand. It helps to balance, and balance is required for sanity and empathy. The uncomfortable gives body to the comfortable. Experience and emotion are playmates, for emotion is the coating that we wrap around an event to describe it as one to be cherished or regretted.

To White Feather's mind came another event that pained him, a time of arrogance and superiority. How could he take Eonah's girl to play with and discard? Eonah had been his friend. As children they roamed the hills and valleys, inseparable. Losing Eonah's respect was worse than losing his legs.

White Feather was told by the ancestors that men of knowing make mistakes, but it is men of wisdom that learn from them and that this bad time and his foolishness would make him stronger, to guide with compassion. And so, we choose our own emotions and therefore select our own worth. One person may see a lesson in an experience, while another may be crushed by it. We are who we are because of our experiences or rather the emotions we attach to them.

White Feather remembered a story from of his youth – a story that burned sadness. The elders call the time the *Trail of Tears* (this did happen). This was during the winters of 1838 and 1839. It was a forced relocation from their Ancestral Home in present day Oklahoma.

As a child, White Feather could not understand how his tribe could tell the story with a forgiving heart. Although the Trail of Tears was generations before White Feather's time, anger rose, like a strong wind. How could the whites be so cruel?

White Feather was told that, 'As the white settlers encroached upon our lands, President Andrew Jackson proclaimed his intention to shift us. Our leaders took him to the highest court in the land. We won our case, but Jackson defied the court order and instructed the army to carry out the order.

We were rounded up like cattle and not allowed to carry possessions. We were forced to walk 800 miles through snow and ice – many had no shoes. We do not know how many of our brothers and sisters perished. Some say 4000, others think it is closer to 8000. They died of exposure, starvation, disease and exhaustion. The white people called it "Indian Removal" – but it was a death march. We were dragged from our spiritual and sacred place of tradition to a land of desolation, and so the dark night fell.'

When the elders spoke of this, it was so vivid that White Feather felt he was there. The people were not given any warning and were told, 'Go. Go now, with only the clothes on your back.' Even much of their food was kept from them.

Yet they spoke about it without bitterness – as if there was no reason for forgiveness. 'When you feel the need to forgive, you judge the person from a position of authority. We remember the Trail of Tears, not from anger or hatred but for the lessons that it has taught us. All humans are good but some do bad things. Even our own have done bad things.'

His visions were interrupted by the need to drink a mug of water from a supportive elder.

As White Feather got older, his grandmother taught him that, 'Not only is there evolution of the body and species but there is spiritual evolution, and we are moving into a new era. The Trail of Tears episode was wrong, but there was a lesson as it was a lens through which all saw more clearly. It may have been in the past but the effect is still felt. It is a reality for the present, and for the future in as much as the emotion is a tool that reveals anger or allows for forgiveness. The way we think about the Trail of Tears indicates our level of spiritual growth. The white folks started to see the folly of domination from one race upon that of another. Our dark night helped some on their spiritual way.'

The elders' chants continued to the slow beat of the drum, sometimes faltering in a dry throat: (drum) he hayuya haniwa (in truth I was conceived) (drum) he hayuya haniwa (drum) he hayuya haniwa, (drum).

Bowed legs just supported a body depleted and exhausted.

On the third day he vomited but there was nothing to bring up. He shuddered violently and gagged. Acid burnt his mouth and the ferocity of it left him weak. So far away was his mind, the sickness and weakness seemed to have happened to someone else.

As a child, White Feather's grandmother told him that he would one day take over the teaching of the right mind.

'But how do I do this Grandmother?' he had asked.

'My child, you do it with awareness. It can only be with awareness that you can be with right mind. When in right mind there is no need for forgiveness as you are at one with all. But when not with right mind, anger can take you. White Feather, do you not remember the teachings of the Eagle? I shall remind you – Eagle is strong and flies to far stars. But Eagle has a weakness. If angry, his tail feathers fall out and he is Earth bound. Only when he buries his anger will he be able to fly again.'

His next vision was one where he was taken by his ancestors to a flat area at the top of a rise. The view over the valley was long and wide. A deep vertical hole had been dug. It was an old hole and had been used many times in days long past. It was in this hole that White Feather stood, his neck at ground-level. The Ancestors filled the hole with dirt so that only his head remained to be seen. Thus incarcerated, White Feather was immobilised and powerless to do anything.

The ancestors told White Feather, 'This is how you see your life, powerless to do anything. It is now time to call back your will. By doing so you will live. By not doing so you will perish. White Feather, we leave you with one tool. The tool is the most important tool you have been given. You have always had this tool. Like all tools it can be put to useful service but used incorrectly it can damage you. That tool White Feather is your mind.' Then they were gone.

White Feather panicked at the thought of this slow death. 'This is not learning... this is torture.'

It was for good reason that the Ancestors had White Feather face the valley. However, to start with he did not see the view, so consumed with the fear his mind fed him.

It was not long before an ant found him, drawn by the smell of meat. It climbed up White Feather's left cheek and took a bite to assess the value of its find. Exploring further, it entered the moist cavity of a nostril, where it paused and drank before going higher up the passage.

White Feather felt the ant climb on his face. He tried to shake his head to dislodge it but there was not enough movement. The bite released a fresh avalanche of fear. He had two points of awareness, the one that death was going to be long and painful. The other was that he felt every footfall of the ant as it scaled his cheek and entered his nose.

The ant expressed pheromones that other ants could smell, and so it was not long before a legion of ants came, first in ones and twos, then by the dozens.

White Feather wondered if he would go crazy before he died. Now, his face was swollen from the toxins that the ants injected. He squeezed his eyelids together to try and keep them from entering his eye-sockets. The ants were in his ears and mouth, everywhere they went they bit and tasted. It seemed that there were fifty marching in an out of his nostrils. Some seemed to go up as far as his brain. He cried in anguished self-pity and pain, 'This is no way for a human to die. I have been forsaken by my own people.'

He opened his eyes as if to gain inspiration. Once his eyes adjusted to the harsh sunlight, he saw the home of his upbringing. He saw the animals and nature that had surrounded his childhood...

As he took this in, an eagle flew into his view. He watched and longed for its freedom. The lesson of the eagle as told by his mother and grandmother came to him. For the first time the strength of the story claimed a ledge in his mind to strengthen and grow. For the first time he understood how weak of mind he had become. He saw that its effect was slow forming, like moss growing on a wet rock.

Somehow, seeing the eagle, and remembering the story brought clarity. 'No more,' he shouted. He looked at the eagle and shouted, 'I see you Eagle... I may die here but I will die with character and clear mind.'

He forced to his mind gratitude. If he was going to die, he would do it with gratitude. He brought many memories to his mind. Each was examined and turned around and looked at from all angles. He released the anger from the Trail of Tears and other things that plagued him. Although the ants were still there, he had less awareness of them.

Not only did he look at the happy memories, he looked with gratitude at the sad events of his life for what they taught him. He sent love to his friend Eonah, and was grateful to have learnt the lesson of self-forgiveness. He apologised to Eonah's girl and asked for forgiveness.

Hours passed as he examined the hurts and sadness of his life. He gave love to all of them and took responsibility.

He was purged and prepared for death. *Death I am ready with clear mind.*

Without realising it, White Feather had claimed his will. As he did, there was a surge of power and optimism.

The Ancestors smiled and were pleased. They knew that White Feather had called his will, called his happiness. They reminded him that it was the Eagle who came to help him. They went on to tell him that it was known that Eagle was his totem animal, and it is for that reason he was given the name White Feather, and that Eagle's wing feathers are white. 'Like Eagle, you lost your tail feathers when you became angry and like Eagle you were grounded. Now that you have called back your will you can fly to far stars.'

White Feather knew that the initiation was over when the dreams and visions ceased and the awareness of his surroundings returned. The lessons ended as quickly as a summer storm leaves, its power spent.

Although weary, White Feather was grateful for the time shared with his ancestors. Concerned elders supported his tortured body and gently cut the thongs. He was supported to a specially constructed wigwam to rest and reflect.

It took him weeks to recover physically, but what he learnt remained with him for the rest of his days. There would come a time when he would take his place amongst his people, to guide and lead, he was ready.

Metamorphosis

The grub lay in its cocoon and watched the world go by through a hole in the wall. He felt rotten. 'Blah, why me? Why am I stuck in this darkness? Am I ever going to get out of here?'

Suddenly a beautiful creature floated towards him. For a moment, the grub was transfixed and forgot his woes. As he watched, he delighted in the colourful wings, the smile on the creature's face and the way in which it joyfully floated from here to there in a dance of joy. Grub thought *you can afford to be happy, you're stunning and free* but shouted in a disgruntled way to the creature, 'Hey you, come here!'

The creature stopped and approached the cocoon. Peering into the hole, it said in a gentle voice, 'Why, hello… I'm a butterfly.'

Without any formality and with irritation the grub asked, 'Why are you so happy?'

The butterfly, in that same soft voice, answered, 'I'm happy because I choose to be happy and you're grumpy because you choose to be grumpy.'

'Thanks for nothing,' moaned Grub. 'It's okay for you to talk. Look at how magnificent you are with your amazing orange wings with their black tips, while here I am stuck in this dungeon, all trussed up and unable to move. I don't even have legs, let alone wings.'

'Gee, you *are* sad! You might like to know that I was once in a dark hole just like you. I remember how horrible it was.'

'So what did you do to get out of *your* hell?'

Butterfly smiled to herself as he remembered that time and then said, 'You know Grub, it is so simple that you are unlikely to believe it.'

Grub became agitated and said, 'If it's so simple, for caterpillars' sake, tell me before I go nuts!'

'Well,' the other said gently, 'If I tell you, do you promise to take the advice no matter how simple it may seem, and try it every day for two weeks?'

'I will, I will,' said Grub urgently.

'Okay, if you are willing to give it a go, the first thing is to stop struggling to get out of there – just relax.'

'How does not struggling help to get me out of here?'

Butterfly answered, 'When we force things to happen out of fear or impatience, we tend to push that which we want away. Trust me on this. Do you think you can do that?'

'Easy peezy,' said Grub.

'The second thing to do is to see yourself, not as a grub in a hole but a beautiful butterfly with the breeze at your back and the sun on your wings. And can you do that as well?'

'I'll try,' he said, but with a tinge of doubt in his voice.

'You'll have to do more than try… you'll have to believe it. If you don't believe, you will not become it.'

'Hmm, how can I be it, if I'm not it?' Grub pondered.

'It's as I said, very simple. The third thing to do is to be happy. To glow inside.'

'Now you've really lost me,' Grub said. 'You try being happy living in this grotto!'

'But you can, and you have to if you want to change.' Butterfly paused, rubbing her wings together in a way that seemed natural to Grub.

'Tell me Grub, do you think I am beautiful?'

'Oh Butterfly, you are magnificent. I wish I could be just like you.'

'Well, you can if you do as I say but let me tell you that the outward beauty you see is a result of inner beauty. You know, when my time is up and I pass on, the first thing that my body loses is its colour. Now I must float off. Remember, it is up to you to change yourself. If you don't, you will just remain a grub forever.'

She fluttered away but suddenly returned, and as an afterthought, said, 'I will come in a day or two and check on your progress. Bye for now.'

This time she did go. Grub watched Butterfly float, first this way and that, in a waltz of delight and joy. Higher and further she went until she disappeared into the dark green foliage of the trees on the mountain.

Grub turned over, and staring at the black nothingness of his home thought about what Butterfly had told him. 'Could it be so easy?' he wondered. 'Yes, it is true that I am more concerned with my worries than with happiness and I do moan a lot.' He decided to try what Butterfly suggested. For two weeks he would chase unpleasant thoughts from his mind and let it be filled only with happiness.

He started the process by marking fourteen days on his ceiling and set about being happy – seeing himself as beautiful, and, as Butterfly said, 'with a gentle breeze behind him and the sun at his back'.

It was hard but Grub was determined. As he ticked off day one, he wondered if he had changed in any way. He was not sure but felt a little happier within himself; he even laughed a bit.

On day three, the light from the hole was suddenly darkened. He heard Butterfly say softly, 'Hey, Grub. I can see you are happier and that you have a smile on your face.'

Grub returned the greeting and asked, 'How are you doing, Butterfly?'

After a chat, Grub watched Butterfly take off, thinking, 'It is nice to have a friend like Butterfly to help me.'

By day five, Grub woke up with an odd feeling on his back. Something was stirring. He quickly turned around to catch it but saw nothing.

On day six, that strange feeling was even more pronounced, but he could not figure it out. When the light from the hole disappeared, he became excited as he was sure that Butterfly had popped over to visit. 'Is that you, Butter?'

'Yes. How are you doing, Grub?' When Butterfly's eyes adjusted to the dark light, she could see partially developed wings on Grub's back. Chuckling to herself, she said, 'Well, well, you are metamorphosing.'

'What's metamorphosing?' asked Grub.

'Just be patient and you'll see. You certainly have made great progress.'

'Do you think so?' asked a grateful Grub.

On day ten he noticed that his home was unravelling. With this, he panicked. 'What will happen if I have to leave this place? It's all I know!' He could not work it out but was sure that it had something to do with his new way of thinking.

As if reading his thoughts, Butterfly appeared and said, 'Hey, Grub, you are almost there. In fact, I can't call you Grub any more. You are glorious.'

'What do you mean, glorious? I'm just me.'

'Well, now you are, but you weren't before.'

'Oh, so what does it all mean and what am I supposed to do now?'

'Nothing,' said Butterfly happily. 'You'll know what to do when the time comes. Just remain positive.'

The day slid to a close with Grub feeling happy.

It was all too soon that the cocoon disintegrated. 'Oh oh, what now?' thought Grub, and sat waiting for inspiration. 'There it goes again, that fluttering!' It was stronger than before.

Suddenly, he felt himself rising. 'Help! What's happening?' he shouted. In panic he froze, causing himself to fall back to the ground. When he landed, he let the fluttering start again and he rose again. It was then that he realised that he could fly, but soon crashed into a tree and flopped to the ground.

'Whoa, I can fly, but now I have to learn to steer,' he thought with joy. And so off he went, happy and free.

Butterfly glided beside him, and with quickly vibrating wings said, 'What does it feel like to be a butterfly?'

'It feels wonderful,' Grub laughed, as he scooted all over the place.

Butterfly asked, 'Have you seen what you look like?'

'No!' he replied.

Butterfly suggested that he float to the pond to look at himself. Grub did, and gently landed on a twig suspended over the water. He was scared to look at his reflection and instead took note of the glen he was in. It was magical; the rays of the sun searched through subdued light, and water lilies in the pond exuded a tranquillity that suggested, 'It's OK, look down.'

After taking a deep breath, he lowered his gaze and took in the most beautiful sight he could imagine. 'No, it can't be me,' he thought, and to see if it was he moved his head. As the reflection moved, his heart quickened with excitement. It was then that he noticed his wings – turquoise with white spots that gave him a fresh and clean look. A tear rolled down his cheek and splashed away his image – he was more beautiful than he could ever have hoped for!

And so it was that with understanding, that by being what he wanted to be, and by just letting it happen, Grub metamorphosed into his true potential, a butterfly – and so can you, if you allow it to happen.

THE TWENTIETH SEED

The Solution

I worked at A. P. Welling and Co for forty-eight years as an accountant. For all that time, I sat in the same chair, at the same desk, in the same lime-green office. I had the same secretary working with me. We aged together doing the same work.

At first, I was enthusiastic, but after several years, the gloss diminished. Yet I continued at A. P. Welling and Co because I was too insecure to experiment with other things.

I caught the same bus home that I caught to work. As an accountant, I knew I had done this 25,442 times!

25,442 times I came through the same gate, into my small and tidy garden and through my front door. On 23,851 of those occasions, Anna was there to greet me with a kiss on the cheek. 'Did you have a nice day, Dear? Let me take your coat; you must be tired. Come on in and sit down while I make you a nice cup of tea.'

One day I came home and she was not at the door to greet me. Unusual, I thought. 'Anna!' I called. There was silence in the cottage. I walked in thinking perhaps she was on the phone. She was, but slumped over it – dead. The doctor said it was a heart attack.

The house, which in the past had been neither friendly nor unfriendly, became sombre in its silence, a place of gloom and nothingness. After my work, I would sit there in a kind of stupor, while the walls seemed to close in on me.

I tried to find solace in my work, but one dismal Friday morning I was given my marching orders. New blood is what they said they needed bright young minds to take the firm forward.

Oh yes, they thanked me for my contribution, gave me a good retirement package and a gold watch. I don't wear watches as for some reason my body electrics play havoc with their workings. And so onto the sideboard it went, as did all the personal memorabilia of Anna's and my boring life. I thought, *I have a cupboard full of junk, and a mind bursting with regrets.*

I was lonely and continued the same routine as if still at the office. At 10.00 I would have tea and a biscuit. At 12.00 I would read the paper with my lunch. More tea and another biscuit followed at 3.00, and at 4.30 I would get up to go home – except I was already home! An hour later, my mind walked through the front door where I heard her say, 'Did you have a nice day, Dear? Let me take your coat; you must be tired. Come on in and sit down while I make you a nice cup of tea.'

Then, some twenty years ago, it all changed. A friend suggested that I be a Santa at the local supermarket. At first, I resisted, thinking it foolish, but my friend persisted. In the end, he almost shoved me into the Santa chair just before the kids arrived.

As the first tiny tot clambered onto my lap it was like a new dawn. His little face looked up at mine, with eyes so large and round they seemed to take over his entire face. They showed his vulnerability, his trust and innocence, and in that moment a lump formed in my throat. He was only about three and half and was as frightened as I was. When I 'ho-ho-ed' and asked him what he wanted for Christmas, he just stared at me in awe and panic.

The prompting from his smiling mother got him going as she said, 'It's okay, Willie. Tell Santa what you would like for Christmas.'

'I, I, I wanna teddy bear,' he blurted. But, once started, he told me all sorts of things and had to be prised from my arms. I am still not sure who held on tighter, he or I.

And then he was gone, and another boy sat down; his smile was wide, toothy and cheeky. Then a girl who looked like a little fairy with black hair fringing a face with a freckled nose sat down.

Ever since then, during the festive season, there has been a stream of these beautiful and trusting young humans in my life, all blessing me with their untainted eagerness and searching for answers in my hairy face.

Oh yes, I have had my beard tugged and fat pillow tummy punched. Many a time I have been told, 'Santa doesn't exist; you are a fake,' or asked, 'Where are your helpers?' I have been asked, 'Do you really live in the North Pole? And is it very cold there?' One impish four-year old asked me, 'Did you come by taxi because I can't see your reindeer?'

Some of those children are now grown up and bring their own offspring. We chat and share in a mutual love of these little beings.

When it is over for the year, I relish the thought that the following year I will again glow like the brightest star and have my time of love and joy. It will be with happiness that I pull on the Santa pants, top hat and itchy beard. Getting older as I am, I lose concentration, my voice quavers and I am not sure if my 'ho-ho-ing' is as rich as it should be. Nevertheless, I will do this work until they stop me or my clock ceases to tick.

After all of those years I have finally found the work I love.

Giving; Social Psychologist, Dr Elizabeth Dunn, of the University of British Colombia, Canada, in an effort to understand how we feel about giving, researched 200 000 adults. The research showed that those who gave money to charity were happier than when they did not. She even showed that toddlers gained joy from giving. Dunn postulates that with children and adults alike, where most feel better for giving, then is this a natural way for humans? The research pinpointed that when people gave (either money, gifts, or of themselves) knowing that the recipient would be better off, that is when they felt the happiest – it was also the connection that they made to that person or those people.

Based on her research, if you want to give, then give knowing that the connection is the best part, and not just giving from a moral obligation. It is getting to know the impact of the gift.

How We See Ourselves

Can you imagine leaving your home and life to go somewhere else to adopt a new persona? Where pretending to be different would gain you instant happiness?

You change your clothing and create a different hairstyle. In this new city you may start the process at the local hotel and act as if you were someone else, wiser or richer, maybe more confident than who you really are. Later you walk, or stagger out, feeling smug and that you really impressed the audience.

It may be fun for a while, but like a bubble finding its way to the surface, the way you saw yourself in your old life will merge into the new. You may look and sound different but the insecurities will be the same. The excitement of a new life and friends will diminish while your original fears will reassert themselves. Your strengths will remain strengths, and your weaknesses will be just as prominent, irrespective of how many times you change your identity. The philosophies and beliefs collected throughout your life will still assert themselves in conversations with your newly acquired friends. Your loves, hates and prejudices, of God, man and country will cling to you as fleas cling to a dog.

The acting of a new life would, like last year's coat of paint, fade. The way you see yourself will place you with a new set of friends but friends much the same as those left behind. You would attract the same sort of luck and circumstances that you ran from into the new life.

You are who you are because of the way you see yourself. You cannot change yourself by external trimmings. You have to change from within. It can be a slow process, much the same as chipping away at raw granite, until an approximation of who you are emerges. Unlike art, we are never completed, always a work in progress. You cannot run away from what you have become, *but you can grow towards what you want to be*.

Yes, perhaps it could be fun being someone else in a new town or country, but it would be just an act. Our little selves will still cry out, 'Here I am, please see me!'

The Creator Within

Sitting in the cold house late at night, he ponders his life. His marriage had been rocky for a while but when he ran out of money, she left him. She could not understand... how could she? He had quit a well-paying position to follow his dream.

With only one light on in the hall to give form to the interior, he sits in semi-darkness and sips a beer – a small man with closely cropped hair and strong sharp features, his jaw wide and strong, jutting out in a defiant way. His large eyebrows giving him a serious but kind look.

For a while he felt sorry for himself, and a bit lonely, but still, determination surges and that he will prevail. He knows no one can help him. This is his calling, and he has to be strong. It was his driving self, and when he felt it, he knew why he was doing this – to create something that was not there before. He also knows that most do not have the fortitude – they're too scared to follow their hearts and dreams, as if pinned to the spot.

Sipping his beer, he acknowledges how tough it is, but has faith in himself that he will win. After all, what else can he rely on, if not himself? Surely that is the only basis any of us can work on? Trust is what allows us to go out on a limb.

His dream and his life are not for everyone. If it were easy all would do it. But they don't, and after an eight-hour day working for someone else, they head home to a family and a cooked meal.

As a creator, he is one in a thousand, and has the strength to see it through. All the hardships and solitude are of no account because he is a builder, a creator, a dreamer – and so he builds and creates his dreams. He has learnt that there is no greater satisfaction than to achieve, and to do so because he trusts and backs himself.

It has been the same since the sun first appeared over the horizon. Man painted and wrote. They were laughed at, but their pictures and words are still with us today. Men thought thoughts that were not in line with the ideologies of the time and were imprisoned or butchered. Yet their thoughts are also with us today to remind us that alternative ideas are good. Look out of the window of your city house or office and you will see the creation of man. Everything you see is a testament to man's ingenuity.

As he finishes his beer and heads towards the kitchen to prepare a simple meal, he is focused. He does not care how many hardships still lie between him and his target; he will overcome them.

Later, he turned on the TV and clicks on the sports channel. He sees a golfer, idolised by millions – he knows what the millions do not, that the golfer has had thousands of lonely hours of practice. When the golf is over, an athletics meet comes on and the winner of the 10,000 metres makes it look easy. However, most do not know about the pain – for years leading up to the race, driving his body beyond what would be considered breaking point. If the runner or the golfer had quit, they would never have tasted the sweet success of pushing themselves into uncharted territory or the trusting of themselves.

He, like the runner and golfer has faith that his rewards are just around the next corner, and like the writer, painter and thinker – he cannot suppress that which is within him. His drive has scared many away but attracted even more.

He remembers a conversation with some buddies about *What is Creativity?* He feels strongly that it comes from within, that it is not derived from external factors. This was a hard concept for him to get across and he believes that he failed to do so. He explained that creativity comes from the same place that intuition does. They both come from the Source that sustains us, the Source that we are connected to, and which can therefore be called upon if one is open to it. After all, it was the Source that created all that there is, and we are of the same form.

He goes to bed content with his direction but wonders why more are not like him. All it takes is trust – trust in your ability to win through, trust that there is a fair Universe that lets winners win, and losers make their own way.

He sleeps well in the comfort that he is the painter, the thinker, the writer and the builder.

Self-worth

Jenny was fourteen and clumsy, always tripping and dropping things. This made her feel worthless, especially when her family good-naturedly joked about it, calling her names; 'butter fingers' or 'dropsy drip.'

Her worst time of the day was cleaning up the dishes after dinner. It made her mad when she heard her mother say in her singsong way, 'Now, Jenny, be careful; that dish is very old, and of good China.' She tried so hard not to drop anything but as usual, she did. Whilst cleaning up a thousand pieces of China's finest, she thought *gee, it was not my fault that I tripped over the toy on the floor.*

There were times at night when she could not sleep as the words 'butter fingers' or 'that plate was a present from my Uncle Lewis' played through her mind. She felt rotten and on occasions wanted to run away, but she never did.

Jenny loved soccer, and one Saturday morning while putting on her kit, she anticipated the game against the Gladiators and pretended to be a top footballer putting on her uniform.

The coach came into the change-room and interrupted Jenny's thoughts, saying, 'Bad news girls. Liz is sick, one of you will have to play goalkeeper. Now, let me see.' She thoughtfully put a finger against her lip as she scanned the team.

Jenny's stomach lurched as she had a premonition that she would be the one picked, and so tried to merge with the clothes hanging from the pegs on the wall. The coach said, 'Jenny, take off your shirt and put this goalie jumper on.'

Jenny froze as the words 'butter fingers' reverberated through her mind. 'Well, come on,' she heard the coach say, 'it won't bite you.'

Jenny was numb as she ran onto the pitch and shook hands with the opposition players. 'Why on this day did this happen to me?' She remembered the speech her coach made at practice on Thursday. 'If we are to win the competition, then we must win this game. It's the last game of the season and the Gladiators have twenty-nine points, while we have twenty-eight. A draw is not good enough, we have to win!'

Standing in the goal, she looked at the spectators. The grounds were green with flashes of colour from the wintry clothes of the London crowd and the bright uniforms of the players. As it was such an important game, it was a pre-game to the Manchester/Liverpool game, the ground was packed with thousands of people. There were shouts of encouragement and people clapped and blew trumpets. The atmosphere was high voltage.

'Damn, damn, damn,' thought Jenny, 'I am so much better with my feet than with my hands. What if I let the team down because I drop the ball? and in front of all these people.'

The first half of the game was even, as both teams were tense and played with caution. The ball scooted up and down the field at quick and regular intervals, while fans cheered and seemed to be part of the game. Many a sideline kick was made, as if to help the team. At half time, the score was nil all.

As Jenny headed to the change-room, she wondered if perhaps there was a God because her prayer, 'God, please keep that ball away from me,' seemed to have been answered; only a few easy shots and back passes came to her.

The intensity picked up in the second half and the opposition seemed more determined, with many forays into Jenny's half. Miraculously, all shots were wide or did not reach the goal area.

With fifteen minutes to go, Samantha the best player on Jenny's team, displayed brilliant footwork by dribbling past three defenders and powered the ball into the back of the opposition's net. The crowd erupted as one, as if the ground had risen, earthquake-like, from underneath them. Spectators jumped up and down, either with glee or frustration.

Jenny jumped with them, until she remembered her position in the goal and excitement turned to dread – so, a new round of pleading started, 'God, please ...'

A few minutes later the voice of the opposing coach boomed out in a slow way, 'Come-on-Gladiators-you-only have ten minutes.' This seemed to galvanise them, as if they were real Gladiators and their lives depended on that one goal. Their attacks became relentless as wave after wave saw the ball ping-ponging around Jenny's penalty box. The atmosphere was so intense that Jenny's adrenaline rose and threatened to burst out of her body. She forgot about broken cups and smashed plates; only one image occupied her mind, and that was herself and the ball – a ball that was not going to cross her goal line.

The first time she stopped it, it was with a diving save to the right, where, with her body horizontal and an arm outstretched, she just managed to finger the ball wide of the post. The crowd erupted again. Two minutes later, she tipped a thunderbolt of a shot over the bar. Soon after that, a Gladiator forward broke through and at almost point-blank range, let rip a shot that nearly took Jenny's hands off, but she held on.

She heard someone shout with urgency, 'Nearly there girls, only a minute to go!'... And then it happened – the opposition winger fell over in the penalty box.

Whether it was a trip or a stumble, the penalty was given.

Jenny was stunned. She knew the entire season was to come down to one kick, a kick that she had to save. Although it was a cold day she was sweating. Her heart thumped so hard, she wondered if it would smash the rib cage of her chest.

It seemed to take hours for the referee to place the ball on the white spot, only eleven short steps from her goal. Jenny was determined and crouched down in readiness, but just as the kicker ran to the ball, the words, *butter fingers* flashed across her mind.... and then everything happened in slow motion...

... Within seconds, Jenny's teammates were all over her. Some were slapping her on the back and others were shouting, 'Jenny, you're the best!'

She realised that she still had the ball clutched tightly to her chest after a spectacular save. The coach ran over and shouted, 'Jenny, Jenny, Jenny that was the best diving-save I've ever seen! I knew I could trust you as goalie!'

Even some of the opposition players came over and grudgingly muttered, 'Well done, Goalie. If it weren't for you, we would have won the competition.' That night Jenny slept in her goalie shirt.

Years later, Jenny is less fit as she watches her own son play soccer for the Wembley Tormentors. She could not help the smile that came to her face when she recollected that, not once since that day had she broken a glass, a cup or any crockery. It still amazed her, just how brittle our self-worth can be and how we let a lack of it can damage us as a result of our thought processes.

Jenny has become financially comfortable as a motivational speaker, teaching people about *self-worth*.

The hero's journey

In days of old, when knights were bold, there lived a knight in not too shiny armour. He went by the name of Alphonse.

Alphonse, a poor knight, could not afford servants to clean his armour. He was so poor that he used to sleep in the woods. It rained a lot, which beat down with a drumming sound on his metal suit.

One bright summer's day, while birds were singing, Alphonse emerged from the forest to forage for scraps in the palace garbage bins. Not watching where he was going, he bumped into a damsel.

'Wach whare y goen, y big oaf,' she screeched. Alphonse was thunderstruck – it was love at first sight. Other than a pea-sized wart, massive beaked nose, hair like a sucked mango pip, and pointy little chin, he thought her lovely. Her name was Fracilla, and she was a chambermaid of the Royal Guard. This was considered a lowly position, but there were perks!

A courtship followed and marriage was discussed. It did not matter to her that he was a bit rusty; she had managed to secure her very own knight. He did not mind her always castigating him. Before the wedding day arrived, Fracilla suggested that he go off on an adventure, not only to prove himself, but mostly in search of a fortune they could live on. 'But I won't be able fight in rusty armour,' Alphonse squeaked.

Considering the problem, she said, 'I done a faver fo the blacksmif, I'll git im to elp. Eel getcha clean.'

What sort of favour? Alphonse wondered but preferred not to know the answer.

She left, and by and by arrived back with a sooty-skinned man, dragging a bag of tools. Introducing them, 'Blacky, this is me hubby to be Alphonse... Alphonse, Blacky.'

Blacky got right to work, polishing, scraping, scrubbing and painting and after a day and a half, our knight in shinier but still battered armour, and with a borrowed donkey was ready to set off for those distant shores to seek his fortune. Avoiding the wart, he kissed Fracilla and rode off into the wild-blue yonder.

Here we pause in our metaphor of life and its lessons.

- *We started the story with Alphonse emerging from the forest rather worse for wear. Clearly his life did not work.*

- *An event, a catalyst, forced him to improve himself or stay stuck where he was. Being an intrepid knight he took on the challenge. Often it takes such an event to "get us going".*

- *The cleaning of his armour is a metaphor for the cleaning up of his act.*

- *Riding off was where he set out to find himself – the hero's journey.*

Now, we will not go into all his trials and tribulations (lessons in life) in his search; suffice to say, there were many.

We pick up the story some eight years later, when ...

Alphonse returned, resplendent in brand new armour that would make any knight of the Round Table proud. He rode regally upon a mount of such breeding and grace that he would become the talk of the land. Following Alphonse was an entourage of some fifty people. Clearly Alphonse had found his fortune.

Back to the metaphors.

Many of us have this image that tomorrow we will find ourselves. That sometime in the future we will be happy and all will be well. In the story, this is what Alphonse accomplishes as he returns a hero. Unless we do something today to improve our tomorrow, tomorrow will be just like today. Remember, this is a fairy tale, and unless we solve our issues, our armour will remain dull and tainted.

To continue ...

Fracilla was beside herself with the anticipation of wealth. She batted her eye-lashes at Alphonse as he dismounted. He seemed taller and stood with eminence, full of confidence.

Avoiding the wart, he kissed her and said, 'Fracilla, we must talk...'

Back to the metaphors.

In finding himself, Alphonse knew that he had grown beyond Fracilla. He learnt that he did not need her to make him happy, and that he was in charge of his own destiny. Besides, there always has to be a twist in the tale, doesn't there?

Let see how it all ends up ...

And so it came to pass that the King issued a decree awarding Alphonse a parcel of land, and a stipend for his service to the crown.

Fracilla continued her position as a chambermaid, where many a time, late at night, a knock on her door could be heard at her quarters, and the clunking of metal as a sword was removed from some lonely knight.

They both lived happily ever after.

THE TWENTY-FIFTH SEED

Impermanence

Ever wondered what happened to that doll or train set that you nagged your parents for when you were little? 'I need it,' you moaned. Yet, later, the item just drifted out of your life.

And what about people? How many 'best friends' have you had? Dozens, I'll bet, but where are they now? Moreover, what about the thousands of people who have come and gone? Some impressed our memory, but most have been forgotten, almost as if they had never been there.

Even our bodies let go of youth and vitality. What was considered good looks become old looks. Robust health gives way to incapacity. Nothing remains the same.

There are so many examples of impermanence in life. There have been loves that have come and gone – your food, here today and eaten or rotten tomorrow. You've had houses that you thought you would never leave, that have ultimately been passed to others – you start a great job, but in time its appeal wanes. So does our life, here now, but tomorrow... well, yes, tomorrow. Time is like a storm sweeping a beach clean, all traces gone.

So what does impermanence mean to us?

It means nothing, absolutely nothing. It does however help to understand how to live with the knowledge that nothing remains as it is.

Imagine, for a moment if there were permanence. Life would be boring – the same clothes, the same car, and working at the same job all your life. One reason why you may love your partner as much as you do is because of the potential of impermanence.

With permanence, there would be less value in possessions. You would be like a spoilt kid who receives too many presents on a birthday. With impermanence there is greater appreciation. Whilst things last, they are not taken for granted. Surely, it is the impermanence of this season's flowers that make them so stunning to look at? Is it also not the short-lived life of those flowers that makes us appreciate their bouquet even more?

Our children… born to us, but not belonging to us – separate in their own right. They, like the seasons come, change and go.

Is there anything that is not immune to change?

Impermanence spotlights the one and only thing that seems permanent – the Universe that supports us, but even that is changing.

As you go about your day, it may help to be aware of the impermanence of everything. By doing so, your appreciation of things will heighten.

Many freak out at the thought of impermanence. It is through their permanence they think they gain some sort of security. This though, is a false security. There is no permanence, therefore, there is no security. You can only get security from your own sense of self. Not through others, nor possessions, qualifications, vocations – through your own sense of self.

My advice is – don't take things too seriously. Remember you are part of something bigger than the impermanence of life. Slow down a bit, lower your sights. After all, what is the point of over-working for something that ultimately slips from your grasp?

All of those things I mentioned above, the impermanence, are there as a reminder of our own very short and fragile existence. The impermanence reminds us to appreciate the beauty to our lives, if only you take the time to enjoy it.

THE TWENTY-SIXTH SEED

Robbed at Gunpoint

(Written from Johannesburg, South Africa in about 1998)

When I set out for an evening walk yesterday, without a care in the world, I had a shock – I was set upon by two robbers. Before I knew it, I was involved in a scuffle.

It was already dark in the quiet, tree-lined streets of the Johannesburg suburb. The robbers threw me to the ground, where the thumping on the tar shattered my sense of reality.

There was a scuffle but it was mostly me trying to squirm my way out of there. The scuffle was brief for when I saw the gun I gave up resisting. At the time, I expected a boot to the head. The gun bought calm; now they were able to frisk me for cell phone, wallet, or any other goodies they could get their hands on. To their annoyance, this walker carried no such valuables, which incited them again to aggression. They shouted 'Phon, phon, (cell phone) money!' in a foreign accent, possibly Nigerian. They got nothing from me.

As fast as it happened, it was over in a flash... or was it? The actual time could only have been a few minutes but in the stunned 'present moment' of the unfolding of the event it seemed longer.

When I analyse the attack and my resultant thought processes, I know what it feels like to be a deer powerless in the path of a lion. The fight or flight was more like fright – yet, unlike the deer, I instinctively felt that I was not in any real danger. I was aware of helplessness, but that can be a good thing as there will always be times when we have no control over a situation. We must just see it through.

When it was over, they shouted, 'Run, run!' as if to intimidate me into a panicked retreat. I, in response, walked away with dignity, without turning around to see if they were following me or raising their gun. When only about four steps away from them, I remember taking time to be grateful that I was alive and unharmed, as in South Africa most die or are beaten for low value items. It went something like, 'Thank you, thank you, thank you,' about twenty times in quick succession.

My next thought, once I was about one hundred steps away was, *why did I attract this into my life?* I know that I alone must take responsibility for this happening.

Further pondering led me to feel empowered. I think the general response from people who are attacked would be, 'Why me, why did this happen to me?'

By making this statement we become a victim or reinforce victim consciousness. As a practitioner of positivity, I know that what we put out we get back. If you put out victim mentality, circumstances will arise to perpetuate that belief. If I were a victim then it is likely that there would have been anger, resentment and frustration. I felt none of these feelings. A victim is powerless to ward off unfavourable circumstances. Not being a victim I attached no emotion to the event. I do not have to live my life in fear, as the victim does.

As this happened only yesterday, I have not had enough time to process my response or gain clarity as to what I have done or not done to create what happened. Nor do I understand the lesson my higher self thinks I need to learn. Sometimes there is no lesson for us to learn, just an experience to be had. As I own the reason for this happening and refuse to be a victim, it is unlikely to happen again or, at least, with any regularity.

The above event was a true one. Because it was true and the lesson learnt from it, I wrote the above article and submitted it to a magazine as I hoped that it may help people. Lots of people in South Africa have similar or worse attacks.

The magazine published it – good I thought. Then I received the first telephone call. It was from a lady in Port Elizabeth who had had a similar episode and was a nervous wreck. She phoned to thank me for the article as it helped her understand the process better.

Over time, there was a steady stream of calls or emails, all from people who wanted to tell me how the article gave them comfort, and to thank me. The most memorable though, was one that came about eighteen months later. It came from a young mother who had just been robbed. Of course, her baby was with her. Amazingly, at the time of it happening, with a gun at her head, she remembered my article, and it gave her the strength to get through the robbery. Luckily, she and the child emerged OK, but shaken. Upon getting away, she was determined to get home and find my article, which she did. She reread it again about three times before phoning me.

Although still panicked, she was grateful that I had written the article. She said that when she read it all that time ago it made an impact, but she did not really know why she kept it. For her, I'm glad she did – that is why I love writing.

Grabbing your potential

This child, six hours old, fought bravely for his place as a human. So determined, he arrived three weeks early – but why? Is it because he, on an inner level, knows how precious human life is? Perhaps it is because life is a lesson.

He will double his weight and Earth knowledge exponentially so that he can cope with the rigors of life on this planet; a planet that has its share of difficulty. It will not be easy for him, but therein contains the lessons he is to master. He will learn to love, he will learn to hate. He will learn of war and friendship, feast, famine, anger and sadness, extreme joy, grief and suffering. Yes, it will be difficult. This tiny bundle, full of passion, knows the big picture, and will get on as best as he can. There will however be times when the big picture gets muddied and he will forget his place in the grand scheme of things. He will lose sight of just how precious life is.

On occasions, I have forgotten life's value, and I suspect that you have as well. Like this baby, you, and my deepest self, knew it would be exhilarating, but we forget. It is beautiful here, but we forget. And, what of the possibilities? So many that it boggles the mind, yet we forget. They are still there waiting for us to reach out and pluck them from where they wait, like ripe apples on a tree. To be happy… we forget.

This child, innately knows the value of every second of every day, and will waste no time to reach out and grab his possibilities... is this not wonderful? You, in turn also need to reach out and grab life and its possibilities.

Oh, I forgot to mention, that this child is my first grandchild! And, his name is Spencer.

THE TWENTY-EIGHTH SEED

The boy without fear

A certain father had two sons, one was sharp and sensible. The other was deemed to be stupid. They were rural people, where the land was considered neither beautiful nor ugly. It just was. Their days in the fields were long, just is as it should be.

It was often asked of the father, 'Why is that one stupid, as looking at him he appears normal?'

The father was always quick to answer, 'The boy is stupid as he holds no fear.'

'No fear,' they would say. 'Why that's absurd… we all must have fear… after all, it is fear that keeps us little… keeps us from being too grandiose… we can't be too big for our boots, can we? We do have a class system, and it would not do to try and exceed our expectations.'

Gustoff, the boy to whom they referred, heard these comments and wondered, *why must I have fear? Having fear is stupid, not the other way around. If I don't want to be fearful why must I?*

His brother Kurt, on the other hand, was deemed normal, as he was full of fear so he was full of promise, so the clan thought. There was a time when it was suggested that he would be the captain of the tug-of-war team but he declined because he was scared of what people would say of him if his team lost. No, he would not take that risk. Then, when it was clear that Maggie had eyes for him, he hid because he feared that she might like him – but he also feared that she might not like him. What if she leaves me for another? Yes, fear does that to people. So Kurt was normal, and lived life to all his fears.

Gustoff, who perhaps was smarter than all, could see how his big brother Kurt was held back from a marriage to Maggie. If he overcame the fear, Maggie would be good for him.

As Gustoff was soon to meet maturity, a family gathering was called for. This was not a celebratory gathering, as one would hope but a discussion. The discussion was about Gustoff, and his so-called "stupidity" because of his lack of fear. The family wondered what could be done about it.

The day came and the long table was put out under the Magnolia tree in the village centre. This tree was large, and umbrella-like that shaded all from the burning summer sun.

Fifteen chairs on either side were all filled with the wisest of the family and villagers. The discussion had been going for about an hour, and as more wine was consumed, louder became the voices. One, about six chairs away, was shouting up and across the table. Likewise, another was shouting and gesticulating to others who seem to be shouting and gesticulating to others. Every so often some words of order could be heard that offered sympathetic solicitations to the stupid boy's father. Also, the words, such as, 'If my boy was stupid and did not have fear, I would adopt him out.' Or, 'That poor man, how hard it must be to have a child to be debilitated without fear. It's normal to have fear, we are bought up to carry our fear. It has been this way for thousands of years, and so it must be right – surely.'

Gustoff's father was at one end of the long table. Gustoff was told to sit at the opposite end. He was told to listen to all the wise talk with the hope that some sense would settle into him. To know that there is good reason why we need fear in our lives.

As Gustoff was without fear, and was also intelligent, he was not afraid to articulate his thoughts, he had enough, and banged on the table. 'Silence!', he shouted. He had to do this three times until gradually the voices dwindled, became a murmur, and finally shut up in disbelief. Gustoff rose, and with confidence, looked at each at the table until finally saying, 'You think I'm stupid because I am without fear. Well, I say this to you, you are the stupid ones because you all allow your fear to rule! ... too fearful to try this, or too fearful to be that.'

All were stunned with these words, but all too fearful to say anything in reply. This made no difference to Gustoff, who continued, 'Like me, all of you were born without fear but your fear-carrying family members and society taught you to live your life with fear... in fear, cringing from possibility. Although living this way is folly, I do not judge you, as you do not know any better.

Look at you, raucous, inebriated, and here for one purpose only – to belittle me. That is what fear does to people. They do not focus on their own strengths and virtues but on trying to reduce another... in this case, me. Well, you will not make me smaller, in fact, your weakness moves me to strength. I see in you everything that can be bad for humanity. I choose to be the exact opposite. Where you have fear, I have belief... where you shrink, I grow... where you say it can't be done, I say, let's try anyway.

I do not know why my intelligence resisted me to live in fear, but thankfully it did. It is not that I have no fear, I just do not let it stop me, as it stops you. I think that right from my earliest thoughts there was something in me that knew that to live a life of fear was a life of reduction. I am not afraid to stand tall and weather any storm that life sends. Nor am I afraid to make mistakes for actions that I commit to, after all, all actions have an element of the unknown, and if I'm to hold back because of these unknown factors, then surely my life will not have as much success or interest as it deserves. Certainly, like now, and at any other time when needed, I shall stand and I will say my piece without fear and with conviction. Unlike you, I will not join the rabble in senseless debate of shouting across tables to belittle another. After all, that is the difference between you and I. My mind is in order... it is clear, crystal clear. Yours, on the other hand is much like that senseless babble across the table where clarity and understanding can never reside. Normally, you would ridicule me behind my back, but the wine gives your tongue power.

I'm leaving you as I can't live with people who are fear based... He who has conquered doubt and fear has conquered failure. I want to be worthy of the life that has been gifted me... I am sure there must be more out there like me who are not afraid to be themselves and to strive for what we believe is right... to claim our right as a unique individual. To be with people who have replaced fear in their heart with character. I'll find these people, and together we will not be afraid to live life the way that it was intended to be lived. That is, to not be afraid of who we are. Nor will we be afraid to share our riches, knowing we can always create more. We will live with respect for the other, because we respect ourselves.

So family, I bid you farewell as I am off to a life of happiness knowing that I live without fear.'

And so Gustoff walked away without a backward glance, without possessions. He had all that he needed – himself.

When he had gone, the dumbfounded silence continued for a while until someone spoke, 'Stupid, I told you, didn't I. Pass more wine... You hear him rave, not be afraid to be ourselves... nonsense, absolute nonsense.' It was not long before all were again screaming and gesticulating, 'Yes, he should be more like us...'

Quantum physics and growth

It takes time to swing from non-success to success. From ignorance to knowledge. From non-awareness to awareness – from fear to love.

There has been much ado about quantum physics and that with the right attitude you will place yourself in its "slip-stream" and achieve immediate benefit. This, according to many, will happen in literally the blink of an eye. Or in the same blink, you will have achieved success. I have known many people who have striven for that quantum physics miracle. None to my knowledge found it. Perhaps it is possible, but for those who are less mortal than you and I.

From a point of view of the growth in our life and circumstances, I am sorry to disappoint you, but quantum physics does not work that way when it comes to healing or lessons in our lives. If it did, where would be the lessons to life? Where would be the growth? Where would the mental preparation be? You need to be mentally prepared for what you are trying to achieve, and if you are not prepared, you will not achieve it. If you are not prepared, and a quantum physics miracle did occur, you would not be able to handle it. The experience gained from your growth is probably the most important, for with the experience comes understanding. How can one understand love, if they instantly were thrust from fear to love? To truly understand love, one must have understood fear, then one must learn about it and be compassionate.

As a teacher or guiding light for other people, it is an empathy, not instant illumination.

Remember, life is not so much about achievement, it is more about growth. First you grow from point A to point B. And then you grow to point C, and then to D and so on. You consolidate knowledge and embody those truths before moving to the next stage.

Your job is to maintain the momentum by constantly working on your mind-set and spiritual growth so as to move from fear to love.

Self Punishment

He walks along the broken cobble stones of life, head bowed, eyes towards his feet, never daring to look up. Somehow, he knows that this self-punishment is a denial of his loving essence. Why instead did he choose to become a victim of his own life? *Do I hold guilt, based on false perceptions?* He wonders. *Why am I so inadequate? I've been told that I am perfect. Arrrraggg, if I am, then why am I bereft of self-belief?*

He trudges for endless hours, bowing to fear, desperately seeking the love that he believes is missing and continues his internal dialogue of misery. *It seems like I live in a tiny box that imprisons, and so I can never fly and soar like the others.* He wipes his face of tears and snot. *How can I, a child of creation, have allowed this to happen?*

In his role of a victim he sees others as different from him. In them, he sees their strength and fortitude. He sees their happiness and joy, tenderness and caring. He sees warmth of character... and friendship. He sees... that somehow it all passed him by. He berates himself further. *I am not good enough to receive the gifts of love.* Instead, he searches all the faces that he passes for this precious gift, hoping... for just once... that someone would share it with him... but alas, for all his searching none could not be found.

'Why me?' He shouts to the heavens. *Why were most given something, and I missed out?* With no answer, despondently he trudges on. His feet take him, to who knows where.

This young man walks the broken cobblestones of life, and each step is as difficult as the one before. His day's experienced little sunshine, for there always seems another hill to climb. The chill of winter is his constant companion.

'Where is the warmth you gave the others?' He cries. Still no word can be heard, nor comfort given. Forsaken, he bows his head even further and looks through tears at the world that he has created – and sees no hope.

Now consumed by the bitter memories of those who tried to share their love with him, but all were shunned because he turned away from them. His broken dreams scattered in a never-ending trail behind him... *my hopes for a better life... like pieces of broken glass blocking my way. I cannot turn in any direction without stepping on these shards of glass, I'm trapped, nowhere to go!*

It is raining and he stops and feels cold trickling down his hair, chilling his neck – icy trickles invade his back. He shivers and shouts once more, 'Was I so bad that love would forsake me?'

A soft voice was heard. It called, 'Child of Creation...' and as he turns around he sees an old man, standing upright, supported by a walking stick. He had a long white beard that came to his belt. 'You are me, as I am you, nothing separates us. All was given to you, and nothing was ever omitted, for you are complete. You are perfect and you will find yourself. Long ago you chose to stop believing in yourself but now you are ready to listen. You are love and have no fear, other than the fear that you create for yourself. These fears that you now believe you are, have denied you the love, which is your natural inheritance. You were never really lost, you simply have not found yourself. When you know who you are, you have found that which you can freely give to others. When you give of yourself you are giving of me my child.'

The rain is forgotten, as for the first time he understands that it was he who had punished himself, and that it was not anyone else's fault. He knew that he had been given the same as everyone – but chose to see fear, and so did not see the love within. About to thank the man for his wisdom, he started to speak but there was no man there. He was alone in the cold rain swept street.

Now oblivious to the rain and cold, he sat on a bench and considered. He realised that no one is any more special or different from him. The only difference was how much each believed in fear and how they allow it to rule their lives. In fear he could not find his love, and so realises that love and fear cannot co-exist. For all those years he chose fear. At last, the rain felt good because his journey is to stop punishing himself by living in the shadow of fear and resolved to step into the light where he can feel the love within.

When he does, he will know that he is complete and perfect in the knowing of who he is. It will give him freedom from self-bondage and suffering. In time, he will see the true essence of his being, which is simply love. In the realisation, he will able to share the most precious of all gifts with another. Gone will be the need to feel that something is missing, for it was always inside of him. Love was simply waiting for him to reach within, to offer its embrace.

His role in life is simple; it is to stay with love, and give this love to all he sees, to bring happiness into the lives of all he encounters. Thus, to take someone by the hand and restore them with love as love restored him.

Excited, he quickens his pace, straightens his shoulders, and stands tall and knows he can give this precious gift to another and enrich their life, and by doing so, he will learn that love returns to enrich in ways he cannot begin to understand. For the love he shares with those that are bereft, those who see no light in their day, he will open his heart so that they can start to believe again; and start their journey to find their missing love and heal their broken heart.

What he learnt, he shared with others, but it was more than that, it was the love that filled him that shone into others. To them, it was warm, and it felt like home.

THE THIRTY-FIRST SEED

The wisdom of the ancients

Once upon a time in lands far away and up in the Pizhahu Mountains there lived a young prince. The prince was loved by his family and the people as he was intelligent and good looking – this they thought was all that was required to be a good emperor – as one day he was to be the emperor.

Intelligence and looks was not enough for the prince, and so one day as he was walking the castle grounds, he pondered at being the emperor in time to come. He knew that this was a privilege, and wondered, *what if I am not a good emperor? What if I am not good enough for my people?* The challenge was great and he knew it. Sitting down he was pensive as he considered the challenge.

As he sat, a swallow darted here and there, consuming insects. It was towards evening when the insects were most plentiful. With its little red head and blue body it was a pretty sight. Noticing the prince, the swallow landed and asked, 'What ails you Prince?'

'Oh, you wouldn't understand little swallow but I shall tell you anyway because I have no one else to confide in. I'm worried that I will not have the wisdom and knowledge to rule when I am emperor.'

'I see,' said the swallow. 'It must be very hard to gain wisdom. But I think there is a way.'

'How swallow, please tell me how?'

The swallow continued, 'My search for food takes me far and wide, and in the warmer months I go further up, and deeper into the mountains. There are stories that I have heard of three wise folk who know all that is to be known. If you could meet these wise folk they might offer you the wisdom you need.'

Exhilarated, the prince jumped to his feet and started running towards his quarters. Not forgetting his manners, he stopped and turned around and shouted back to the little swallow, 'Thank you swallow… you have greatly helped me.' With that, he ran to make his preparations.

He knew that his father, The Emperor, and his mother, The Empress, would be afraid for him if they knew that he was to go into the mountain as it was rumoured to be inhabited by the ancients, and so he planned to leave early the following morning before they arose.

He prepared two horses and enough food and supplies to last for two weeks. He did not know if two weeks would be long enough but hoped it would be.

His next task was to write his father a letter to state he was to visit some of the outreaches.

The next morning, long before the sun rose, he headed towards those high and distant mountains. *Hurry* he thought to himself. *I have no time to waste.*

Just before the sun rose, the prince heard the musical tweet of the swallow, and looked up and saw it flying above him. Before he could say anything the swallow said, 'Prince, I have come to guide you to the ancients. If we hurry we will be there by tomorrow afternoon.'

And so… the following afternoon they came to a place in the forest. The swallow said, 'Prince, you must go on your own. Climb this peak and meet the wise man up top.'

Setting off, the prince determinedly marched up the mountain. Crawling and scrambling on his knees, he finally reached the apex. Looking for inspiration as to where the wise man could be he noticed a cave. It was in this cave that he saw a bearded man. The man was sitting on a rock, a small fire at his feet. 'Well,' the old man said, 'I don't know why you are here but it must be important to scramble all the way up. Would you like a cup of soup that I have just made?'

The prince was too busy for food but knew it would be impolite to refuse. He settled with a large shell as his bowl, full of steaming soup. Like the old man did, he half sucked and drunk from the shell. It tasted surprisingly good.

Without prompting the old man, the old man said, 'The message that I am to give you is one of forgiveness. Too many people live in fear that they will be wronged again. Compassion is a better way. To break the cycle you must be of gentle heart and loving spirit and forgive that person, or those deeds, from that gentle heart and loving spirit. When you can do that with all of your foes, you will be a great ruler.'

The old man paused for a minute to let the prince take in this important message before continuing, 'In discussing the act of forgiveness it is important to appreciate how the process of forgiveness releases one's own fear and moves the mind to a state of peace. Holding on does not release our fears, so without forgiveness, the mind is confined to live in a state of conflict. In this mental battleground, there comes suffering and misery.

For you to rule with compassion, you must have a forgiving heart.'

The prince was soon on his way back down the mountain with the wisdom – be *forgiving, and you will be on the way to becoming a great ruler.*

The prince did not wait long before following the swallow towards the next wise man. Early the next morning the swallow said, 'He is in that bush somewhere. You go down that narrow track... use your instincts.'

The prince looked in the direction that the swallow indicated. If there was a path, he could not see it, only impenetrable bush. Not concerned, he took out his sword and formed his own track, and within minutes was in darkness. The vines were thick and full of thorns that scratched his exposed skin. Although it was day, it could have been night. 'Just follow your instincts,' the little swallow had said. He was wary but continued nevertheless as somehow, someway, he knew that he would endure the thorns and uncertainty until he reached the wise man.

Exhausted, he found a bit of shelter at the base of a tree and rested. Later he continued, and an hour or so later he saw a woman, and so approached her. The woman, although stooped, was imperious and full of confidence and humility. She had small brown eyes that shone with humour. Clad in animal skins and carrying a club, the prince heard her voice, 'Who are you and what brings you to my forest?'

The prince asked, 'I'm looking for the wise man. Can you direct me to him?' The woman replied, 'You fool. You think there is not a wise woman here?... Come.'

Suddenly, they were out of the forest and in a clearing – the sun shone and warmed. The open space was liberating. The wise woman said, 'You must carve your own way in life... just as you carved the path in this forest that bought you to me. We each have a path to carve, but most go in the wrong direction, and be ready for any circumstances.'

'But how do I know which is the right way?' the prince asked.

'Prince, you already have your message... What did the swallow say as you headed into my forest?'

'To use my instincts?'

'Yes.... When you left the castle to follow your heart, leaving the security of the known for the unknown, and set off, not so much as to find wisdom, but to find character. Do you really think it is a little swallow that has guided you? It is you and your instincts. Listen to the little voice within, it may be little but it says a lot... it is your treasury of wisdom, your inner university. Listen to it as it will give you the best advice you can get.'

The prince tried again, 'But I am still uncertain, perhaps I don't trust myself or that little voice… or the swallow, or whatever it is.'

The woman offered, 'Okay think of your people, your subjects for a minute…What do you feel?'

The prince did and felt happy and warm. He was not sure of what word to call it. The woman, seemingly reading his mind, said it for him, 'It's compassion you feel. With compassion always guiding your heart, you will do well when the emperor.

Now go, I bid you well. You have one more wisdom to gain.'

It was easier leaving the forest as all he had to do was to follow the path that he had hacked open on the way in.

As the prince rode with the swallow guiding him to the next and last wise elder, he thought of the wisdom he had been given. The first taught him to learn to forgive. The second was to listen to the inner voice, the one that says so much, and rule with compassion. *What next* he wondered?

Stopping at a stream for a drink he noticed a funny little man peering at him. To have a better look he moved closer.

He was only about fifteen centimetres high and looked shrunken. He wore a baggy robe that crossed over on the right and held in place by a cloth belt. His hat was long, pointed and tilted at a funny angle. Underneath the hat his face was bright and fun looking, with big red cheeks. A short white pointed beard gave him an impish look.

'Welcome prince,' said the ancestor in a forthright way.

'How do you know who I am?'

'We ancients know all that goes on. In fact, the elders sent me to talk to you.'

The prince had never greeted an ancestor before and was not sure what to do. He need not have worried, for the ancestor gave a hearty laugh, extending his hand up towards him. 'Prince, I am pleased to meet you, my name is Wardlaw but you can just call me Law.' He finished off with another laugh.

The prince also chuckled, bent down and gave the hand a hearty shake. 'And I am pleased to meet you Mr Law.'

'Oh Prince, do call me Law. Don't you think that we are too formal these days?'

'I guess so,' said the prince, thinking of his father rushing to his affairs each day.

He continued in a conspiratorial tone. 'Prince, you are not the first human to come here to seek wisdom. But sadly most don't listen.'

The prince became serious and said, 'I will listen, yes I will.'

'I believe you... Your lesson from me is to understand what strength is. Not the strength that you use to lift a heavy log... it is strength of character... fortitude in all things that you undertake. The question is, to understand with courage, your convictions.'

The prince was thoughtful before asking, 'You mean that every time I do something, I need to apply fortitude. Is that correct?'

'Indeed, that is correct. Law had a rather large mid-section, and with his arms tucked behind his back, he had a studious but comfortable look. His head was bowed towards the ground, and he occasionally nodded in an animated way like a foraging pigeon. He nodded now as he said, 'Come, Emperor to be, let us sit over by the waterfall and let the mist gently refresh us.'

The prince sat on a rock. He noticed a rainbow from the spray of the waterfall. The elder following his eye said, 'Did you know that the rainbow was formed by The Ancients to remind us to be grateful for water?' Then he seemed to be lost in thought for a moment before continuing, 'As you rule your kingdom, there will be many that will not agree with you, and they will plot your downfall. You need the courage of your convictions, to stand on your feet, and not let others stand on yours. With your courage, you will know what course will give you peace and happiness, and what behaviour will create resentment and conflict? This is the choice we make for every moment of our lives.'

Even though the discussion was a serious one, Law's jovial manner made the prince realise that even serious topics can be approached in a playful way.

The elder continued, 'This is probably the most important principle for all of us.' The elder paused and smiled, 'Do you understand?

'I... I think so', mumbled a hesitant prince.

As he thought about this, the Elder interrupted his thoughts and said, 'Indeed that's right, believing in yourself, that is courage... and then sticking to it. All it takes is a willingness to be yourself and keep an open and enquiring mind. Each act is a call to courage.

After this last piece of advice, Law stood and stretched, whilst saying, 'For now, Prince, I think that we have talked enough. You have your messages.'

'Please Law, can we meet again?" asked the Prince.

'Indeed we shall,' said the ancestor with a chuckle. Then, folding his arms behind his back, he waddled off but with a final call, 'Remember, the courage of your convictions.'

The prince sat for a while after the ancestor had gone and thought of all that he had learnt, of forgiving, instinct, and courage. It was now time to return home. He had what he came for.

Back home, two days later, he went out to find the swallow, and to thank it once again. As he went he passed his father who was about to go and perform some stately business. They stopped in greeting, and the Emperor asked, 'Did you have a pleasant walk son?'

Pleasant walk? Thought the prince in surprise, but said, 'Father, I have been away for ten days, did you not miss me, or see my note to you?'

'Ten days, what on Earth are you talking about. It was only this morning you said you were to walk the grounds... ... but never mind, I must be off as I have pressing concerns that await.'

How odd thought the prince and went out in the courtyard to look for the swallow.

He waited most of the morning until the forester came past. 'Forester, have you seen the swallow? I have been waiting all morning.'

'Young Prince, there are no swallows at this time of the year. Some three months ago they flew south, to a place far away where they have their young.' With that, he went on his way.

The prince was flummoxed by the events of the morning. Checking his hands there were no scratches. Just clean skin. For a time he stood, contemplating these events, and then it dawned on him, a fourth lesson! He remembered the words of the woman in the animal skin with the club, 'Do you really think it is a swallow that guides you? Most knowledge is internal.' Then he realised, *I do not have to go anywhere to get wisdom. It is within me* – when he needed it, it came to him. The inner knowledge is no less than the knowledge from the wisest of beings.

Ahhh, a fifth lesson, listen and look for the council of women, as they have so much to teach me.

THE THIRTY-SECOND SEED

My Mug Runneth Over

The young scholar was filled with joy. It seemed that everything in his life worked perfectly and so often, he would quote the words in the ancient language – "My cup runneth over". He remembered the time of his life when things were difficult and nothing seemed to work, and so he made an appointment with the village elder to gain his wisdom.

'Ahh my boy,' the elder said upon hearing the question of the student, 'Many are inflicted with lives that are chaotic and wonder what the answer is.' The elder spent an hour with the student and gave him a simple but profound method for living. This is based on not wanting too much in life, and not desiring after excessive assets and material possessions. There was a curious term that he used as he spoke about these things, and the term was to be in "flow". He kept saying that when people try to achieve too much or work too hard, or covet illicit things, then they are not in flow with life.

Slowdown, and have your mind on what you are doing now, not what you did yesterday or could do tomorrow. Nor have your mind agitated with need. For when the mind is cluttered with all this extraneous rubbish you cannot be in flow. For you to have the life that you want, whereby you are able to attract those things in your life that you want, you must be in flow. After all, trying to pour water into a spinning cup will only fling the water hither and yon.

That was six years ago. It took the young man several years for him to work his mind in the way that the elder told him. It was hard at first as there was much resistance, like swimming against the hardest current. For a long time he thought he was getting nowhere but little by little he could see the changes, and as the changes came his life improved. The things that he desired in his life, slowly at first, started to show up. It dawned on him one day that all of a sudden he now knew the feeling of what it meant to be in flow. Of course, he cultivated this, and the more that he was in flow the better his life became.

Two years later the young man returned to the elder, and so enamoured with his progress his openings words were, 'Sir, I love life... I love living life, and I'm so grateful for what you have taught me. I now know the meaning of being in flow and I am forever grateful... However, I have a question Sir... How does it work that my being in flow allows my life to be as smooth? Yes, I still have problems... Remember my barn burnt down last year. I don't know what set it off, and at the time I was distraught because I had lost my harvest. Soon enough I reeled in my frantic thoughts and replace them with thoughts of gratitude and happiness, as you taught me, so that I could be in flow again. Then I had more harvest than I did before the fire. Getting back to my question, how does being in flow make such a difference to one's life?'

The elder smiled with candidacy and said, 'To be honest, I don't know. I do know it works, as you have found for yourself. We know the sun rises every day, but don't know how. How do we know the workings of the nature? We don't, we can't ... it's too vast, too mysterious, and I suspect that we are not ready to know the mind of that one. Well not yet anyway.' He laughed at his own wit as he poured himself water from the earthen jug.

The young man sighed and said, 'Yes, you are probably right and I suppose that knowing how it works does not necessarily mean it will work any better or that I am in more awe of nature.'

There was silence for a while, as both thought about this principle, and then the elder said, 'Perhaps an example may be of assistance. When you want to grow your vegetables, as a farmer you know the things that you have to do. Don't you?'

'Yes of course, I know all of that,' said the young man with interest.

'Although you do these things, is it you who really grows the vegetables?'

'What do you mean?' Replied the young man, 'I am the farmer and so I grow them.'

'Really? Chuckled the elder, 'You may put in the seed, and water the garden on a regular basis. You may also pull out the weeds and apply nutrients, and other things. But that is the extent of what you do to grow the vegetables. The reality is, you contribute to growing vegetables but it is nature that does the rest. Unless you plant the seeds, the vegetables will not grow, so it is a relationship. As always, it is a relationship between you and nature. Nature is well beyond our understanding. Or, put another way, you can do all of these things but without the mysterious power of nature nothing will grow.

So I can't tell you how being in flow works but you have your part to play in that, and then you get out of the way and let that mysterious nature of all things do the rest. It's the same with flow, be in gratitude, support others, do your work, then get out of the way.'

Another few years pass, and once again the young man found himself walking towards the elder's house. Upon arriving the elder gave him a hearty welcome before sitting under a tree. After chatting about the young man's family and the price of corn, the elder asked the young man how could he help?

It took the young man a moment to compose the way he wanted to present his question. 'Sir, I do not mean to sound ungrateful or unhappy with my life, as you know it is with flow, and I'm truly blessed. I know that my cup runneth over. My question is; even though I have a good life, I would like more of it. Oh, it's not material possessions or wealth or anything like that, but I would like to be able to still do what I do, but to do more of it, perhaps study more. Alternatively, help young people in the village. But I can't do this because I don't have the time, nor can I be in two places at the same time. After all, it takes time to walk from my land to the village... I guess I'm asking for something that may not be possible, that is to have what I have now but to be able to have more, so I can experience more. Does that sound selfish... or stupid?'

'No not at all, I can understand that you want to fill your life with new and interesting things, otherwise we become stale. And yes, we can do this, providing you don't scatter your brain, as per my first lesson to you, and that you remain in flow.'

'How Sir, how do I do this?'

'Oh... it is easy enough,' said the elder... 'and you do it by growing your cup.'

'Growing my cup, what do you mean?'

'Well several times you have shown your gratitude and you have used our term that my cup runneth over. So grow your cup... extend its size.

The way that you are seeing your cup of life is that of a teacup in size. For you to increase your attendance to life even more, you need to see in your mind your cup more like a mug, one that is bigger than a teacup. So at the moment your tea cup runneth over, from now on make your mug runneth over.'

That is what the young man did, instead of seeing his cup of life being teacup size, he saw it, mug size, a large mug, and as a mug that runneth over. By doing so, he had all the flow he needed.

To my knowledge, that was the last time that the farmer came to visit the elder with questions. However, he did come and chat with him as often as he could, where they shared the wisdom of life.

Years later, the elder had passed on, and the young man, now, well into his middle years, had a deep path towards his door, where many young men, and women, came to him for advice.

THE THIRTY-THIRD AND LAST SEED

As a Man Thinketh

By James Allen

(with comments by Pat Grayson)

INTRODUCTION

As a Man Thinketh by James Allen is an essay published some 114 years ago. The essay deals with the power of thought, and particularly with the use and application of thought for a happy life. He wrote, "*I have tried to make the message simple, so that all can easily grasp and follow its teaching, and put into practice the methods.*" His message is simple, primarily saying that "*each man and woman holds the key to every condition, good or bad, that enters into his life, and that, by working patiently and intelligently upon his thoughts, he may remake his life, and transform his circumstances.*"

I revere the work of James Allen. His eloquences of stating deep truths in so few words was his real brilliance. Phrases such as "*As he thinks, so he is; as he continues to think, so he remains*", Or, "*Man is made or unmade by himself*" or "*Thought and character are one.*" His words on positivity reveal this simple truth, as to just how easy it really can be.

For my own experience, I learnt years ago that when I held positivity and uplifting thoughts, my life "worked" better. There is a story (seed) below called my *My Mug Runneth Over*, which talks about the concept of our life being in flow. Well, my life is in flow when filled with positivity. Conversely, when I allowed insidious negativity into my mind my life did not work, and was out of flow. I have also seen this with literally hundreds of people. There is only one way to know this for yourself, and that is to try it.

Although Allen wrote *As a Man Thinketh* all those years ago, his principles are still valid, as natural law never changes. It was the same a thousand years ago and it will be the same in a thousand years' time – when you are positive, life is better. Therefore, the value of his teaching is everlasting.

When he wrote the work, it was a truth but a truth that (seemingly) had no scientific evidence behind it. Since that time, science has proven much of what Allen contended – I present some of that science, such as The Higgs Bosan experiments (or what is considered as the God Particle). You will read about this further below. And, all those years ago when I learnt that principle, my mind asked *how does thinking positively work?* At the time, and for many years I had no answer. The science that is reflected below explains how it works.

To make the work accessible to all, I have taken much of Allen's brilliance and bought the words in line with modern usage (Allen's work is in the public domain, and therefore available to all). I have also, with humility, taken the liberty to extend some of his concepts based on my own experience and research.

I hope that by reintroducing his short work in this volume on anthologies on positivity, I hope to extend the life of Allen's creativity for another 114 years.

ABOUT ALLEN

James Allen was born in 1864 in England. He was a philosophical writer and poet who wrote nineteen books. His best known was *As a Man Thinketh*. However, Allen's early life was indeed difficult, which is often the door to wisdom and learning.

Life in England in the late 1800s was harsh. Allen was fifteen when his father took the family to America for a better life. However, two days after arriving in New York, his father died. It was thought he was murdered for his wallet.

Without his father's income, Allen quit school and worked as a framework knitter to help support the family.

Although working long hours, he kept up his study and education by reading things like: The Light of Asia, Shakespeare, Milton, Emerson, the Bible, Buddha, Whitman, Trine, and Lao-Tze. Later, he returned to England.

Along with the nineteen books that he wrote, Allen also became a publisher by creating and publishing a monthly magazine, *The Light of Reason*. As the publisher, he was the editor and contributed many articles. The magazine continued even after his death, where it was run by Allen's life-long friend and wife, Lily.

Allen died at the age of forty-seven of unknown causes.

As a Man Thinketh

(Allen's words are in normal text.

My commentary is in *italics and between paragraphs*)

Mind is the Master power that moulds and makes... and evermore he takes The tool of Thought, and, shaping what he wills, Brings forth a thousand joys, a thousand ills. He thinks in secret, and it comes to pass, the Environment is but his looking-glass.

It is interesting to see that Allen regarded thought as "a tool", and indeed it is. It is at your disposal for as often as you want to use it. However, there is a key, or a trick that you must employ, and that key or trick is awareness.

Briefly; we have thoughts, we can't help but have, the mind can never be a vacuum, there is always activity. The prominent thoughts that occupy the mind are what shape our lives. The mind, like a delivery man, delivering whatever is in his van, so being a faithful servant, it will deliver what you have in it – good or bad.

Another point he makes is that life will reflect, like the looking-glass to mirror its state as a result of the contents of your mind.

CONTENTS of As a Man Thinketh

Foreword

Thought and Character

Effect of thought on circumstances

Effect of thought on health and the body

Thought and purpose

The thought factor in achievement

Visions and Ideals

Serenity

As a Man Thinketh by James Allen – **Foreword**

This little volume is not intended as an exhaustive treatise on the much-written-upon subject of the power of thought. It is suggestive rather than explanatory, its object being to stimulate men and women to the discovery and perception of the truth that "They themselves are makers of themselves." by virtue of the thoughts, which they choose and encourage; that mind is the master-weaver, both of the inner garment of character and the outer garment of circumstance, and that, as they may have hitherto woven in ignorance and pain they may now weave in enlightenment and happiness.

James Allen. Broad Park Avenue, Ilfracombe, England (circa 1904)

Seldom do we "normal" people, have any influence on world events. We come and we go, and if we are lucky, there are a handful of people who morn us at our funeral. Then that fades.

However, there is an opportunity of a personal nature, one that is universal. One that every human who has ever lived has, and that is to be the best version of ourselves. How do we be the best version of ourselves? That is what this book is about.

As a Man Thinketh by James Allen – **Thought and character**

The aphorism, "As a man thinketh in his heart, so is he," not only embraces the whole of a man's being but is so comprehensive as to reach out to every condition and circumstance of his life. A man is literally what he thinks, his character being the complete sum of all his thoughts.

As the plant springs from, and could not be without the seed, so every act of a man springs from the hidden seeds of thought and could not have appeared without them. This applies equally to those acts called "spontaneous" and "unpremeditated" as to those, which are deliberately executed.

Another way of saying this is that if you are this – it is your fault. If it went that way – it is your fault. The mind continues, whether you feed it intentionally or not. Therefore, it is always your fault. It is about knowing that it is always you who defines your life – you, or the lack of your involvement – your full intention or external circumstances. Once again, if it works, or doesn't work, you did it!

Act is the blossom of thought, and joy and suffering are its fruits; thus does a man garner in the sweet and bitter fruitage of his own husbandry.

Science states, there is an equal and opposite reaction; the reaction is that your life is the result of your thoughts. My goodness, if only I understood the implications of this when I learnt it at about the age of twelve. Or, conversely, most science teachers do not understand the powerful implication of this rule. They should have taught it in relation to the mind!

Thought in the mind hath made us. What we are by thought was wrought and built. If a man's mind hath evil thoughts, pain comes on him as comes the wheel of the ox behind....If one endures in purity of thought, joy follows him as his own shadow – sure.

Vibration; everything is a vibration. Quantum physics proves that substance is nothing more than vibration. All creatures emit a consistent range of frequencies – in general; the more primitive the organism the lower the bandwidth. Advanced animals have higher frequencies. For instance, the range that an ant emits is around 1500 KHz, while a human's range starts from about 9000 KHz. For this discussion, what we are interested in is the fact that frequencies can be measured. Each human has their own unique frequency. These adjust according to our moods. That's why music (which is also a vibration) can change our mood. A human in a specific mood would emit a specific vibration or frequency.

To recap thus far, as your mind-set changes, so does your vibrational frequency.

You may ask, so how do I know what is a good or bad vibration? The answer comes from the amazing revelations of Masaru Emoto and his work on water and crystals. In his bestseller, The Hidden Messages in Water, he proves beyond doubt that our moods affect our enzymes and biology.

Masaru, a Japanese scientist, discovered that the molecules of water are affected by thought, words and feelings. Masaru and his team of researchers froze water and took photos of the resulting crystal patterns. Before doing this, they offered the water words or thoughts of either a positive or negative nature and then measured the crystalline results. For instance, the word 'hate' produced deformed crystal patterns, whereas words or thoughts like, 'love' and 'gratitude', generated patterns as delicate and lovely as the best crystal or jewellery. Music resulted in different crystal patterns. Soft and gentle sounds offered the most beautiful patterns, whilst heavy metal fragmented the patterns.

As his work developed, he learnt that water expresses itself in a vast variety of ways that is consistent with the medium fed to it. 'Clearly, water has intelligence,' Emoto says. 'To understand water is to understand the very cosmos and life itself.'

Moreover, as up to 60% of our human body is water (the brain and heart are composed of up to 73% water), it is obvious that as thoughts and words affect the water, it also affect us as well.

When I read his work I realised that he had discovered the most profound truths and was further proof that our thoughts influence our very being right down to a cellular level (which is 60% water). The impact that love and gratitude have on water, and therefore on us, and the world beyond ourselves, is a major breakthrough in the development of mankind. Words and thoughts flow from an intent. That intent results in a vibration. Water on its own does not change anything, it is merely an intelligent medium that mirrors our internal state or that of the planet. Our collective vibration is a result of our collective thought. Therefore, the condition of the world is a direct result of our collective consciousness.

However, let's return to the matter at hand — you. Motivational teachers as well as spiritual masters have been telling us for hundreds of years just how important it is to remain positive and loving. Emoto's work, coupled with the understanding of how vibrations function, is all the proof that any rational human would need to understand the importance of remaining positive and loving.

Man is a growth by law, and not a creation by artifice, and cause and effect is as absolute and undeviating in the hidden realm of thought as in the world of visible and material things. A noble and saint like character is not a thing of favour or chance but is the natural result of continued effort in right thinking, the effect of long-cherished association with saint like thoughts. An ignoble and bestial character, by the same process, is the result of the continued harbouring of grovelling thoughts.

Vibration again; what you put out you surely get back. Put out respect, and respect will return to you in kind.

Man is made or unmade by himself; in the armoury of thought he forges the weapons by which he destroys himself – he fashions the tools with which he builds for himself heavenly mansions of joy and strength and peace. By the right choice and true application of thought, man ascends to the best he can be; by the abuse and wrong application of thought, he descends below the level of the beast. Between these two extremes are all the grades of character, and man is their maker and master.

Here Allen's language is pretty heavy, but it represented the speech of those times. Nevertheless, he speaks a plain truth.

Of all the beautiful truths pertaining to the soul which have been restored and brought to light in this age, none is more gladdening, more fruitful of divine promise and confidence than this – that man is the master of thought, the moulder of character, and the maker and shaper of condition, environment, and destiny.

As mentioned at the start of this book, most of us have no individual effect on the maker and shaper of condition, environment, and destiny (as stated by Allen) but collectively we humans do. The world is in the state that it is in – war or peace, riches or poverty, honesty or greed –through the collective thought process of all of humankind – the collective vibration. That is; when more people think greed, then there is more greed in life than honesty.

For me though, I know that I rather be at peace than war, be honest than greedy, and with riches than poverty, then my own life will be better than most, whilst adding to the collective vibration of the masses.

As a being of Power, Intelligence, and Love, and the lord of his own thoughts, man holds the key to every situation, and contains within himself that transforming and regenerative agency by which he may make himself what he wills.

Man is always the master, even in his weaker and most abandoned state; but in his weakness and degradation, he is the foolish master who misgoverns his "household." When he begins to reflect upon his condition, and to search diligently for the Law upon which his being is established, he then becomes the wise master, directing his energies with intelligence, and fashioning his thoughts to fruitful issues. Such is the conscious master, and man can only thus become by discovering within himself the laws of thought, which discovery is totally a matter of application, self-analysis, and experience.

Allen is also saying here, that irrespective of how negative a person's mind is or how bad his resultant life is, that he can change it. It may take time and a lot of retraining the mind, but it is possible. It is up to each of us as individuals.

Only by much searching and mining, are gold and diamonds obtained, and man can find every truth connected with his being, if he will dig deep into the mine of his soul; and that he is the maker of his character, the moulder of his life, and the builder of his destiny, he may unerringly prove, if he will watch, control, and alter his thoughts, tracing their effects upon himself, upon others, and upon his life and circumstances, linking cause and effect by patient practice and investigation, and utilizing his every experience, even to the most trivial, everyday occurrence, as a means of obtaining that knowledge of himself, which is Understanding, Wisdom, and Power. In this direction, as in no other, is the law absolute that "He that seeketh findeth; and to him that knocketh it shall be opened;" for only by patience, practice, and ceaseless importunity can a man enter the Door of the Temple of Knowledge.

Although the above is old fashion speech, it says, it is up to you. If it is good, you did it!

As a Man Thinketh by James Allen – **The effect of thought on circumstances**

Man's mind may be likened to a garden, which may be intelligently cultivated or allowed to run wild, but whether cultivated or neglected, it must, and will, bring forth. If no useful seeds are put into it, then an abundance of useless weed-seeds will fall therein and will continue to produce their kind.

If you want to grow cabbages, you do not plant tomatoes. The mind is like a garden and will produce what you plant – plant secure, you will get secure – plant sad and sad is what you will get back.

It is interesting that both Allen and I discuss seeds as a tool for growth. Yet, I had derived my name for the book long before working through Allen's treatise.

Just as a gardener cultivates his plot, keeping it free from weeds, and growing the flowers and fruits which he requires, so may a man tend the garden of his mind, weeding out all the wrong, useless, and impure thoughts, and cultivating toward perfection the flowers and fruits of right, useful, and pure thoughts. By pursuing this process, a man sooner or later discovers that he is the master-gardener of his soul, the director of his life. He also reveals, within himself, the laws of thought, and understands, with ever-increasing accuracy, how the thought-forces and mind elements operate in the shaping of his character, circumstances, and destiny.

We return to the concept of awareness, for without it we do not know what thoughts we have, nor the weeds that grow. Awareness is a habit, one that you must continually strive to have. In fact, awareness of what thoughts you have is probably your best habit. Conversely, the worst habit, and the one most detrimental to your life, is a lack of thought-awareness – non-awareness is limitation.

Thought and character are one, and as character can only manifest and discover itself through environment and circumstance, the outer conditions of a person's life will always be found to be harmoniously related to his inner state. This does not mean that a man's circumstances at any given time are an indication of his entire character, but that those circumstances are so intimately connected with some vital thought-element within himself that, for the time being, they are indispensable to his development.

There is a lot of research on the Internet and in books, about the plasticity of brain. Essentially, this is the brain's capacity for adaptation through a given stimulus. For instance, if a person starts to learn to play the violin, with constant practice, there will be growth and development of synaptic paths – especially the Prefrontal Cortex.

Another example; if a child has two fingers that are taped together, and if they were left taped for a long time, then the brain will adapt and amend, believing that there is only one finger, not two separate fingers.

On the Plasticity of the brain; Research carried out by Associate Professor Pilyoung Kim, of the Department of Psychology, University of Denver, showed that mothers to be also utilised the plasticity of the brain to thicken the Prefrontal Cortex as a better coping mechanism. Again, this research shows that the brain has an adaptation process.

With focus in a specific direction, the brain can change. The focus of self-criticism stimulates the threat system, releasing negative endorphins and enzymes and amends the biology accordingly. Whereas, focused self-belief will stimulate that part of the brain, releasing dopamine (the happy endorphin), and like the violin player develops those centres, so they become ingrained. What was once hard to do, becomes natural. What once felt bad, feels good. When I speak of awareness, and I do often because it is so important, its constant use will also allow those brain paths to adapt and strengthen, and so, awareness will also become ingrained, and therefore more at the forefront of your mind.

The key to amending the synapsis in a positive way is the emotion and belief behind it. You have to trust that you are good enough, be enthusiastic, and above all, be positive and uplifted.

Once again, science, this time with the plasticity of the brain, proves the imperative of a positive mind set.

As a Man Thinketh by James Allen – **Negative Affirmations**

Most people unknowingly use affirmations, but in a negative way, i.e. 'I'm no good at making speeches'. Through negative affirmations we are brainwashed into sickness, money problems, relationship issues and unwanted modes of behaviour.

The longer we have been in a negative state, the greater we will need to be uplifted to reverse the negative influence.

Every man is where he is by the law of his being; the thoughts which he has built into his character have brought him there, and in the arrangement of his life there is no element of chance, but all is the result of a law, which cannot err. This is just as true of those who feel "out of harmony" with their surroundings as of those who are contented with them.

As a progressive and evolving being, man is where he is that he may learn that he may grow, and as he learns the spiritual lesson, which any circumstance contains for him, it passes away and gives place to other circumstances.

Man is buffeted by circumstances so long as he believes himself to be the creature of outside conditions, but when he realizes that he is a creative power, and that he may command the hidden soil and seeds of his being out of which circumstances grow, he then becomes the rightful master of himself.

This last paragraph is beautiful wisdom and states in a handful of words that life as we create it is entirely in our hands. If we take responsibility for our own circumstances and success or failure, then, and only then, do we improve our life.

That circumstances grow out of thought every man knows who has for any length of time practised self-control and self-purification, for he will have noticed that the alteration in his circumstances has been in exact ratio with his altered mental condition. So true is this that when a man earnestly applies himself to remedy the defects in his character, and makes swift and marked progress, he passes rapidly through a succession of vicissitudes.

It is scientifically recognised that like-vibration attracts like-vibration. For instance, take two magnets; when you place the North Pole of one magnet near the South Pole of another magnet, they are attracted to one another. When you place like poles of two magnets near each other (North to North or South to South), they will *repel each other.*

The personality attracts that which it secretly harbours; that which it loves, and that which it fears; it reaches the height of its cherished aspirations; it falls to the level of its unchastened desires, and circumstances are the means by which the soul receives its own.

Every thought-seed sown or allowed to fall into the mind, and to take root there, produces its own, blossoming sooner or later into act, and bearing its own fruitage of opportunity and circumstance. Good thoughts bear good fruit, bad thoughts bad fruit.

I like his term "thought-seed" as every thought you have ever had has the potential to produce. Perhaps get into the habit of calling your thoughts "thought-seeds".

The outer world of circumstance shapes itself to the inner world of thought, and both pleasant and unpleasant external conditions are factors, which make for the ultimate good of the individual. As the reaper of his own harvest, man learns both by suffering and bliss.

I am sure that Allen would be quick to agree with the following; the crisis that the world finds itself in, is not so much from inadequacy, corruption, or an inept government, nor the greed of commerce and the falseness of advertising – it is a crisis of consciousness, and inability to recognise the power that each of us welds, in all things that we do. We all need to awaken.

Following the inmost desires, aspirations, thoughts, by which he allows himself to be dominated, (pursuing the will-o'-the-wisps of impure imaginings or steadfastly walking the highway of strong and high endeavour), a man at last arrives at their fruition and fulfilment in the outer conditions of his life. The laws of growth and adjustment everywhere obtains.

A man does not come to the alms house or the jail by the tyranny of fate or circumstance, but by the pathway of grovelling thoughts and base desires. Nor does a pure-minded man fall suddenly into crime by stress of any mere external force. The criminal thought had long been secretly fostered in the heart, and the hour of opportunity revealed its gathered power. **Circumstance does not make the man; it reveals him to himself.** No such conditions can exist as descending into vice and its attendant sufferings apart from vicious inclinations or ascending into virtue and its pure happiness without the continued cultivation of virtuous aspirations, and man, therefore, as the lord and master of thought, is the maker of himself the shaper and author of (his) environment. Even at birth the personality comes to its own and through every step of its earthly pilgrimage it attracts those combinations of conditions which reveal itself, which are the reflections of its own purity and, impurity, its strength and weakness.

Allen says – Circumstance does not make the man; it reveals him to himself. *By accurate analysis of your circumstances, and awareness, you can determine the prominent thoughts that you have.*

Men do not attract that which they want, but that which they are. Their whims, fancies, and ambitions are thwarted at every step, but their inmost thoughts and desires are fed with their own food, be it foul or clean.

The "divinity that shapes our ends" is in ourselves; it is our very self. Only himself manacles man: thought and action are the gaolers of fate, they imprison, being base; they are also the angels of freedom. They liberate, being noble. Not what he wishes and prays for does a man get, but what he justly earns. His wishes and prayers are only gratified and answered when they harmonize with his thoughts and actions.

In the earlier story about Anthony (the Australian), he spoke about fate as a copout. Allen just said thought and action are the gaolers of fate.

In the light of this truth, what, then, is the meaning of "fighting against circumstances?" It means that a man is continually revolting against an effect without, while all the time he is nourishing and preserving its cause in his heart. That cause may take the form of a conscious vice or an unconscious weakness; but whatever it is, it stubbornly retards the efforts of its possessor, and thus calls aloud for remedy.

So what is negativity thinking? People who moan are negative, as are people who unduly worry about things. Self-esteem issues usually derive from negative thinking, as does a lack of confidence. If you (mostly) think others can achieve more, you are negative. Jealousy (generally refers to the thoughts or feelings of insecurity, fear, concern, over relative lack of possessions) is the result of thinking other people can get more, do more, make more, or are better than you. The same applies to envy. A lack of trust of people can be because once someone treated them badly. They tend to be a disgruntled employee, where all that the company does is bad for the employees, where they tend to be sneaky and do as little as possible, or just doing enough to get by on. Many people think themselves into disease through negative thinking. Pessimists are negative thinkers. Those who always think that things are too good to last are negative, and so do people who think they are unlucky. The negative thinkers of the world fit into the, "I'm not good enough, I'm never good enough; it is too hard; I could not make that happen; I don't deserve this; why me?" They are the victims, the meek and the downtrodden. They are sadder than most, hanging on to past difficult episodes and living them as if they were still there today; nor can they forgive others. They seem to think that the world is against them, and that life will always be hard. They think it is all because of fate, and that they have no control over life and its events. They are the ones who wish bad luck or misfortune on others and are quick to offer words of hate. Negative people fret a lot of the time and are more risk adverse. Emotive people are usually negative people, or negative people are usually emotive people. Cynicism and suspicion are part of their makeup, and they tend to be selfish (what's mine is mine and you must go and get your own). They also take pleasure in shooting other people's ideas or enthusiasm down. People who over eat and drink too much alcohol tend to be negative, and certainly once they have over eaten or consumed too much alcohol, they are pretty much always in remorse from doing so.

If you want to confirm what the opposite list is, that is of positivity, go back and read the first seed in the book, What would you do if you knew you cannot Fail?

As a Man Thinketh by James Allen – **Men are anxious to improve their circumstances but are unwilling to improve themselves**. Therefore, they remain bound. The man who does not shrink from self-crucifixion can never fail to accomplish the object upon which his heart is set. This is as true of earthly as of heavenly things. Even the man whose sole object is to acquire wealth must be prepared to make great personal sacrifices before he can accomplish his object. How much more so he who would realize a strong and well-poised life?

How are we influenced? When you were born you did not care if you were white or black? Nor did you care if you were not yellow or white or black? When born, you had no hate but you were smart enough to learn it fairly quickly. Nor did you worry about money. As you aged you learned to be in fear of not having enough. Were you concerned with your appearance, or rather, did it worry you if you did not look good in the eyes of others? The truth is, you didn't give a damn!

When you were born, you were less complex and knew what you wanted. Your mind was not cluttered with numerous things because your focus was always on one thing at a time. When you wanted food, you only wanted food. There were not ten wants cluttering your mind.

When you had food in you, were dry and not tired, you were content – there was no scheming for more – nothing was missing – or greed or need for excess.

When you fell over, you got up. There was no moaning, you just got up – there was no aggravation – you got up – and let it fade from your memory. It was only later that you learnt to hang on to aggravation.

At that young age, the thing that drove you was wonderment – all was exciting. It still can be. A child is not stuck in one direction – is happy to change direction at any time and is able to let go.

A new born does not strive for identity — she or he is enough.

At that time you did not think you were better than others. Nor did you think they were better than you — can anyone be better than anyone else?

You were not afraid to learn, and learn you did. It was later in the classroom where you compared yourself with others, where you learnt to be small.

When did you concluded that you were not good enough? When you were born you did not think this, so when did you decide you are not perfect just as you are?

What happened to you — from that excited, adventurous and fearless child?

Influence happened. You were influenced by people and society. That was when you stopped trusting that you would receive. It was then that you moved from love to fear.

For your first years of life you trusted that all your needs would be supplied. You knew food, warmth, comfort and love would be there. Somewhere you lost that trust. By doing so your vibration changed.

Here is a man who is wretchedly poor. He is extremely anxious that his surroundings and home comforts should be improved, yet all the time he shirks his work, and considers he is justified in trying to deceive his employer on the ground of the insufficiency of his wages. Such a man does not understand the simplest rudiments of those principles, which are the basis of true prosperity, and is not only totally unfitted to rise out of his wretchedness but is actually attracting to himself a still deeper wretchedness by dwelling in, and acting out, indolent, deceptive, and unmanly thoughts.

Here is a rich man who is the victim of a painful and persistent disease as the result of gluttony. He is willing to give large sums of money to get rid of it, but he will not sacrifice his gluttonous desires. He wants to gratify his taste for rich and unnatural viands and have his health as well. Such a man is totally unfit to have health, because he has not yet learned the first principles of a healthy life.

Here is an employer of labour who adopts crooked measures to avoid paying the regulation wage, and, in the hope of making larger profits, reduces the wages of his workpeople. Such a man is altogether unfitted for prosperity, and when he finds himself bankrupt, both as regards reputation and riches, he blames circumstances, not knowing that he is the sole author of his condition.

I have introduced these three cases merely as illustrative of the truth that man is the causer (though nearly always is unconsciously) of his circumstances, and that, whilst aiming at a good end, he is continually frustrating its accomplishment by encouraging thoughts and desires which cannot possibly harmonize with that end. Such cases could be multiplied and varied almost indefinitely, but this is not necessary, as the reader can, if he so resolves, trace the action of the laws of thought in his own mind and life, and until this is done, mere external facts cannot serve as a ground of reasoning.

Again, awareness is the key here. The things that you tell yourself are the things that you become. So does it not make sense to become aware of what you think?

Circumstances, however, are so complicated, thought is so deeply rooted, and the conditions of happiness vary so, vastly with individuals, that a man's entire soul-condition (although it may be known to himself) cannot be judged by another from the external aspect of his life alone. A man may be honest in certain directions yet suffer privations; a man may be dishonest in certain directions, yet acquire wealth. The conclusion usually formed that the one man fails because of his particular honesty, and that the other prospers because of his particular dishonesty, is the result of a superficial judgment, which assumes that the dishonest man is almost totally corrupt, and the honest man almost entirely virtuous. In the light of a deeper knowledge and wider experience such judgment is found to be erroneous. The dishonest man may have some admirable virtues, which the other does not possess. The honest man obnoxious vices which are absent in the other. The honest man reaps the good results of his honest thoughts and acts. He also brings upon himself the sufferings, which his vices produce. The dishonest man likewise garners his own suffering and happiness.

The facets of our character are like boxes. You may have twenty-three boxes, while I may have thirty. There is no fixed number. We are strong in some boxes and weak in others. In some areas of our life we may exude great ability, and therefore confidence. In others, we may be weak and timid. Our task is to understand each and every box. Where we are strong, we must remain strong; where we are weak we must attend to those weaknesses.

In your twenty-three boxes, fifteen may have good positive aspects in them, five could be neutral, while the remaining three are negative. Nevertheless, it could be that the negative three exert a massive influence on how you see yourself. It is imperative to identify your boxes and strengthen those that are weak. The number of boxes as well as the positive or negative influence will change throughout your life. You will have to scrutinise your boxes constantly.

Good thoughts and actions can never produce bad results; bad thoughts and actions can never produce good results. This is but saying that nothing can come from corn but corn, nothing from nettles but nettles. Men understand this law in the natural world, and work with it, but few understand it in the mental and moral world and they, therefore, do not co-operate with it.

Suffering, that is long-term and ongoing suffering, is always the effect of wrong thought in some direction. It is an indication that the individual is out of harmony with himself, with the Law of his being. The sole and supreme use of suffering is to purify, to burn out all that is useless and impure. Suffering ceases for him who is with a pure mind. There could be no object in burning gold after the dross had been removed, and a perfectly pure and enlightened being could not suffer.

The circumstances, which a man encounters with suffering, are the result of his own mental in harmony. The circumstances, which a man encounters with blessedness, are the result of his own mental harmony. Once again, this is referring to continuous suffering.

Blessedness, not material possessions, is the measure of right thought; wretchedness, not lack of material possessions, is the measure of wrong thought. A man may be cursed and rich; he may be blessed and poor.

There is no law, other than silly man-made laws, that state that for a person to be happy they must not have riches. Riches and a positive mindset can work together like a horse and carriage. Money and wealth do not by themselves corrupt a man. Only the mind of man corrupts himself through his thoughts.

Blessedness and riches are only joined together when the riches are rightly and wisely used; and the poor man only descends into wretchedness when he regards his lot as a burden unjustly imposed.

If a person is rich but dissatisfied – then he did it. If there are not a lot of material possessions, but the person is happy – he did it.

Indigence and indulgence are the two extremes of wretchedness. They are both equally unnatural and the result of mental disorder. A man is not rightly conditioned until he is a happy, healthy, and prosperous being, and happiness, health, and prosperity are the result of a harmonious adjustment of the inner with the outer, of the man with his surroundings.

Here is a good time to talk about fate and destiny. Many allow their lives to run any which-way and then moan that is was fate or destiny that gives them a poor life. We must take responsibility for our own lives, through our thought process. It is our thought process that will determine if our life has value or not – not some preordained plan. Further to this, I believe that the creative force gave man "free will", which opposes fate or destiny. If fate or destiny plays a part in a person's life, it is only an influence that can be utilised for good or overruled if not good by our free will.

Fate and destiny have been popularised through some of the eastern beliefs, such as: the four pillars and astrology, whereby your destiny is determined from the alignment of the planets at the time of birth, the date of birth, time of birth, and geographical location. These things may have an influence, but they are not the categorical reason for a good or bad life, a wealthy or poor life, a happy or sad life. They are merely influences. For instance, the alignment of the planets at the time of your birth propose or suggest a positive influence, will always be overruled or diminished if you are of a negative mindset. So it is not fate, it is thought that rules with the greatest power.

To define it; destiny is where a person is born to do or achieve a specific thing. I believe we are born to be the best person we can be, which entails being happy, and so destiny has nothing to do with our reason for being here. Whilst we are growing, we can attune to the talents that we have been blessed with. The universe is not interested in what you do, it is only vibration, negative or positive, that influences. It really is not worried if you are a baker, butcher or banker as long as you are trying to live life with seed-thought awareness, the right vibration.

A man only begins to be a man when he ceases to whine and revile and commences to search for the hidden justice, which regulates his life. As he adapts his mind to that regulating factor, he ceases to accuse others as the cause of his condition and builds himself up in strong and noble thoughts; ceases to kick against circumstances, but begins to use them as aids to his more rapid progress, and as a means of discovering the hidden powers and possibilities within himself.

Law, not confusion, is the dominating principle in the universe; justice, not injustice, is the soul and substance of life. Righteousness, not corruption, is the moulding and moving force in the spiritual government of the world. This being so, man has but to right himself to find that the universe is right. Whilst, during the process of putting himself right he will find that **as he alters his thoughts towards things and other people, things and other people will alter towards him.**

We attract what we put out via our vibration. The vibration of positivity will bring opportunity, whereas the vibration of negativity will negate opportunity, it will only bring hardship.

The proof of this truth is in every person, and it therefore admits of easy investigation by systematic introspection and self-analysis. Let a man radically alter his thoughts, and he will be astonished at the rapid transformation it will affect in the material conditions of his life. Men imagine that thought can be kept secret, but it cannot – it rapidly crystallizes into habit, and habit solidifies into circumstance. Bestial thoughts crystallize into habits of drunkenness and sensuality, which solidify into circumstances of destitution and disease. Impure thoughts of every kind crystallize into enervating and confusing habits, which solidify into distracting and adverse circumstances. Thoughts of fear, doubt, and indecision crystallize into weak, unmanly, and irresolute habits, which solidify into circumstances of failure, indigence, and slavish dependence: lazy thoughts crystallize into habits of uncleanliness and dishonesty, which solidify into circumstances of foulness and beggary. Hateful and condemnatory thoughts crystallize into habits of accusation and violence, which solidify into circumstances of injury and persecution. Selfish thoughts of all kinds crystallize into habits of self-seeking, which solidify into circumstances more or less distressing.

On the other hand, beautiful thoughts of all kinds crystallize into habits of grace and kindliness, which solidify into genial and sunny circumstances. Pure thoughts crystallize into habits of temperance and self-control, which solidify into circumstances of repose and peace. Thoughts of courage, self-reliance, and decision crystallize into manly habits, which solidify into circumstances of success, plenty, and freedom. Energetic thoughts crystallize into habits of cleanliness and industry, which solidify into circumstances of pleasantness. Gentle and forgiving thoughts crystallize into habits of gentleness, which solidify into protective and preservative circumstances. Loving and unselfish thoughts crystallize into habits of self-forgetfulness for others, which solidify into circumstances of sure and abiding prosperity and true riches.

A particular train of thought persisted in, be it good or bad, cannot fail to produce its results on the character and circumstances. A woman cannot directly choose her circumstances, but she can choose her thoughts, and so indirectly, yet surely, shape her circumstances.

Nature helps every man to the gratification of the thoughts, which he most encourages, and opportunities are presented, which will most speedily bring to the surface both the good and evil thoughts.

Let a man cease from his sinful thoughts, and all the world will soften towards him, and be ready to help him. Let him put away his weakly and sickly thoughts, and lo, opportunities will spring up on every hand to aid his strong resolves. Let him encourage good thoughts, and no hard fate shall bind him down to wretchedness and shame. The world is your kaleidoscope, and the varying combinations of colours, which at every succeeding moment it presents to you are the exquisitely adjusted pictures of your ever-moving thoughts.

You are bombarded with thoughts every second of every day. Most steal your clarity and unconsciously mould you into a form that you do not like, that you are not even aware of. They rob you of your innate power and control your life. Negative or unconscious thoughts make you do and say things that are not compatible with who you are or who you want to be.

If you knew how many thoughts direct your life you would be stunned. In just one year there can be millions and each and every one of them has the power to reduce your focus and stifle your potential, or hopefully to assist you to gain what you want. Most thoughts however are of a revolving theme – themes that recur thousands of times, thereby creating your circumstances. These can be emotive issues, frustrations, impatience, anger, peevishness and defensiveness, all taking you down the wrong route.

As a Man Thinketh by James Allen – **The effect of thought on health and the body**

The body is the servant of the mind. It obeys the operations of the mind, whether they be deliberately chosen or automatically expressed. At the bidding of unlawful thoughts the body sinks rapidly into disease and decay. At the command of glad and beautiful thoughts it becomes clothed with youthfulness and beauty.

Positive body language may change your life. Scientists call this Non Verbal Communication (NVC). Most of the work on NVC by scientists show how one person's body language affects others and how they respond. Sometimes we can be "small" or "large" with others, and our being this will affect those others as to how they respond to us.

Amy Caddy (Social Psychologist), a researcher from the USA, has spent years on understanding how our body language affects ourselves, and has discovered what she calls "power posing", a method that can make us feel more confident and happier. That is to stand in a posture of confidence, even when we do not feel confident to help boost feelings of confidence, therefore it is likely to have an impact on our chances for success.

Essentially, what the above says is that the way we carry ourselves affects our thoughts, feelings and physiology, and so Caddy calls the process "power dynamics". A lot of her research comes from the animal kingdom and primates, where she (and many others, such as Jane Goodall) study animal behaviour. The findings have been researched and confirmed with groups of people.

Consistently, people with success or power will display a different body language to those of people who fall short of their potential. A part of the research was on people who had not fulfilled their potential, that if they changed their body language, would it help to move closer to that potential. For this to be applied, those studied would have to "fake it until they made it". The results of behavioural changes were overwhelming, where people's lives turned around for the better. So clearly, positive NVC affects our thoughts, feelings and physiology.

A simple example, one that has been researched for well over 100 years is that when smiling, even pretending to smile, we actually feel better. Try it for a day or so, you will see that it works. Conversely, try the opposite, that is, to frown and feel small. This is not good!

It has been known that our mind changes our body, but Caddy's research has shown that the body, and the way we carry it, affects our mind. People who have changed their body language have become more assertive, confident, optimistic, they tend to think more creatively, are happier, and take more risk (that is changing jobs or taking on jobs that previously they did not consider themselves worthy of).

As this section of Allen's essay in on health, body language (as Caddy's research has proven) has an effect on testosterone, the power hormone, and cortisol, the stress hormone. By adopting positive body language (and I suspect a more positive mindset) testosterone increases and cortisol decreases. Whereas, most unfulfilled individuals have low testosterone and high cortisol. Obviously higher testosterone and lower cortisol is of benefit. Caddy's research showed that as little as two minutes of positive body language can change the hormone level, and that body language can change the mind. This, you talking to yourself, through your body language (and positive self-talk) has long-term implications. This tool is becoming better known, where body language changes the mind, and the mind changes outcomes.

Back to the health; research consistently shows that high cortisol levels that remain in the body for long periods of time affect the physiology in the form of disease. By increasing testosterone, disease can diminish. Therefore, a feel good smile may keep you out of the hospital.

Now, Allen told us decades ago that positive thinking affects outcomes, and now science is showing us that body language affects outcomes. Allen knew that being positive affects our health in positive ways.

For more on Amy Caddy's work go to TED or many other websites.

Disease and health, like circumstances, are rooted in thought. Sickly thoughts will express themselves through a sickly body. Thoughts of fear have been known to kill a man as speedily as a bullet, and they are continually killing thousands of people just as surely though less rapidly.

I knew of a husband and wife team. The husband died in a car accident. Two months later the wife died. Yet before the accident, she was in perfect health. How, why? Clearly of a broken heart. A broken heart is an emotional issue. All emotions derive from thoughts – so she literally thought herself to death. However, this would not have been on a conscious level as she would have literally fretted herself to the grave. I am sure that you have also seen this with pets. Perhaps there are two dogs or two cats within a household. One dies, then in a short time the other dies.

Thought equals vibration. Vibration equals results.

Anxiety quickly demoralizes the whole body and lays it open to the entrance of disease, while impure thoughts, even if not physically indulged, will soon shatter the nervous system.

Strong, pure, and happy thoughts build up the body in vigour and grace. The body is a delicate and plastic instrument, which responds readily to the thoughts by which it is impressed, and habits of thought will produce their own effects, good or bad, upon it.

Men will continue to have impure and poisoned blood, so long as they propagate unclean thoughts. Out of a clean heart comes a clean life and a clean body. Out of a defiled mind proceeds a defiled life and a corrupt body. Thought is the fount of action, life, and manifestation; make the fountain pure, and all will be pure.

This is such a truism; I have known many who are on a pristine diet, yet, they remain sick. I have also known many who eat badly and are relatively healthy. In both cases, it was not so much the food they ate, it was the belief they had.

Change of diet will not help a man who will not change his thoughts. When a man makes his thoughts pure, he no longer desires impure food.

Clean thoughts make clean habits. The so-called saint who does not wash his body is not a saint. He who has strengthened and purified his thoughts does not need to consider the malevolent microbe.

If you would protect your body, guard your mind. If you would renew your body, beautify your mind.

Thoughts of malice, envy, disappointment, despondency, rob the body of its health and grace. A sour face does not come by chance – it is made by sour thoughts. Wrinkles that mar are drawn by folly, passion, and pride.

The above thoughts Allen refers to creates that vibration.

I know a woman of ninety-six who has the bright, innocent face of a girl. I know a man well under middle age whose face is drawn into inharmonious contours. The one is the result of a sweet and sunny disposition; the other is the outcome of passion and discontent.

As you cannot have a sweet and wholesome abode unless you admit the air and sunshine freely into your rooms, so a strong body and a bright, happy, or serene countenance can only result from the free admittance into the mind of thoughts of joy and goodwill and serenity.

More on brain plasticity. The brain has an amazing ability to heal itself of health issues and to overcome inadequacies. The research has two reasons; the first is to understand how or why this works. The second reason is that by understanding the process, then with human intervention the brain can be supported in its self-healing process (but there must be human intervention).

Our mental state can affect the brain. I remember reading (sorry, but I cannot remember the source) about some research done on people, whereby before and after, measurements of the pre-frontal cortex had been taken. The subjects were to regularly sit and focus on being positive, hopeful and calm. The results were amazing; in just about all of the hundreds of people who were measured, the prefrontal cortex had thickened. When a muscle, and or the brain weakens, we say it has atrophied or emaciated, so the fact that there was a thickening of that part of the pre-frontal cortex proves the brain's plasticity to development.

So my thought, and I suspect this is true, is that by living a life of gentleness, calm compassion, respectfulness, and positivity, will change the way that you see life through the functioning of a different brain, and you will probably live longer, and healthier.

At first, it may seem strange trying to live that way, but as research has shown, repeatedly, that by faking it you will make it. You will change your brain, and you will change your attitude towards life and people.

On the faces of the aged there are wrinkles made by sympathy, others by strong and pure thought, and others are carved by passion. Who cannot distinguish them? With those who have lived righteously, age is calm, peaceful, and softly mellowed, like the setting sun. I have recently seen a philosopher on his deathbed. He was not old except in years. He died as sweetly and peacefully as he had lived.

There is no physician like cheerful thought for dissipating the ills of the body; there is no comforter to compare with goodwill for dispersing the shadows of grief and sorrow. To live continually in thoughts of ill will, cynicism, suspicion, and envy, is to be confined in a self-made prison. To think well of all, to be cheerful with all, to patiently learn to find the good in all. Such unselfish thoughts are the very portals of heaven. To dwell day by day in thoughts of peace toward every creature will bring abounding peace to their possessor.

At the end of this section on thought and health, I have two comments;

I'd like to remind you of Masaru Emoto's water experiments and their results. As our body is made up of a high percentage of water, it is easy to draw the conclusion that feeding the body-water with the right vibration will support health. Conversely, feeding the body with hate and envy will render the body with impurities and dysfunction.

And the second comment is; though people are living longer (there is no doubt of that), but they are no healthier than decades ago. Why?

Health systems, all over the world are over burdened because there are so many sick people. I can't help but think that if people changed their thoughts there would be less sickness.

As a Man Thinketh by James Allen – **Thought and Purpose**

Until thought is linked with purpose, there is no intelligent accomplishment. With the majority the bark of thought is allowed to "drift" upon the ocean of life. Aimlessness is a vice, and such drifting must not continue for him who would steer clear of catastrophe and destruction.

They who have no central purpose in their life fall an easy prey to petty worries, fears, troubles, and self-pity, all of which are indications of weakness, which lead, just as surely as deliberately planned sins (though by a different route), to failure, unhappiness, and loss, for weakness cannot persist in a power evolving universe.

Above I wrote — In action there is hope.

A man should conceive of a legitimate purpose in his heart and set out to accomplish it. He should make this purpose the centralizing point of his thoughts. It may take the form of a spiritual ideal, or it may be a worldly object, according to his nature at the time being. Whichever it is, he should steadily focus his thought-forces upon the object, which he has set before him. He should make this purpose his supreme duty, and should devote himself to its attainment, not allowing his thoughts to wander away into ephemeral fancies, longings, and imaginings. This is the royal road to self-control and true concentration of thought. Even if he fails again and again to accomplish his purpose (as he necessarily must until weakness is overcome), the strength of character gained will be the measure of his true success, and this will form a new starting-point for future power and triumph.

Apathy causes disease, unhappiness, boredom, all of which can lead to a life of little value.

Those who are not prepared for the apprehension of a great purpose should fix the thoughts upon the faultless performance of their duty, no matter how insignificant their task may appear. Only in this way can the thoughts be gathered and focussed, and resolution and energy be developed, which being done, there is nothing which may not be accomplished.

In thought, there is energy, and that is where our potential is,

The weakest soul, knowing its own weakness, and believing this truth, that strength can only be developed by effort and practice, will, thus believing, at once begin to exert itself, and, adding effort to effort, patience to patience, and strength to strength, will never cease to develop, and will at last grow perfectly strong.

Science and what is known as the God Particle supports this.

The following is from the pen of Australia writer John Lovell; There is compelling evidence that matter is not what it appears to be. At the atomic level, electrons, which orbit the nucleus, form the perception of matter, and only manifest as particles when observed. Remember these words, "when they are observed."

Furthermore, electrons are not static in one position and constantly rotate around the nucleus. Thus, the term solid, when referring to matter, is an illusion. If matter is an illusion, and if we as humans are considered to be of matter, then surely, we are also an illusion. The further we descend through the sub-atomic level to the planck scale; matter does not exist or behave as we know it as it acts as a wave, in fact there is virtually nothing to matter. Even the nucleus of the atom, once thought to be solid, exists as a wave that materializes in a specific location in time and space when being observed. There is a belief that molecules, which are the building blocks for cell tissue, do the same thing. It appears that we can never really know the true nature of the Universe because every time we observe it, it turns to matter.

The notion that matter has intelligence is naturally a compelling concept as this would imply that the Universe has innate internalised governance. It also raises conceptual notions of the possibility of it being self-aware and perhaps self-determining. It is considered that all past and future knowledge is already stored on waves of potentiality that constitute pure intelligence.

*Matter appeared to express intelligence, (*as shown*) when observed in the double split screen experiment. When fired from a particle generator, and passed through a split screen, a particle splits into two identical particles. However, when the same process was observed (*by the scientists*), the effect of the observer collapsed the wave function or entanglement of the particles and produced two clear images instead of the diffracted multiple images. It appeared that the particle, in a state of entanglement, was aware it was being observed and changed its function from a wave to solid matter. The inescapable conclusion is that all matter, holds and can express intelligence.)" Unquote.*

For us wanting the best of life, this is an important concept. If thoughts create vibration, and if vibrations are the building blocks of life, then it is imperative that positive thoughts are had, thereby producing a more positive outcome — and as just given, when matter is observed it changes. Therefore, when we observe in a positive way the goings on in our life, the outcomes will be better.

As the physically weak man can make himself strong by careful and patient training, so the man of weak thoughts can make them strong by exercising himself in right thinking.

It is here that the importance of the plastic brain comes to the fore.

To put away aimlessness and weakness, and to begin to think with purpose, is to enter the ranks of those strong ones who only recognize failure as one of the pathways to attainment. It is they who make all conditions serve them, and who think strongly, attempt fearlessly, and accomplish masterfully.

Having conceived of his purpose, a man should mentally mark out a straight pathway to its achievement, looking neither to the right nor the left. Doubts and fears should be rigorously excluded as they are disintegrating elements, which break up the straight line of effort, rendering it crooked, ineffectual, useless.

As the above given research shows, what we focus on is what we get. If we focus on being not likely to win, then for sure, we will lose.

Thoughts of doubt and fear never accomplished anything, and never can. They always lead to failure. Purpose, energy, power to do, and all strong thoughts cease when doubt and fear creep in.

The will to do springs from the knowledge that we can do. Doubt and fear are the great enemies of knowledge, and he who encourages them, who does not slay them thwarts himself at every step.

He who has conquered doubt and fear has conquered failure. His every thought is allied with power, and all difficulties are bravely met and wisely overcome. His purposes are seasonably planted, and they bloom and bring forth fruit, which does not fall prematurely to the ground.

Thought allied fearlessly to purpose becomes creative force. He who knows this is ready to become something higher and stronger than a mere bundle of wavering thoughts and fluctuating sensations. He who does this has become the conscious and intelligent wielder of his mental powers.

As a Man Thinketh by James Allen – **The thought factor in achievement** (As he thinks, so he is. As he continues to think, so he remains).

All that a man achieves and all that he fails to achieve is the direct result of his own thoughts. In a justly ordered universe, where loss of equipoise would mean total destruction, individual responsibility must be absolute. A man's weakness and strength, purity and impurity, are his own, and not another man's; they are brought about by himself, and not by another; and they can only be altered by himself, never by another. His condition is also his own, and not another man's. His suffering and his happiness are evolved from within. As he thinks, so he is; as he continues to think, so he remains.

It is the total weight of your thoughts that make you who you are and direct the circumstances that you live in. One negative thought will not change your life, but if you have twenty negative thoughts in a day, then the weight of negativity will outbalance the positive.

Imagine an empty bottle attached to a tap, where the tap drips every few seconds. After the first hour, there is virtually no water in the bottle, but by the end of the day, there will be a great deal of water in the bottle. Thoughts, negative or positive, accumulate one thought at a time, like the water accumulates, one drop at a time. You need to ensure that there are more positive than negative thoughts.

A strong man cannot help a weaker unless that weaker is willing to be helped, and even then the weak man must become strong of himself. He must, by his own efforts, develop the strength, which he admires in another.

Reading this book will not give you the knowledge to have a great life, unless you apply the principles, you will stay as you are... all the telling will not make one bit of difference to your life. Only you, through your effort and awareness, will change your circumstances.

None but himself can alter his condition.

Success is fulfilment, and when you consider yours, do not listen to what society suggests as the standard. You must understand what is important to you.

Identifying with money or power is not nearly as precious as identifying with happiness, love and contentment. When you create your own understanding of success, be true to yourself, not what society expects. Flattery is an ego issue, as are the labels that go around. Be careful of your illusions, cravings and ambitions.

To be successful, you need to take time to evaluate. You need to know in your mind what is important and what is not. By doing so, you begin the process that will take you to that fulfilment. As there are likely to be many different topics, set goals and time frames for each. Know that these aspirations may take time, and do not attempt to make too many changes at once.

It has been usual for men to think and to say, "Many men are slaves because one is an oppressor; let us hate the oppressor." Now, however, there is amongst an increasing few a tendency to reverse this judgment, and to say, "One man is an oppressor because many are slaves; let us despise the slaves."

The truth is that oppressor and slave are co-operators in ignorance, and, while seeming to afflict each other, are in reality afflicting themselves. A perfect Knowledge perceives the action of law in the weakness of the oppressed and the misapplied power of the oppressor; a perfect Love, seeing the suffering, which both states entail, condemns neither; a perfect Compassion embraces both oppressor and oppressed.

He who has conquered weakness, and has put away all selfish thoughts, belongs neither to oppressor nor oppressed. He is free.

When you feel better about yourself, it is easier, you will be happier to take measured risks; or change where appropriate, experiment with your creativity, and make new friends who are like-minded. In my experience, people who do these things, have more friends and have greater happiness than those that do not.

A man can only rise, conquer, and achieve by lifting up his thoughts. He can only remain weak, and abject, and miserable by refusing to lift up his thoughts.

Failure is giving up; failure is temporary unless you let your mind say otherwise. Failure is not fatal unless you believe that it is.

Before a man can achieve anything, even in worldly things, he must lift his thoughts above slavish animal indulgence. He may not, in order to succeed, give up all animality and selfishness, by any means; but a portion of it must, at least, be sacrificed. A man whose first thought is bestial indulgence could neither think clearly nor plan methodically; he could not find and develop his latent resources and would fail in any undertaking. Not having commenced to manfully control his thoughts, he is not able to control affairs and to adopt serious responsibilities. He is not fit to act independently and stand alone. He is limited only by the thoughts, which he chooses.

There can be no progress, no achievement without sacrifice, and a man's worldly success will be in the measure that he sacrifices his confused animal thoughts and fixes his mind on the development of his plans, and the strengthening of his resolution and self-reliance. The higher he lifts his thoughts, the more manly, upright, and righteous he becomes, the greater will be his success, the more blessed and enduring will be his achievements.

The universe does not favour the greedy, the dishonest, the vicious, although on the mere surface it may sometimes appear to do so; it helps the honest, the magnanimous, the virtuous. All the great Teachers of the ages have declared this in varying forms, and to prove and know it a man has but to persist in making himself more and more virtuous by lifting his thoughts.

Confucius was one such great teacher. He stood for the people, and nothing changed his desire to help them. He scorned riches and the power structures of the day. He died in virtual poverty, preferring to share all that he had through growing his schooling facilities, to share education to the masses. Confucius was a big man, with a body that was slightly deformed, and a head larger than normal.

Intellectual achievements are the result of thought consecrated to the search for knowledge, or for the beautiful and true in life and nature. Such achievements may be sometimes connected with vanity and ambition, but they are not the outcome of those characteristics; they are the natural outgrowth of long and arduous effort, and of pure and unselfish thoughts.

By understanding what success means to you and setting your goals, you will always have a shining light to head for, one that offers guidance. By having a strong moral code and knowing who you are, will also allow you to be the best person that you can be.

And when we talk about success, what about money? You need it, but how much? Many preach against greed, many are hungry for it. Most authors when talking about money tell of its evil. I will tell you what is evil about money — it is not having enough!

Just about every creature on the planet, including man, must make some effort to obtain food to sustain their life. Some, like spiders, make a web and wait for the food to come to them. Other species hunt, bees go from flower to flower, cows graze all day. We humans used to hunt or grow our food, but now we mostly earn money that we trade for food. Not only is it food that we need, we also need shelter. This puts pressure on us to secure it.

It is therefore an inherent right of life for all creatures to have the capacity to sustain ourselves. We all deserve our sustenance. In terms of setting your goals, money must be a high priority because without it you will be miserable. There will be limitation in what you can do in life, anxiety and ill-health. A shortage of it prevents us from eating properly and leads to sickness and an early death. A shortage of funds reduces our vision when we should have glasses or ruins our teeth because we did not have the money for dentistry. A lack of money embarrasses us with tatty clothes or reduces our education, thereby keeping us in poverty. Not having enough money ensures that young girls, really young, have babies that they cannot afford, thereby extending the poverty trap, and living with husbands who they hate. We collect garbage or beg instead of being a schoolteacher or a hairdresser. Because of little money, people become drunks and destroy their lives and the lives of their loved ones. Girls sell their bodies to men because of no money, parents fight and separate because of a lack of money, and husbands beat their wives from the pressure of not having enough money. Our friendships are reduced, usually to those who also have little money. Many sleep in little more than a shed without proper bedding to keep them warm... they are wet and cold, uncomfortable, and full of resentment. The bill in the post brings worry and tension that knots up the gut. Not able to broaden our horizons by seeing the Great Wall of China or the magnificence of Sydney Harbour. Without money it is hard to be of a noble character and generous to others with less than we have. There can be no entertaining or entertainment as life is a constant battle for survival.

A shortage of funds can plague you all your life, embarrass you from birth to death, humiliate you a million times. Our lives were never our own, they were pulled this way and that by the bosses and the system.

And if that is not enough, knowing that you never supplied enough to your children, or the feeling of failure because you had no money – they are the worst feelings of all.

So money is important, very important. Love what it gives you, do not be greedy, it is not a god. Know its need and place, it is though, your inherent right, just as seeds are the rights of birds.

He who lives constantly in the conception of noble and lofty thoughts, who dwells upon all that is pure and unselfish, will, as surely as the sun reaches its zenith and the moon its full, become wise and noble in character, and a position of influence and blessedness.

There is a universal law, one that perhaps has not been proven by scientific research, but one that has been practiced for hundreds of years, and through that practice has repeatedly, anecdotally shown to be true – when you give goodness, you receive goodness back. That when you are generous, generosity will follow you, when you give to a good charitable cause, then goodness will be returned to you. Remember, the second story of Gawa who went to find happiness from Princess Wencheng?

This law, which I shall call it, the law of giving and receiving, does work, as it hinges on the scientific law of equal and opposite reaction. So of course, when you give goodness out, goodness will return. If you give out greed, then an equal reaction will diminish you in some way. (From an esoteric perspective, Karma is also; what you place out there is what you will receive back, what you sow is what you reap. All the same laws but from the perspective of different cultural groups).

This law is also the law of vibration. Equal vibrations attract in likeness, so if you vibrate generosity, then you will be the receiver of generous acts. By vibrating anger, then harshness will be returned in kind.

When Allan wrote his principles, he knew this through practice, and through reading ancient treatises.

Achievement, of whatever kind, is the crown of effort, the diadem of thought. By the aid of self-control, resolution, purity, righteousness, and well-directed thought a man ascends; by the aid of animality, indolence, impurity, corruption, and confusion of thought a man descends.

A man may rise to high success in the world, and even to lofty altitudes in the spiritual realm, and again descend into weakness and wretchedness by allowing arrogant, selfish, and corrupt thoughts to take possession of him.

Victories attained by right thought can only be maintained by watchfulness. Many give way when success is assured, and rapidly fall back into failure.

All achievements, whether in the business or intellectual, are the result of definitely directed thought, are governed by the same law and are of the same method. The only difference lies in the object of attainment.

These laws are run in conjunction with the highs and lows of life. We cannot live without experiencing the death of friends or loved ones, feeling grief so deeply, it is like a punch in the stomach. Nor can we live without disease or accidents, physical pain. Nor can we live without the act of people stealing or being greedy against us. Nor can we live without friends turning on us, hurting or betraying us in some way. Nor can we live without us hurting others in some way. Nor can we live without disappointment in our career or desires. Nor can we live without making mistakes. Nor can we live without experiencing our own anger.

These things I talk of are life. They are the experiences of life that we cannot avoid. Their effects shape us, if we let them. It is how we think of these things that shape us. They break us, or make us stronger, they make us perpetually sad, or we can emerge happy through them. Whatever effect they have on us, is predicated from the constant thoughts we have of them. Have sad thoughts about them for too long and we be become sad – it's embedded through brain plasticity. We can let circumstances rule us, or we can overcome them and use them as lessons to give us clear sight. Remember above the story called Life, does it have to be fair? The wild dog being taken by the young hungry lion. From this story you learnt that life is not fair, not for any of us. Accept this principle and get on with being positive.

Know now that you cannot go through life without difficulties, we all do, but many are destroyed by them. But many grow from them, they recognise that, still they will succeed, still, they will be happy, still they will be generous of heart and nature, still they will strive to be the best they can.

Moreover, do you know what makes all this so? It is the thought that you bring to things.

He who would accomplish little must sacrifice little; he who would achieve much must sacrifice much. He who would attain highly must sacrifice greatly.

As a Man Thinketh by James Allen – Visions and ideals

The dreamers are the saviours of the world. As the visible world is sustained by the invisible, so men, through all their trials and sins and sordid vocations, are nourished by the beautiful visions of their solitary dreamers. Humanity cannot forget its dreamers. It cannot let their ideals fade and die – it lives in them. It knows them as the realities, which it shall one day see and know.

Such beautiful and profound writing. Why not read it again.

Scientist, Tali Sharot highlights the need for optimism. Her research shows that people who are optimistic for a certain outcome were essentially happier than those who were not. This is irrespective of the hoped for event succeeding or failing. Not only that, those who are generally more optimistic have a higher success rate than those who don't. Those measured, who had a low optimism, tended to be people of a low achievement rate. So, regardless of the outcome, those with high optimism felt happier – and if the outcome was not as hoped, the optimism encouraged those to greater effort, and were able to get on with their life with less disillusionment. Optimism, therefore, helps with wellbeing, and health (stress and anxiety are reduced). According to Sharot, optimism changes reality and can act as a self-fulfilling prophesy – it not only relates to success but leads to success. Lowering your expectations does the opposite.

Using a method called Functional MRI, Sharot and her team were able to measure changes to the brain (that plastic brain again) when subjects were asked to be optimistic or unoptimistic. (See Ted talks for more information in Sharot's work).

Composer, sculptor, painter, poet, prophet, sage, these are the makers of the after-world, the architects of heaven. The world is beautiful because they have lived. Without them, labouring humanity would perish.

He who cherishes a beautiful vision, a lofty ideal in his heart, will one day realise it. Columbus cherished a vision of another world, and he discovered it. Copernicus fostered the vision of a multiplicity of worlds and a wider universe, and he revealed it. Buddha beheld the vision of a spiritual world of stainless beauty and perfect peace, and he entered into it.

Confucius envisioned education to the poverty-struck, and he made it happen.

Cherish your visions; cherish your ideals; cherish the music that stirs in your heart, the beauty that forms in your mind, the loveliness that drapes your purest thoughts, for out of them will grow all delightful conditions, all, heavenly environment. Of these, if you remain true to them, your world will at last be built.

It is here that I remind you of the very first story in this book, What would you do if you knew you could Fail? It was of the visionary Dr Jardine's who had achieved so much because he had the words in his mind, I cannot fail.

To desire is to obtain. To aspire is to achieve. Shall man's basest desires receive the fullest measure of gratification, and his purest aspirations starve for lack of sustenance? Such is not the Law. Such a condition of things can never obtain. Call for it, and it will come.

Dream lofty dreams, and as you dream, so shall you become. Your Vision is the promise of what you shall one day be; your Ideal is the prophecy of what you shall at last unveil.

The greatest achievement was at first and for a time a dream. The oak sleeps in the acorn; the bird waits in the egg. The highest vision of the soul a waking angel stirs. Dreams are the seedlings of realities.

Earlier in the this work I wrote my take on luck, and I finished off that section by saying; Irrespective of your belief in luck or no luck, it will happen according to the positivity you hold.

Your circumstances may be uncongenial, but they shall not long remain so if you but perceive an Ideal and strive to reach it. You cannot travel within and stand still without. Here is a youth hard pressed by poverty and labour. Confined long hours in an unhealthy workshop; unschooled and lacking all the arts of refinement.

I remind you that Allen had a menial job but studied at night to improve his lot.

But he dreams of better things. He thinks of intelligence, of refinement, of grace and beauty. He conceives and mentally builds up, an ideal condition of life – the vision of a wider liberty and a larger scope takes possession of him. Unrest urges him to action, and he utilizes all his spare time and means, small though they are, to the development of his latent powers and resources. Very soon so altered has his mind become that the workshop can no longer hold him. It has become so out of harmony with his mentality that it falls out of his life as a garment is cast aside, and, with the growth of opportunities, which fit the scope of his expanding powers, he passes out of it forever. Years later, we see this youth as a full-grown man. We find him a master of certain forces of the mind, which he wields with worldwide influence and almost unequalled power. In his hands, he holds the cords of gigantic responsibilities. He speaks, and lo, lives are changed; men and women hang upon his words and remould their characters, and, sun-like, he becomes the fixed and luminous centre round, which innumerable destinies revolve. He has realized the Vision of his youth. He has become one with his Ideal.

You too, youthful reader, will realise the Vision (not the idle wish) of your heart, be it base or beautiful, or a mixture of both, for you will always gravitate toward that which you, secretly, most love. Into your hands will be placed the exact results of your own thoughts. You will receive that which you earn, no more, no less.

Whatever your present environment may be, you will fall, remain, or rise with your thoughts, your Vision, your Ideal. You will become as small as your controlling desire, as great as your dominant aspiration. In the beautiful words of Stanton Kirkham Davis, "You may be keeping accounts, and presently you shall walk out of the door that for so long has seemed to you the barrier of your ideals, and shall find yourself before an audience – the pen still behind your ear, the ink stains on your fingers and then and there shall pour out the torrent of your inspiration. You may be driving sheep, and you shall wander to the city-bucolic and open-mouthed; shall wander under the intrepid guidance of the spirit into the studio of the master, and after a time he shall say, 'I have nothing more to teach you.' And now you have become the master, who did so recently dream of great things while driving sheep. You shall lay down the saw and the plane to take upon yourself the regeneration of the world."

Everything that man has ever created started off as a thought. Thoughts are creative energy which become matter – if you can dream it, if you can see it, it will become reality.

The thoughtless, the ignorant, and the indolent, seeing only the apparent effects of things and not the things themselves, talk of luck, of fortune, and chance. Seeing a man grow rich, they say, "How lucky he is!" Observing another become intellectual, they exclaim, "How highly favoured he is!" And noting the saintly character and wide influence of another, they remark, "How chance aids him at every turn!" They do not see the trials and failures and struggles, which these men have voluntarily encountered in order to gain their experience. They have no knowledge of the sacrifices they have made, of the undaunted efforts they have put forth, of the faith they have exercised, that they might overcome the apparently insurmountable, and realize the Vision of their heart. They do not know the darkness and the heartaches. They only see the light and joy and call it "luck". They do not see the long and arduous journey, but only behold the pleasant goal, and call it "good fortune," do not understand the process, but only perceive the result, and call it chance.

In all human affairs there are efforts, and there are results, and the strength of the effort is the measure of the result. Chance is not. Gifts, powers, material, intellectual, and spiritual possessions are the fruits of effort. They are thoughts completed, objects accomplished, visions realized.

The Vision that you glorify in your mind, the Ideal that you enthrone in your heart, this you will build your life by, this you will become.

As a Man Thinketh by James Allen – **Serenity**

Calmness of mind is one of the beautiful jewels of wisdom. It is the result of long and patient effort in self-control. Its presence is an indication of ripened experience, and of a more than ordinary knowledge of the laws and operations of thought.

Self-help and positivity are tools of power but what good would they be if you are not happy? To be happy, you need to be positive. As it is impossible for sugar to remain solid in water, it is impossible to be negative and happy. This book on positivity is really a treatise on happiness. That is why there is so much emphases on working on your happiness, through positivity.

A man becomes calm in the measure that he understands himself, of knowing himself, as a thought evolved being, for such knowledge necessitates the understanding of others as the result of thought, and as he develops a right understanding, and sees more and more clearly the internal relations of things by the action of cause and effect he ceases to fuss and fume and worry and grieve, and remains poised, steadfast, serene.

To know thyself is to seek to know what you are not. When you know what you are not, and accept that fact, only then are you likely to be satisfied with who you really are. There is freedom in accepting your limitations. We all have them, know yours, for without knowing them you are not living to your truth. It is only when living your truth can you have a calm mind, therefore be joyous.

The calm man, having learned how to govern himself, knows how to adapt himself to others. They, in turn, reverence his strength, and feel that they can learn of him and rely upon him. The more tranquil a man becomes, the greater is his success, his influence, his power for good. Even the ordinary trader will find his business prosperity increase as he develops a greater self-control and equanimity, for people will always prefer to deal with a man whose demeanour is strongly equable.

The strong, calm man is always loved and revered. He is like a shade-giving tree in a thirsty land, or a sheltering rock in a storm. "Who does not love a tranquil heart, a sweet-tempered, balanced life? It does not matter whether it rains or shines, or what changes come to those possessing these blessings, for they are always sweet, serene, and calm. That exquisite poise of character, which we call serenity is the last lesson of culture, the fruitage of the soul. It is precious as wisdom, more to be desired than gold, yea, than even fine gold. How insignificant mere money seeking looks in comparison with a serene life. A life that dwells in the ocean of Truth, beneath the waves, beyond the reach of tempests, in the Eternal Calm!

How many people we know who sour their lives, who ruin all that is sweet and beautiful by explosive tempers, who destroy their poise of character, and make bad blood! It is a question whether the great majority of people do not ruin their lives and mar their happiness by lack of self-control. How few people we meet in life who are well balanced, who have that exquisite poise which is characteristic of the finished character!

Yes, humanity surges with uncontrolled passion, is tumultuous with ungoverned grief, is blown about by anxiety and doubt only the wise man, only he whose thoughts are controlled and purified, makes the winds and the storms of the soul obey him.

Tempest-tossed souls, wherever you may be, under whatsoever conditions you may live, know this in the ocean of life the isles of Blessedness are smiling, and the sunny shore of your ideal awaits your coming. Keep your hand firmly upon the helm of thought. In the bark of your soul reclines the commanding Master; He does but sleep, wake Him. Self-control is strength. Right Thought is mastery. Calmness is power.

If you have enjoyed Pat Grayson's words, perhaps you like to read some of his other books;

The Intelligence
Oh Hell
Chinese Down Under
Yogi, the tails and teachings of a suburban doggy
Know ThySelf (parts one and two)
Gruffian's, Bare Teddy Bear (book for Children)
Trees, the guardians of the soul
How to write – right!

To contact Pat Grayson for workshops,
email: pat@heartspacebooks.com

www.ingramcontent.com/pod-product-compliance
Lightning Source LLC
Chambersburg PA
CBHW021421110726
47901CB00008B/2255